'No helpless female would dare to board my ship alone, and with nothing on her person for protection.

'You deserve a commendation for sheer guts, Rowena. I salute your courage and your boldness. You are undeniably brave—as well as beautiful. But your father is in debt to me up to his ears. Would you compound that debt by adding to it?'

'There is something I could give in payment.'

'Could you, indeed? You mean that you and I could have a very delightful arrangement?'

His voice was like silk, and his eyes had become a warm and very appreciative blue, and Rowena knew immediately what price he was asking her to pay. She felt fury rise up inside her—not just with him, but with herself and at the excitement which stirred at the very idea…

Helen Dickson was born and still lives in South Yorkshire, with her husband, on a busy arable farm, where she combines writing with keeping a chaotic farmhouse. An incurable romantic, she writes for pleasure, owing much of her inspiration to the beauty of the surrounding countryside. She enjoys reading and music. History has always captivated her, and she likes travel and visiting ancient buildings.

Recent novels by the same author:

MISTRESS BELOW DECK

Helen Dickson

All the characters in this book have no existence outside the imagination
of the author, and have no relation whatsoever to anyone bearing the
same name or names. They are not even distantly inspired by any
individual known or unknown to the author, and all the incidents are
pure invention.

First published in Great Britain 2009
Harlequin Mills & Boon Limited,
Eton House, 18-24 Paradise Road, Richmond, Surrey TW9 1SR

© Helen Dickson 2009

ISBN: 978 0 263 86795 4

Set in Times Roman 10½ on 13 pt
04-0809-75498

Harlequin Mills & Boon policy is to use papers that are natural,
renewable and recyclable products and made from wood grown in
sustainable forests. The logging and manufacturing process conform
to the legal environmental regulations of the country of origin.

Printed and bound in Spain
by Litografia Rosés, S.A., Barcelona

MISTRESS BELOW DECK

Prologue

The open solitude of the land above Falmouth beckoned fifteen-year-old Rowena. She rode with reckless abandon away from the house as though the devil himself pursued her. Her scarlet skirts covered the horse's flanks and her unbound dark brown hair streamed behind her like a ship's sprightly pennant. Her cheeks were poppy red, the colour heightening the intensity of her eyes, their blue-green aglow with the excitement and exhilaration of the ride.

Did not her father call her a gypsy, a vagabond—all because she was too restless to be caged within the house? Her father was right. She did look like a gypsy and she was a gypsy at heart, for in her soul there was a wildness, a yearning to be free of all constraints, that made her feel like one.

When the attack came it seemed to come from nowhere. She had no time to defend herself as she was dragged from her terrified horse and thrown to the ground. Wrenching herself away from her assailant, she shrieked, but he stifled the sound, clapping his hands over her mouth. She immediately began fighting, blindly thrashing in an iron grip that pinned her to the ground. She pushed against his chest to break free, but his arms became bonds, forcing her arms to her sides, and his mouth grinding down on hers prevented her cries of rage.

Inwardly she raved. It was disgusting to be treated like this, absolutely disgusting. The depraved beast was intent on ravishment, without tenderness, without decency, as without mercy he began tearing at her clothes. Every twist of her body to escape his lust caused him to utter obscenities.

Horror at the abuse gave her frenzied strength. She fought against his brutal strength, her mind somehow refusing to accept what was happening. Tears of outrage streamed from her eyes and her soul screamed against this violation.

'Such spirit, such defiance, my little pretty,' the man said, laughing low in his throat. 'Your protests are useless. It will be better for you if you do not fight me, darlin'.'

Rowena recognised her attacker—it was Jack Mason, captain of the *Dolphin*, her father's ship. Earlier, when her father had introduced her to him, he had squeezed her hand and she had looked openly and without fear into his admiring eyes. His look was heavy lidded, beguiling, hungering, and had she not been a naïve fifteen-year-old, she would have been alarmed and wary, and would certainly not have been found riding alone in the open countryside.

Determined to be free from this nightmare, in one last desperate thrust she brought up her knee into his groin and shoved him away. With a yell of pain he doubled over on the ground, clutching his damaged manhood, and, taking her chance, Rowena wriggled away. On her hands and knees she looked down at him as he writhed in agony. He was seething, his eyes bulging with rage and filled with murder.

'Think again if you intend to ravish me,' she hissed, her eyes glaring her hatred. 'Did you mean to frighten me?'

'I would enjoy frightening you,' he gasped. 'Indeed, I would heartily like to hear you scream for mercy.'

Rowena shot to her feet. 'Do you think to convince me of your brutal ways? Ha!' she retorted, laughing bitterly. 'You are as I shall always remember you—on your knees where you belong.'

Captain Jack Mason's cold grey eyes narrowed dangerously. 'I warn you, Rowena Golding, do not laugh at me.'

'I do laugh at you,' Rowena sneered and flung a further taunt full into his face. 'Do you think I would give myself to the likes of you? You are only fit to mop the decks on my father's ship. Aye, Jack Mason, unfit company for gentlefolk—and, more's the pity, you are too ignorant to know why.'

Turning from him, she hauled herself on to her horse and galloped away. The man on the ground watched her go, cold murder curling round his heart. 'Go, you little bitch,' he ground out. 'But you'll be dealt with, I'll see to that.'

Chapter One

May 1721

Lord Tennant's masquerade balls were famous affairs, which were talked about from Land's End to the Tamar. They were attended by the cream of Cornish society, all in a fantastic display of costumes—some quite outrageous—men in medieval, Turkish, Arab, more than one Henry VIII and Richard III, and much more that quirked the imagination. Some of the ladies had come as Good Queen Bess and two as the tragic Mary Stuart. There were Spanish mantillas, flounced skirts, elaborate wigs and fluttering ivory-and-lace fans.

In keeping with the spirit of the evening, Rowena had danced every dance with this partner and that. Despite being a great success and basking in the admiration that turned every head in her direction and brought an appreciative gleam to each male eye, in her hauteur she had no particular opinion for any of them.

As Queen Cleopatra, she was wearing a plain white linen gown and gold girdle about her slender hips; it revealed more of her shapely assets, which was considered by some to be quite shocking and indecent and would have sent her widower father into a fit of apoplexy had she presented herself for his inspection before they had left Mellin House for the ball.

Matthew Golding was a cripple and unable to attend, but such a grand occasion as this served as a marriage market for all unmarried girls. Facing financial ruin and desperate to find husbands for his two daughters, he had insisted on them attending under the chaperonage of his good friend and neighbour, Mrs Crossland, who had two daughters of her own.

As the evening wore on Rowena became bored and she found that the sparkle with which the evening had begun had evaporated. Her head beneath the heavy black fringed wig felt hot and was beginning to ache, and she was sure the kohl around her eyes beneath the mask was beginning to run in the heat.

'I feel so hot I shall have to slip out for some air,' she told Jane, her seventeen-year-old sister, who was dressed as a Grecian lady.

Jane was as different to Rowena in temperament and looks as it was possible to be. Pretty and small featured, Jane's pale skin was flushed with a lovely rosy glow, her green eyes sparkling. Her whole body was surging enchantingly towards Edward Tennant, who was watching her from across the hall. Rowena intercepted the look that passed between them and her face became thoughtful. Edward was Lord Tennant's youngest son, a handsome youth, and he had danced two dances with Jane. She looked away. Their father would be well pleased if a match could be made between them.

'If you must. Is Edward not handsome, Rowena?' Jane said breathlessly, her eyes shining in his direction.

Rowena's look was keen and Jane turned eagerly to her, her radiance shining from her eyes, her expression that of all those who had found love and longed to speak of it.'

'He is quite handsome, I do agree, and he seems much taken with you, Jane.'

'I do hope so. Who's that with him?'

Rowena's eyes were drawn to the tall, indolent figure standing beside Edward. He met her gaze with the cool expression gentlemen always seemed to assume when presented with an attractive woman, but there was a leap of pleasure in his eyes behind his silver mask, which she knew was answered in hers. His identity was a mystery to her, but his manner bespoke the privileged class, of generations of men of superiority and honour. Averting her gaze, she turned to her sister.

'I'm going outside. If you must know, this wretched wig is making my head hot and unbearable. I have to take it off, else I swear I shall scream.'

'Then go to the ladies' retiring room. I'll come with you if you like. Mrs Crossland was most insistent that we were not to leave the house.'

'I really do need to go outside for a bit. I'll be back before Mrs Crossland notices I've gone.'

Jane watched her go. No one, except perhaps their

father, had ever defied Rowena's dangerous spirit, nor had the courage to try to curb it. Through a succession of governesses had been employed to educate her, not one had had the resolution that was needed to discipline Rowena Golding.

She had a hot temper, had Rowena, which could flare in a second from mere annoyance to a rage from which one would flee in alarm. Without a mother and their father a cripple, Rowena had taken on the mantle of responsibility for her family, which gave her a degree of freedom not experienced by many of her peers. In her spare moments her laugh rang frequently across the hills around Falmouth, where she had grown up as free and wild as an unbroken pony.

Rowena ventured deeper into the gardens, smiling with amusement on hearing whispers and giggles and the odd shriek of laughter coming from the undergrowth—the gardens were full of dark places and dark deeds. Eventually she found herself in an enclosed, secluded arbour, where she tore off her mask and wig and shook her thick, dark brown tresses free.

A moment later she heard a sound. She looked towards it, her senses suddenly alert. Something or someone was watching her. Her heart began to race, urging her to turn and run back the way she had come. But then a man, tall, long-limbed, dark and mysterious in the shifting shadows, stepped into the arbour. It was the man she had seen with Edward Tennant.

She let out her breath, unaware until that moment that she had been holding it. 'You startled me.'

'Do not be alarmed. I mean you no harm.'

His voice was unusually deep and rich in timbre. She could not make out his face, which was hidden by a silver mask and the shadow of a wide-brimmed hat on which a black plume curled with a flourish.

He drew close, his eyes gleaming through the slits in his mask, and as she was about to step back, murmured, 'Dear God! Never have I seen the like!' Lifting his gaze from the gentle curve of her slender hips encased in the gold girdle, he stared into the vibrant beauty of her face. How did she get away with it?

On his arrival he had been a figure passing among the throng, a mysteriously ominous keen-eyed observer of the masquerade. This young lady had not escaped his notice—in fact, she had stood out like a black sheep in a field of white. He had watched her, with a toss of her head and a wide smile on her carmine lips, almost with wild abandon dance first with one gentleman and then another, just two who vied with many for her attention and to make her laugh—too loud at times, causing heads to turn to see what Matthew Golding's undisciplined daughter was up to now.

Like everyone else he had been unable to tear his eyes from her, and he had observed the leap of interest in her own when she had met his gaze. He had thought her outrageous, a young woman who evidently believed she was above every consideration, every rule, every discipline that life and society dictated. He had been amused and strangely stirred by her appearance, as any man with a drop of red blood in his veins would be.

Recovering quickly from her initial discomfort, Rowena stiffened, clutching her mask and wig in both hands at her waist. 'What are you staring at?' she retorted rudely, her eyes dark and dangerous.

'At you, lady,' he answered softly. Deliberately his gaze raked over her from top to toe. 'Did no one think to tell you that your costume is outrageous for a young marriageable lady, who with behaviour such as this will never attract the attention of a husband?'

'And how do you know I don't already have a husband?'

'Had you a husband, I doubt he would allow his wife so much freedom and abandon with every one of your partners.'

She scowled, feeling a certain amount of discomfort at the way he was looking at her. 'Would you please stop looking at me like that? I find it most annoying.'

'If you don't want to be looked at then you shouldn't make a spectacle of what no sane man can resist. You can't expect men to be unaffected by the sights you display so audaciously.' Again he let his gaze wander speculatively over her.

Rowena was angry now without really knowing why. Perhaps it was because his words had a ring of truth to them. She had started to regret her choice of costume the moment she had stepped on to the dance floor and every face she saw was secretly smiling, covertly sneering. Suddenly she had felt stark naked. What she had done was childishly defiant and she wished she had chosen something more demure to wear.

'What right have *you* to lecture *me* on what I should wear? It is nobody's business and certainly none of yours, whoever you are.' The hot flash of temper exploded quite visibly. Her nostrils flared and her soft pink mouth had thinned into a hard line, straining to find the words to punish him.

'Then if anything should happen to you, you will have no one to blame but yourself.'

'Why, you rude, insolent…' Her mouth gaped in amazement and the scathing words with which she intended to berate him stuck in her throat. It wasn't often she was lost for words, as she was now as she confronted this presumptuous stranger.

Her eyes blazed into his while her mind struggled to find something to say to reduce him to his rightful place, but even while she did so, something in the core of her sensibility, independent and wilful, dwelt on his hard, lean body and the pleasing shape of his mouth, and the dark depths of his eyes glinting at her from behind his mask. He was a head taller than she was, with wide shoulders, yet his waist and hips were slim. He stood indolently in front of her, his manner telling her plainly that it was of no particular interest to him whether he offended her or not.

'What a capricious and flighty manner you have, along with courting danger, young lady, being out here alone in the dark.'

'And what kind of danger could there possibly be, surrounded as I am by so many revellers?'

'Precisely—with the majority of the gentlemen so

drunk out of their minds they would not give a jot for your reputation.' He let his amused eyes drift to her flushed face and his smile was mocking. 'You should know better—unless, of course, you have arranged a tryst with one of the young men you danced with.'

'Of course I haven't,' she snapped, her cheeks flushing an indignant red. 'What are *you* doing here? Did you follow me?'

'No, I did not, but I did see you leave.'

Rowena studied him thoughtfully. 'You are unfamiliar to me, and I know most people hereabouts.'

His lips, well cut and firm, lifted at the corners with a hint of humour. 'That's because I'm not from—hereabouts. My home is in Bristol.'

'Then that explains why I've never see you before. I trust you were invited to Lord Tennant's ball?'

'Actually I wasn't. I am in the area for a short time and thought to sample some of the town's novelties. When I was told about the masquerade ball, I thought, why, what a pleasant way to pass an evening. Behind a mask one loses one's identity, so who would know I was not invited? The amusement would help me spend my time until I have to leave.'

'And you are amused?'

He chuckled low in his throat. 'I have heard Lord Tennant's masquerade balls are informal, but this is informality with a vengeance. I also heard that his parties are famous for their diversions—which appears to be correct, for it seems that the accepted way of sitting out a dance is to crawl into the undergrowth with one's partner to indulge in pleasures other than dancing. Like you, after partaking of the revelries I sought a solitary place, wishing to take respite.'

'Then I would be obliged if you would seek another arbour in which to be solitary and leave me to mine.' She frowned at his attire. This man intrigued her. He interested her, and so she satisfied that interest in the only way she knew how—by asking questions. 'Forgive me, but who or what are you supposed to be? It's bad manners not to come in fancy dress to the masquerade.'

His smile deepened into an amiable grin, showing strong white teeth. 'My face is covered, but I am not given to dressing myself up and looking like a complete idiot. I have my reputation and my dignity to uphold.'

'But if no one knows who you are, it doesn't really matter, does it?'

'Not to you, perhaps, but it does to me.'

Rowena regarded him with interest, responding to his completely easy and natural manner. His eyes twinkled wickedly through the slits in his mask, making her wish she could see the man and his expression behind it, suspecting he was grinning wolfishly. 'But if your costume was clever and original, you wouldn't look like a total idiot.'

He laughed, then said, 'You look extremely elegant—and exceedingly provocative. It is clear you have put much thought into your costume—and succeeded in not looking like an idiot.'

'You know who I am supposed to be?'

'How could I not? You have enough kohl painted

around your eyes to supply half the ladies in Egypt. Cleopatra would be envious. But I am curious as to the identity of the real you.'

'It is no secret. Even though I wear a mask, everyone knows who I am. My name is Rowena Golding—and there isn't a man or woman in Devon or Cornwall who doesn't know my father, Sir Matthew Golding.'

He stared at her quite openly, behind his mask his eyes narrowing. 'Miss Rowena Golding?' He should have known, of course, for who else could it be? This was the girl whom the whole of Falmouth gossiped about, the whispers rustling like wind through the bracken on the land, whispers of how Matthew Golding's daughter rode her fleet-heeled mare with all the wildness that was in her, and by God, he could see why. She was undeniably magnificent.

The gentle curves of her body all rippled beneath the fine material of her gown. Any female dressed in such revealing garments was bound to attract attention, but it was not just her lack of clothing that drew every male eye at the ball to her—it was her defiant, direct stare, the way she tossed her imperious head, the challenging set to her shoulders, and the way she moved with a sensual arrogance. But the most interesting—and more than a little surprising—thing of all was that she was Matthew Golding's daughter.

Becoming thoughtful, he considered her apace, then, recollecting himself, took a step back and said abruptly, 'Don't you think you should return to your chaperon, Miss Golding, before she comes looking for you?'

They were the exact words needed to release her from the strange spell his voice and presence had cast upon her. 'I need no one to tell me what to do, sir,' she uttered sharply. 'But it is time I returned to my sister, since it is almost time for us to leave.'

Rowena turned in the entrance to the arbour and looked back. The impact of his gaze was no less potent for the distance now placed between them. As if moved by forces beyond her control, she inclined her head in recognition of the strange contract conjured up between them.

Her companion of a moment before merely smiled intimately and watched her go, with a promise in his eyes that said he would see her again.

Mellin House was set in a sheltered fold surrounded by well-tended, spacious gardens and with a fine view of Falmouth and Flushing across the Haven. It had been built by Matthew Golding's grandfather, the man who had purchased a modest sailing vessel, trading between Bristol and the Channel ports, buying warehouses to store his goods, and expanding to make his business a thriving concern.

He would have been proud of his grandson's exploits. Matthew had become the owner of two trading vessels— the *Rowena Jane* and the *Dolphin,* trading between Cornwall, Gibraltar and the Mediterranean ports, where, taking on cargoes such as wine, lace and polished marble, they would sail on to the West Indies, the ships returning to Cornwall heavily laden with highly profitable cargoes of sugar, tobacco and possibly rum.

Today, however, Matthew Golding was facing bankruptcy. He was also crippled, having been shot in dubious circumstances four years ago on Antigua. Rowena had not been made privy to the details, but she remembered well the time he had been brought home on the *Rowena Jane.* The *Dolphin,* in command of its captain, Jack Mason, had sailed away from Antigua and nothing had been heard of the ship, its cargo or its captain since.

Matthew had expelled a great deal of hot air and vows of revenge against Tobias Searle, the man who had shot him, and Jack Mason, the scoundrel who had stolen his ship.

And now, seated at the table in his downstairs room where he conducted his beleaguered business affairs, he was awaiting the arrival of yet another suitor for his eldest daughter. Rowena had never met Phineas Whelan. He was more than twice her age, but many a lass would be honoured to have attracted the attention of such a man.

Having no need for another's wealth, owning land and property in Cornwall and beyond, he was willing to overlook Rowena's lack of dowry. Matthew hoped she would look on him with more favour than the others she had rejected outright, but she was proving stubborn.

Though Rowena was tempted to ride out of Falmouth to avoid meeting Mr Whelan, she resisted the temptation and instructed Annie, the housekeeper of many years, to have a fire lit and refreshments served in the drawing room. Her lovely face was composed as her mind became locked in bitter conflict with her conscience. Their situation was dire indeed. She felt compassion for her father, a person who by her action to defy him in this marriage to Mr Whelan would be wounded. She must put his wishes and the needs of her family before her own, to curb the wilful need to escape the restrictions marriage to any man would bring.

In the next halting moment, doom descended when a loud knock sounded on the door.

Her mind flew ahead with her nerves. Annie must not have heard because the knocking came again. In frantic haste she went into the hall, meeting Jane as she emerged from the kitchen to answer the door herself.

'It must be Mr Whelan,' Jane said, whipping the apron from round her waist as she crossed to the door.

With calm deliberation Rowena smoothed her troublesome hair from her brow and tried to soothe her anxieties as she watched Jane raise the latch and open the door. The space seemed entirely filled with a tall dark figure.

'Please come in,' Jane said to their father's visitor, flushing prettily when her eyes beheld the handsome visage.

Rowena stepped forward to receive Mr Whelan, halting abruptly when he stepped into the hall. Her gaze travelled up from expensive brown leather boots, over a dark green redingote, to the face beneath the brim of a tricorn hat. Her breath froze in her throat. His face was by far the most handsome face she had seen. How tall he was, she thought, lean and superbly fit. There was an uncompromising authority, an arrogance, to the chiselled line of his jaw, and his aquiline profile and tanned flesh would have been well at home at sea.

Yet humour came quickly, softening the features, and crinkles of mirth appeared at the corners of his eyes. His eyes, compelling, bold, mocking and piercingly blue, were totally alive, as if searching out all life had to offer and determined to miss nothing. They openly and unabashedly displayed his approval as his gaze took in the length of her. The slow, lazy grin that followed and the wicked gleam in his eyes combined to sap the strength from her body.

Rowena knew at once that here was a man unlike any other she had known, a man of power, diverse and complex, who set himself above others. She felt slightly irritated by the intensity of his inspection, yet at the same time stirred by it.

This was no doddering, whiskery old man, she realised, but a man handsome and virile in every fibre of his being. That he exceeded everything she had imagined him to be was an understatement.

The man swept off his hat to reveal a short thick crop of black hair. His rich deep voice was as pleasing as the rest of him, but, when Rowena heard it, it rendered her momentarily speechless.

'Well, well, Miss Golding. What a pleasure it is to meet you again.'

She stared at him in amazement, recognising something in his stance and in the deep timbre of his voice. Realisation that this was the man she had met at Lord Tennant's ball hit her like a thunderbolt. He was watching her steadily now and she was glad she had tied her hair back with a bright red ribbon. If only her father had told her what he looked like, then perhaps she would not have been so reluctant to meet him. She felt her spirits lift and was unable to shake off the thrill of seeing him again.

Dear God, he was so handsome! Perfect. A supremely eligible suitor. Never in her wildest imaginings had she visualised a man quite like this. It just went to show that her wilful, rebellious heart was as susceptible to a handsome face and a pair of laughing blue eyes as the next. Any woman would be flattered, honoured, to be courted and wed to such a man.

'You! So it was you lurking behind a mask at the ball! Oh—I had no idea.'

'Clearly. Do you mind?'

Rowena, who had been paralysed into inaction by the knowledge of his identity, laughed outright, feeling as if a heavy burden had been lifted from her shoulders. *Mind,* she thought, her common sense raging and her heart racing, *surely there had to be some mistake?* As she studied him intently, her face was alight with curiosity and caution.

'Why should I mind? My father said you were coming. You are expected.'

'Indeed?' His eyebrows crawled upwards with a certain amount of amazement, and for a moment he looked somewhat bemused, but then he smiled, a slow, secretive, knowing smile. 'Forgive me if I seem surprised, Miss Golding, but I expected to be received with resentment, not kindness.'

To her annoyance, Rowena found herself flushing scarlet. 'I apologise if I appeared rude on our previous encounter, and if my father told you of my unwillingness to meet you. You see, I'm an obstinate, selfish creature—at least that is what he's always telling me—and for the sake of relieving my own feelings, I care little for offending and wounding others. I am relieved to see you are not in the least as he described you to be, and that you greatly exceed my expectations. Has he told you much—about me, I mean?'

'I know a good deal about you, Miss Golding. I've made it my business,' he murmured, catching a tantalising scent of her flesh as she moved closer, his eye drawn to the scooped neck of her gown and her creamy, perfect skin. For a long moment his gaze lingered on the elegant perfection of her glowing face, then settled on her entrancing soft blue-green eyes. He felt himself stir in sudden discomfiture as his blood began to throb in his veins. 'And I'm looking forward to getting to know a good deal more about you.'

'Oh—yes, of course you are. This is my sister, Jane.'

Jane looked at the stranger before resting her gaze on her sister curiously, and then a knowing smile curved her soft lips. Rowena had shown an interest in no man beyond a willingness to engage in flirtation of the very lightest kind with local boys, and here she was, gazing at this stranger with the air of someone who has been transported to another world, fidgeting like a restless colt and with stars in her eyes, her cheeks a delicate shade of pink to match the roses on the hall table.

'I'll go and get some refreshment, Rowena.' Jane quickly disappeared back to the kitchen where she was helping Annie prepare the evening meal.

The visitor was looking at Rowena in a way that warmed her body and brought a quickly rising sense of excitement. 'I hope you won't be disappointed, and that, along with everything else, you will be satisfied with the arrangement you made with my father.'

The humour vanished from his smile, replaced by a quizzical puzzlement. 'Everything else?' His look became thoughtful, and then into his eyes came a look of understanding, like a sudden flame, and he smiled slowly, as if in secret amusement. 'Yes, Miss Golding. Be assured that I shall be more than satisfied.'

'Never having been properly introduced, you know very little about me.'

He tilted his head to one side as he studied her face, that glimmer of secret amusement in his eyes. 'I know that your name is Rowena, that you are the elder of Matthew Golding's two daughters. You have lived in Falmouth all your life and your mother died several years ago. I know you were a child of unpredictable disposition, that you and your sister were well educated by a string of governesses.

'I also know that your father has a penchant for self-destruction. He's got himself into an appalling financial situation, and once his creditors discover his dire circumstances he will have to run for the Continent or risk facing an unpleasant, prolonged stay in a debtors' prison. As a result he is now striving to procure for you a wealthy husband, regardless of age, status or your feelings on the matter. In short, you are loyal to a fault, left to perform the biddings of your father's avarice. Is this correct? Tell me if I'm wrong.'

Rowena swallowed, her spirit, like her pride, shattered. She acknowledged the truth of his words with a slight, regal inclination of her head, thankful that none of this mattered to him. 'I'd say your information is entirely accurate. I'm the only thing standing between my father and absolute ruin.' Her lips curled bitterly. 'What a pathetic creature you must find me.'

He stood for a moment, his imperturbable penetrating gaze studying the hurt his words had brought to her eyes. The sun filling the hall had brought a bloom of rosy colour to her delicately boned cheeks, setting off a sparkle in her jewel-bright eyes, the blue-green orbs slanting slightly upwards, thickly fringed with black lashes. There was a naïvety about her and an indescribable magnetism that totally intrigued him, as well as something special and fine.

'I'm sure you are many things, Miss Golding, but being pathetic is not one of them. Now, isn't it time you took me to your father?'

'Yes, of course. Please come this way.'

'A moment of your time, Rowena, before we go in.'

She paused and gazed up at him, noting how his expression had hardened. He had used her Christian name for the first time; though she noticed it, she liked the sound of it, the familiarity, and could not protest.

'You may be amazed by what you hear. I apologise

beforehand for misleading you.' Without waiting for a response, he opened the door and strode into the room.

At the sudden interruption Matthew looked up from some papers he was scrutinising. With stupefied slowness his eyes focused on the man who had burst in.

'What the devil…?' He stared blankly, giving no hint of recognition at first, but then he froze, an expression of stunned horror on his face, and when he spoke the first word came out in a sibilant hiss. *'You*. How dare you enter my house uninvited? What do you want—and what the devil are you doing with my daughter?'

Rowena felt a strange slithering unease as she hovered in the doorway. Fear began to congeal in her breast and run its tendrils through her veins as she watched the two men.

The visitor walked to within a yard of where Matthew Golding sat beside the fire in his cumbersome wheelchair and stopped. His eyes flicked over the older man's portly frame with contempt. As Matthew made a feeble attempt to straighten his neck linen, the corners of the taller man's mouth twisted in derision.

'I want answers, not questions, Golding. This is not a social call. I want justice, and by God I will have it. I am here to collect a debt. When I left Antigua I thought you were dead. Imagine my surprise when I discovered you are very much alive. You must have known I would catch up with you sooner or later, that I wouldn't let it pass.'

Matthew's face took on a look of incandescent rage. 'What the devil are you talking about? How dare you force yourself into my house?'

Rowena was speechless, frozen in shock, unable to assimilate what was happening. She gaped at her father in blank confusion. When she moved towards him, bewilderment was written all over her face. 'Father, what is this? And why are you not pleased to see Mr Whelan? Did you not tell me you were expecting him?'

Matthew looked at Rowena as if she had taken leave of her senses. 'You brainless, witless girl,' he snarled. 'This isn't Phineas Whelan.'

Rowena stared at him through eyes huge with horror and disbelief. 'He isn't? Oh, God,' she cried. With sudden, heartbreaking clarity all the pieces of this bizarre puzzle began to fall into place. The whole gruesome picture was suddenly presented to her in every horrendous detail. In the space of two seconds, all those images collided head on with the reality of what it all meant, bringing her whirling around on the stranger in a tempestuous fury.

He smiled sympathetically. 'I apologise.' He cocked a mocking brow. 'I take it that Mr Whelan is a suitor?'

'How dare you?' Rowena hissed with poorly suppressed ire, stepping closer to the intruder. 'How dare you do this? Of all the treacherous, despicable, underhand… How dare you tell me you were Mr Whelan?' Her mind screamed at the injustice of it, and her fury increased a thousandfold when she found his eyes resting on her with something akin to compassion or pity. It was too much to bear.

'I didn't.' His tone was brusque where before it had been soft. 'You assumed. I am sorry. I'm not proud of deceiving you. You do right to put me in my place.'

Rowena's eyes narrowed into slanted slits of piercing green. 'Your place? Just who are you?'

A crooked smile accompanied a slight inclination of his head. 'Tobias Searle—at your service.'

This pronouncement of the name that had bedevilled them all since her father had been brought home close to death was like acid on a raw wound to Rowena. 'You fraud. You disgusting fraud. You're no gentleman, that's for sure, and you are not welcome in this house. How dare you come here hoping to be received?'

Tobias stared at her with a look like a man who has just realised that the fragile flower he has casually picked is in actuality a hornet's nest. It came to him that there was a changeling in the room, for this termagant was not the winsome girl who had let him in. The face that had been so open and radiant was now closed and turned against him.

'I was quite prepared not to be received. I considered it wise not to tell you who I was until I had been admitted to your father.'

'You told me my father was expecting you.'

His lips curved in a cynical smile. 'That was true. He has been—for the past four years, in fact—but I confess I wasn't invited.' He fixed his gaze on the man in the chair. 'Have a care, Golding,' he warned, 'for I would not hesitate to expose your ugliest secret to the illustrious people of Falmouth and beyond.'

'What do you want from me?'

'I would like to say I want recompense for a cargo of rum and sugar you stole from me, but it is as nothing compared to the compensation you owe to the families of the men who perished on one of my ships—the *Night Hawk*—when it was fired in Kingston Harbour four years back. The lengths you went to to prevent the ship collecting the cargo you coveted for yourself was nothing short of murder. Men who were asleep on board didn't stand a chance of saving themselves.'

Purple veins stood out on Matthew's forehead, his eyes protruding from their sockets as he glowered up at the other man. 'That was not my doing,' he said hoarsely. 'I swear it. Jack—Jack Mason—'

'I know Jack Mason. *Captain* Jack Mason, the master of the *Dolphin*—your vessel, I believe.'

'Aye—and Mason, renegade that he is, made off with it and left me to rot on Antigua.'

'Perhaps like everyone else he thought you were dead—myself included. Had I known you had survived the shooting, I would have been here sooner.'

'Mason's the one you should be looking for, not me. I had nothing to do with what happened to your ship.'

'I am looking for him, only I'm having a little difficulty in tracking him down. But I shall—be assured of that. You were there that night. You saw what happened. As owner of the *Dolphin,* who had command of his own crew, I hold you responsible. Believe me, Golding, I am no respecter of your standing in society and I would gladly see you ruined and your house razed to the ground for what you have done, so do not think for one minute that my threat is idly voiced.'

Matthew's usually florid features had become chalk

white and his breathing shallow and rapid, as he felt the ghosts of the past begin to claw at him with savage fingers. 'What is it you want from me?'

'I've told you. Compensation for dead men. It's a matter of human decency. Compensation for their families and for those men who were badly burned, some blinded, some with life-limiting injuries, men who will never work again, who are unable to support their wives and children.'

Appalled by what she was hearing, Rowena stared at him. 'What are you saying?' she cried. 'That my father killed those men?' The look he gave her said it all. 'But that's outrageous.' She looked at her father. 'Tell me it's not true. Tell me he's lying.'

'Rowena, I did not do what he accuses me of. I may not always have done what I should, but at least I have no man's death on my conscience.'

'But you were there. You sailed on the *Dolphin* to the West Indies. I would like to know the truth of it.'

'Damn you, Rowena. You think your father a killer, do you? I was there, I admit that, but I was nowhere near the *Night Hawk* when the fire started.'

Rowena believed him. She knew what Jack Mason was capable of—she hadn't forgotten his attack on her before he had sailed for the West Indies. She directed her hard gaze on Tobias Searle, icy fire smouldering in the green of her eyes. 'You speak of compensation for the families of those men who died. What of my father? Does he not warrant compensation from you, sir, for shooting him in the back like a coward and leaving him a cripple?'

'And that's what he told you, is it?' He looked contemptuously at Matthew with a lopsided smile. 'You have been living under a misconception. I am not a man who would shoot another in the back. God knows I wanted to shoot you; had I done so, I would not have maimed you—I would have killed you. As I recall, you were the worse for drink on the night I ran you to ground on Antigua. I doubt you can remember much of what happened. But that is not what I am here for. The debt, Golding. I do not intend remaining in Falmouth overlong, so it must be paid within the week.'

'And it is thanks to you making me a cripple—despite what you say to the contrary—and unable to conduct my business as I would like, that I lack the wherewithal to pay,' Matthew said, refusing to believe Searle innocent of shooting him.

Slowly, distinctly, the younger man said, 'I have heard you soon won't have a pittance to your name. Do you think I don't know you have money lenders and creditors hounding you—and I don't doubt you have even used your daughters' dowries to put towards paying them?' His smile was sarcastic. 'They are like sacrificial lambs to your ambitions, are they not, Golding? However, after meeting your eldest daughter—' he turned his head, his gaze leisurely sweeping over Rowena appraisingly '—I'm somewhat surprised there have been no takers. She would make the most charming companion. Perhaps I should make a bid for her myself. 'Tis obvious she doesn't take after you.'

Matthew clenched his hands into tight fists. 'Keep

yourself away from my house and your filthy hands off my daughter. She'll have nothing to do with the likes of you.'

Undaunted, Tobias smiled blandly into Rowena's rage-filled eyes. 'I am tempted to try to change her mind—if she would allow it. It would be interesting to see what might come of it.'

Her chilled contempt met him face to face. 'Why? To try to thwart my father? Do not even think of adding me to your long string of conquests.'

He smiled with wry humour. 'Conquest? You mistake me, Rowena. Don't be too hasty. I might be prepared to be—generous.'

'Generous? What are you talking about?'

'Aye,' Matthew said, clearly bemused, 'explain yourself.'

'I am not usually an impulsive man, but in exchange for your daughter's hand in marriage, I would be prepared to reduce your debt to me.'

'Why, you arrogant, pompous oaf!' Rowena gasped. 'Your callousness disgusts me. I would marry the ugliest, oldest man on earth rather than have anything to do with you.'

'Never!' Matthew railed over his daughter's surprised gasp. 'I won't have a daughter of mine married to the likes of you. If you know what's good for you, you'll keep away from her.'

Tobias considered Matthew with open mockery. 'Why not ask Rowena what her pleasure might be?'

'I'd kill you before I'd see her take up with you. So be warned.'

Tobias laughed derisively. 'I'd be careful with my threats if I were you, Golding. The last time you threatened someone, he put you where you are now. I don't think I have anything to worry about.' He looked at Rowena, who was glaring at him with eyes burning with indignation. 'Do not concern yourself, Rowena. I mean you no harm.'

'My name is Miss Golding to you,' she retorted, twin spots of colour growing on her cheeks. 'Take your offers and endearments and inflict them on some other willing ear.'

'And this Mr Whelan you mistook me for—is he someone your father hopes to saddle you with? Rich, is he? Rich enough to get him out of his mess?'

'That is none of your business. One way or another the debt will be paid in full. I promise you that. Now will you please leave. As I said, you are not welcome in this house.'

The muscles flexed in his cheek, giving evidence of his constrained anger. 'I don't intend staying any longer than necessary. I find merely being in this house with the man who murdered members of my crew extremely distasteful.'

He took a step closer to his adversary, his eyes merciless in their intensity, and his next words were uttered slowly, like uncoiling whips. 'But heed me and heed me well, Golding. Were it just a matter of the cargo you stole from me by burning my ship, I might have seen fit to cancel your debt in view of your unfortunate disability—and if you had agreed to my offer to marry your daughter. But since my offer has been rejected, you will pay in full for what you did to those men. I swear, if you try to evade your obligation, I will crush you out of existence. There will be a scandal, but it would be worth the scandal to see you go under. You have a ship for sale—the *Rowena Jane.* I might have a buyer to put your way, which will go some way to settling your debt.'

Rowena stepped forward, her hands clenched in the folds of her dress. She felt sick and more than a little afraid of this new threat to their future security, but her anger and indignation were much stronger. Pride warred with the years of resentment she had harboured against her father's weakness to succumb to his disability, which had seen his once-thriving business slip into a decline, but he was still her father and the ties of blood and duty bound them irrevocably. Loyalty and anger rose like a phoenix out of the ashes of her resentment towards this stranger who had tricked his way into her home.

'I think you've said quite enough,' she said, seething, incensed that this man wasn't who she thought he was.

What a fool she had been, what an absolute idiot. For one mad, irrational moment, when he had arrived, she had been so relieved and happy to find him young and handsome—her suitor, she had thought—that she could scarcely speak. She had let herself hope. No sunshine had ever felt so warm, been so bright, dancing on her face as she had looked at him. Wrapped in that magic circle of enchantment, she had wondered what it was about him that was so in tune with her, with the flesh, the bone and muscle of Rowena Golding. Now her eyes took on a steely hardness.

'I hate you for this. I'll hate you till the day I die.'

'You do right to hate him,' Matthew seconded. 'Now get out of my house.'

Tobias looked at Rowena. Her face was as white as a sheet, and the young woman to whom it belonged was trembling like a flower ravaged in the wind. He nodded slowly. 'I'm sure you do hate me, Miss Golding, and I can't say that I blame you, but when you consider what your father intends for you and your sister, then I would reserve a large measure of what you feel for him.'

After he gave her a curt bow, Rowena watched him stride to the door, where he paused and glanced back over his shoulder. His gaze rested on her, those sharp blue eyes burning with something other than anger, something she could not quite lay a finger to.

Chapter Two

Tobias Searle went out and Rowena stood listening to his footsteps cross the hall. A door opened and closed and then there was silence. A stone had settled where her heart had been, and cold fury and an overwhelming disappointment dwelled where just a short time ago there had been hope.

'What are we to do?' she asked quietly, deeply concerned by Mr Searle's visit, her resentment still running high. Her father rubbed his forehead with his fingers.

'This is Jack Mason's doing,' he mumbled. 'The man's a damned menace.'

'Mr Searle accuses you of setting light to his vessel. What really happened? Where were you?'

'Ashore—at the offices of a merchant I'd traded with before, negotiating the purchase of a return cargo.'

'And Jack Mason was on the *Dolphin?*'

He nodded. 'Due to bad weather we were blown off course and failed to pick up our intended cargo in

Kingston. I wasn't unduly concerned about the cargo we would be taking back because there were always plenty to choose from, but when we put in there was an unusually large number of merchantmen. On a suggestion from the merchant and a letter of introduction, I intended going on to Barbados to pick up a cargo of rum and sugar, but Mason was anxious to leave for home.

'I wasn't on board when the fire on the *Night Hawk* started and it didn't occur to me until we were loaded with the cargo meant for the *Night Hawk* and had left Kingston that he'd been behind it. Under cover of darkness and away from the eyes of the harbour officials, he fired it, knowing there were men on board.'

'Why did you go to the West Indies on that voyage? You'd only just returned from Gibraltar with the *Rowena Jane*.'

'A lot of money would be changing hands on the voyage to the Indies. I felt it might be better if I were to carry out the negotiations. I didn't entirely trust Mason and would have got rid of him before sailing, but it was too late to find another captain.'

'When you found out what he'd done, why didn't you turn back to Jamaica and hand him over to the officials there? Surely that would have been the right thing to do.'

'Had I done that, I'd have had a mutiny on my hands. The crew weren't for going back to a place where they might have been thrown into gaol. Besides, most of them were behind Mason that night.'

'And how did you come to be shot?'

'At a quayside tavern.'

'Was that where Mr Searle found you?' He nodded. 'What happened to his crew was a terrible thing and Jack Mason should have been punished. You can hardly blame Mr Searle for seeking justice and compensation for those who were maimed, but I cannot condone his method of exacting revenge—if that's what it was,' she said, feeling a stirring of doubt since his denial.

Rowena knew the rest, of how the *Rowena Jane* had put in at Antigua and found its owner alive but a cripple. Deeply affected by this latest turn of events, she spun on her heel and stalked to the door.

'Now where are you off to?'

'To see what has happened to Mr Whelan. You are right, Father. For me to marry well is the only way out of this mess. I'll get Tobias Searle off our backs if it's the last thing I do.'

Unfortunately Mr Whelan didn't arrive. According to Jane, who had watching from the window, he had been waylaid by the detestable Mr Searle as he approached the house; after they had spoken together, Mr Whelan had walked away.

Rowena galloped along Falmouth Haven. As she reached higher ground, her dogs, two faithful companions she had reared from pups, raced ahead. They were young and fresh and relieved to be out of the stables, their sleek black shapes pouring over the ground and slipping in and out of the rocks.

The wind ruffled her hair, tugging it loose from the ribbon. Away from the town she dismounted and left her horse free to nibble the short grass. Sitting on the grey-veined rocks, she clasped her arms around her drawn-up knees, one of the dogs settling beside her. The air was sweet, smelling of the spiky bushes of gorse and tasting of the sea.

Her gaze did a sweep of Falmouth's deep harbour beyond the quay. Being the most westerly mail-packet station, with ships stopping on their passage to the Mediterranean, the West Indies and North America and requiring provisions, Falmouth, with its flourishing and increasing trade, was a prosperous, bustling harbour town, full of rich merchants.

As a merchant trader, her father's prosperity had always been inextricably linked to the sea, but like every other trader he was always acutely conscious of the dangers that lay just beyond the horizon. Pirate vessels were a constant threat, and because of it he nearly always sailed in convoy with other merchantmen.

Rowena remembered a time when all over the southern coast, a veritable flotilla of traders and merchants had hoisted their sails and pushed their vessels into the troubled waters of the north Atlantic on trading voyages to Spain, Portugal and the colonies of North America. The hazards of such daring oceanic voyages were considerable, and tempests, hidden reefs and Barbary pirates had taken a grim toll over the previous century.

Her gaze travelled to where the *Rowena Jane* was moored. She was saddened by the thought that her father had put it in the hands of a broker. Her eyes moved on to a sloop anchored out in the bay. She looked sleek and fast with tall, raking masts pointing to the sky and its sails neatly furled. A pennant—a bold, bright gold 'S' entwined with the letter 'T' against a background of bright crimson—flew from its masthead. She stood tall and serene, like a proud queen. A figurehead of a woman graced the head of the ship and the name *Cymbeline* was carved into the stern.

She now knew the vessel belonged to Tobias Searle. It was his flagship, just one of many that he owned, and could outgun and outrun most of those who tried to take her.

Looking inland, she let her eyes dwell on the skeletal, blackened ruins of Tregowan Hall rising high above the trees in distance. Fire had gutted part of the hall ten years ago, its owner, Lord Julius Tregowan, and his wife having perished in the blaze. The Tregowan estate was a prosperous one with vast productive acres. The quiet rural communities in this part of Cornwall flourished on rumours about the family that had lived and died in the great house. Lord Tregowan's heir, who employed a bailiff to administer the working of the estate, remained a mystery. Some said he lived in Bristol and had never been to Tregowan Hall to look over his inheritance. Whether he eventually came to Cornwall remained to be seen, and meant nothing to her anyway.

Her thoughts far away, she did not seem to hear his approach until the dogs bristled and growled low in their throats. Turning her head, she looked up, shielding her eyes against the sun's brightness. A man astride a horse was looking down at her. Her eyes and brain recognised his presence, but her emotions were slow to follow.

'You!' she said, surprised to see Mr Searle.

Mocking blue eyes gazed back at her. 'Aye, Rowena,' Tobias said, swinging his powerful frame out of the saddle, his boots sounding sharp against the rocks. 'My apologies. I didn't mean to startle you.'

Removing his hat, the intruder looked down at her, his face grave, though Rowena noticed one eyebrow was raised in that whimsical way he had and his lips were inclined to curl in a smile. What was he doing up here? she had time to wonder, since he was a long way from his ship.

His gaze swept the landscape, settling for just a moment on the skeletal chimneys of Tregowan Hall, before coming to rest on the young woman who made no attempt to get up. He was surprised to see that she wore a jacket and breeches and black riding boots more suitable to a male than a female. She lounged indolently against the rock at her back, one of her dogs beside her, her long slender legs stretched out in front of her and crossed at the ankles. She was as healthy and thoughtless as a young animal, sleek, graceful and high-spirited as a thoroughbred, and dangerous when crossed.

There was also a subdued strength and subtleness that gave her an easy, almost naïve elegance she was totally unaware of. The sun shone directly on the glossy cape of her deep brown hair, which had escaped the restriction of the red ribbon. Few women were fortunate enough to have been blessed with such captivating looks. Her eyes were as clear and steady and calm as the waters he had seen lapping a stretch of tropical sand and were the same exquisite mixture of turquoise, sapphire and green, their colour depending on the light and her mood. In fact, Rowena Golding was blessed with everything she would need to guarantee her future happiness.

The beauty of her caught his breath, then irritation at her recklessness in being up here alone.

'Have you no sense?' he chided, sitting with his back to a rock facing her, a knee drawn up and an arm dangling across it. Glancing at one of the dogs reclining some yards away watching him closely, baring its teeth menacingly since it did not know him, he made no move to approach it. 'Don't you realise the danger of riding alone up here, where vagabonds and gypsies and all kinds of travellers roam the country looking for work? They would do you serious harm for the pennies in your pocket. What is your father thinking of to allow it?'

She gave him a haughty look, as though to ask what that could possibly have to do with him. 'I don't have any pennies in my pocket, and my father has more important things to worry about than what I get up to. Besides I rarely do what people suggest, as you must have noticed. What did you say to Mr Whelan, by the way? He didn't even wait to see Father. Jane told me you spoke to him and that the two of you left together.'

'I merely told him you were spoken for.'

Her eyes opened wide and her tone was indignant. 'You told him that? It was a lie and you had no right.'

'Surely you would not choose to wed an old man over me.'

'Oh, I shall marry—if it will get *you* off our backs— but never would I consider you, Mr Searle.'

His eyes narrowed. 'Worry not. Before you know it, your father will come up with another suitor.'

Rowena glared across at him, holding a tight rein on her temper. 'It is none of your affair.'

'On the contrary, my dear Miss Golding. Everything your father does is of primary importance to me. I have an investment in your family. I seek only what is my due, and if marrying you to some tottering ancient is his only means of acquiring the money to settle his debt, then so be it.'

'Mr Searle, I may be many things, but I am certainly not your dear.'

A soft chuckle and a warm, appreciative light in his eyes conveyed his pleasure. 'You are by far the loveliest and dearest thing I've seen for many a year, Rowena.'

His gaze swept over her, from her shining head, sliding leisurely over her rounded bosom and down the length of her legs. Her hand went to the ears of the panting dog, which she fondled and smoothed and pulled, to the dog's evident delight, and she was rewarded by the thump of a black tail. It obviously meant a great deal to her the way she was fussing over it. Tobias felt a strange sensation come over him and he could hardly believe it when he realised it was resentment—that he, Tobias Searle, who knew himself to be attractive to women, and not because he was one of the richest merchants in Bristol, but because—and he would make no bones about it—he was handsome and had a certain way with the ladies, could be jealous of a dog.

Casting a wary eye over both animals, he saw they were big dogs, gentle and affectionate, but let anyone make a move they didn't like against their mistress and he suspected they could become fierce as tigers.

A lazy smile dawned across his tanned face, and Rowena's heart skipped a beat. Tobias Searle had a smile that could melt an iceberg. She immediately wished she'd worn her riding habit, which was less revealing than her breeches, for his careful scrutiny left no curve untouched. When his eyes returned to hers, her cheeks were aflame with indignation. He smiled into her glare.

'Yes, Rowena. You really are quite lovely, you know.'

'And you are the most insufferable man I have ever met.'

She fell silent, looking at him openly. His face was virile with a compelling strength, which said that no matter what words she flung at him, he would never yield to them. His dark curling hair was cut short, glossy and thick, dipping across his wide forehead. His eyes were steady and narrowed in a deep brilliant blue when he smiled, and his mobile mouth curved across strong white teeth in his brown face.

'What are you doing here? Were you spying on me?'

'I grew bored with Falmouth and came to see if the sights were better up here.' The corners of his lips twitched with amusement, and his eyes gleamed into hers as he added, 'I am happy to report they are much better.'

'It's a pity you have nothing better to do than go about ogling women.'

'I could find plenty to do, if I weren't waiting for your father to come up with the money he owes me. So, with time on my hands, I can't think of anything more enjoyable than being in the company of a very attractive young lady.'

'So, not only are you a man hellbent on ruining my father, you are also a womanising rake,' she sneered.

Making himself more comfortable Tobias grinned leisurely. 'Don't mind me. It's just my way. You must forgive me. I've been too long at sea and have grown forgetful of how to behave when I find myself in the presence of a lovely lady. It will take a while for me to re-adapt to civilised society.'

Rowena's eyes flared with poorly suppressed ire. 'Then go and re-adapt with some other unsuspecting woman. Falmouth is full of willing wenches. I'm sure you will be able to find one to your taste—or perhaps you already have.'

He laughed softly. 'A gentleman never tells, Rowena, but I'd rather spend my time with you. I'd like to get to know you better. Besides, we have to delve into this matter of how your father is to pay his debt to me.'

'How he does that is his concern.'

'And yours. I hate to think you'll be forced into marriage because of a debt owed to me. You're worth much more than any debt.'

'Mr Searle, you have clearly taken leave of your

senses if you think of me as compensation for my father's unpaid debt to you.'

'That is exactly what you are. To get himself out of his mess, he will have you bought and sold to the highest bidder before you can blink an eye.'

Rowena's jaw dropped with indignation and her eyes flashed like fireworks. 'Please don't insult my father. My father and I might argue like the best of them among ourselves, but when family honour is called into question I can be counted on to unite with him against the world if necessary. So condemn him to others if you must, but do not do so to me.'

Tobias clamped his jaw shut. Apparently he had pricked her defences, for she looked irritated and could not let it lie.

'You don't know him,' she went on, 'what kind of man he is. When he was younger he had the tough-fibred tenacity that every man who tries to make a living at sea, whatever the size of his concern, needs to make a success of it. My father had it, for in his veins runs the blood of the stout-hearted Cornishman who would fight for his own bit of ground until they buried him in it. But ever since he returned home to live the life of a cripple, something inside him has shrivelled and died.

'I've watched the fight drain out of him—the force, the need, or whatever it was that drove him—and with it the means for us to survive. Our house is tottering like a house of cards, Mr Searle, but I will not see my family homeless and forced to manage like the meanest beggars. No matter what you accuse him of, I honour my father and would not deceive him by taking up with the likes of you.'

Tobias considered her seriously for a moment, then got to his feet, slipping his hat on his head. Looking down at her his mockery was subtle yet direct. 'No, I don't imagine you would—and that was a commanding speech, by the way.'

'My father is deeply concerned by your accusations. If you truly believe he was behind that terrible incident with your ship, then there is nothing I can say to change your mind—only that perhaps you don't know the true nature of Jack Mason. With every day that dawns my father's burden—and mine—will become more wearisome, and that is because of you. You set your verdict against a decent, honourable man before he could voice a plea.'

'As he did when he accused me of shooting him in the back.'

'Are you saying you didn't?'

'That is precisely what I am saying.'

Rowena was staring up at him, waiting for him to continue, to tell her more, but he chose not to. He looked back at her, at the tumbling mass of hair swirling about her shoulders. Beneath its fullness dark fringed, smoky blue-green eyes glowed with their own light, the colour in their depths shifting like richly hued jade. Her nose, finely boned yet slightly pert, was elevated, and gently rising cheekbones were touched with a light flush of colour. Her lips, not the pouting lips of some simpering females, but gently curving, were expressive and soft.

She was flaunting, outrageous, and he was sure that

no man could come within sight of her who was not fascinated by her. He drew his breath and then looked away so she could not see the expression on his face. What the devil was the matter with him? Why should he feel this gnawing in his chest, which her words had caused him, for this woman who was nothing to him? He must be off his head. What was he doing here skulking on the high ground when he had work to do?

He stood for a moment then, making a decision which even then he was not sure was right, mounted his horse and rode back in the direction of Falmouth.

When Matthew Golding received an offer of marriage for Rowena from Lord Tregowan, it came in the form of a letter with a red wax seal, brief and to the point. It was brought by Mr Daniel Hathaway, Lord Tregowan's solicitor in Falmouth, a man who was well known to Matthew. If Matthew agreed to the proposal, Lord Tregowan would call and see him in due course when everything would be put in order, and he would not be ungenerous.

Rowena turned the letter over in disbelief. 'What? Is that all?' she murmured incredulously. 'Lord Tregowan must be very sure of himself to write in such terms. But who is he really? How old? What does he look like? What kind of man is he?'

Matthew was excited, unable to believe their good fortune. 'Lord Tregowan? He must be back from foreign parts. It's not every day a lord is admitted into the family. Think of it, Rowena. You could be mistress of Tregowan Hall—Lady Tregowan.' He preened in his chair, his eyes alight with pleasure at this unexpected good fortune. 'Very grand. Annie was only saying the other day that there's been some activity at the house of late and masons have been called in to repair the part that was affected by the fire.' He looked expectantly at his daughter. 'What do you say, Rowena? Will you agree to his proposal?'

Casting all melancholy thoughts aside, Rowena desperately tried to sort out in her mind what the best course of action would be to take. She had reached a crossroads, but with only one route to take, a route on which she was being forced. Tobias Searle was going to crucify her father, and it was up to her to see that he didn't; to do that, rather than be tricked or trapped into an alliance with Mr Searle—such was her attraction to him—she would willingly throw in her lot with this man she had never met.

Rowena stiffened her spine, her eyes hard and resolute. 'Yes, Father, I will marry Lord Tregowan, and the sooner the better.'

While a handsome, dark-skinned man dived into the water from the *Cymbeline* and swam in the rippling deep waters of Falmouth harbour, Rowena was on the busy quay to see Jane off on her journey to St Mary's, the largest of the Scilly Isles, to visit their Aunt Sarah.

Jane wouldn't be gone for more than a month, but Rowena was going to miss her dreadfully. She was to travel with Mrs Garston, a respectable lady who lived not far from them. She was a Scillonian, whose family had been fishermen for generations and still lived there.

'You look very serious this morning, Rowena.' Jane gave her sister a worried look, observing that her eyes lacked their customary lustre. 'I do hope you're not feeling the effects of my leaving. It won't be for long and before you know it I'll be back.'

Rowena was feeling despondent. 'I know. I only hope you don't encounter any of those wretched pirates who constantly prey on honest sailors, kidnap them and carry them off to goodness knows where.'

'You mustn't worry. It's a route the captain regularly takes and I'm sure the *Petrel* is well armed. And don't you go marrying Lord Tregowan until I get back, will you? Aunt Sarah will soon be feeling better and when she is I'll come home immediately.'

'Make sure you do. I'm going to miss you, Jane, and as for me marrying Lord Tregowan, it will be a solution to all our problems.'

'It saddens me that you are having to do this, Rowena.'

'Don't be. Everything will be all right.'

'But changed. You don't have to marry him. You don't have to marry anybody you don't want to, and you mustn't let Father bully you into it.'

'I'm not, but Lord Tregowan's proposal is generous—and it is one way of getting rid of the odious Mr Searle and his wretched debt.' She gave her sister an encouraging smile. 'Now you'd better get on the ship, Jane, otherwise it will leave without you. Mrs Garston is already on board. I hope you have a good journey and that you come home safe.'

Jane was an emotional young woman. She enfolded Rowena in a tight hug and there were tears in both their eyes. 'Don't worry about me. I'm a good sailor, you know that.'

'Of course you are. Give Aunt Sarah my love.' Releasing her sister, she stood back and watched her walk across the gangplank and on to the vessel that was to carry her away from Falmouth.

He appeared suddenly, seeming to come from nowhere. His dappled grey horse tossed its fine, noble head and pranced to a halt in front of her as she rode the high ground the day following Jane's departure—and, out of curiosity, to take an edifying look at Tregowan Hall from afar.

Her mare shied to a halt and reared, pawing the air before landing with a thud and whinnying loudly. For a moment, stunned by her horse's reaction and bringing it expertly under control, Rowena could only stare at the man in front of her, unprepared for the sudden lurch her heart gave at the sight of the handsome Tobias Searle.

He looked quite splendid in his well-cut clothes, his shirt front snowy and his cloak thrown back over his wide shoulders in a dashing way, his teeth startling against his brown skin. Then, gathering her wits, the memory of what she was being forced to do because of him made her go hot, then cold, with anger and she glared at this incursion of her freedom.

Tobias admired the way she handled her horse—a sleek, graceful, spirited, dangerous beast when crossed—very little difference, it seemed, between the horse and its mistress. Leisurely, his gaze wandered over the lovely face that was frowning with indignation. A faint smile of appreciation twisted the corner of his mouth.

'Oh, it's you! I might have known,' she retorted irately into the mocking blue eyes that gazed back at her.

'Aye, Rowena, it's Tobias Searle at your service,' he murmured with a slight incline of his head, sweeping his hat from his head in gallant haste, revealing his thick dark hair, which gleamed beneath the sun's rays.

'Do you have to keep bothering me?'

One eyebrow crawled up his forehead and his smile was almost lecherous. 'So I bother you, do I, Rowena?'

'Like a wasp. Do you wish to speak to me, Mr Searle?' she asked haughtily, her manner implying that, if not, he could take himself off and look sharp about it.

'I was merely riding my horse when I came upon you by surprise. Now we have met, there is no reason why we can't be congenial to each other and converse on a matter that will not give offence to either of us.'

'And what do you suggest? That we should discuss the weather, perhaps, or the latest gossip in Falmouth?' she retorted, her lips twisting with sarcasm. 'I cannot think that you and I have common interests, Mr Searle.'

'I find you to be a more interesting topic, Rowena. Once again I find you courting danger. This track is not meant to be ridden at breakneck speed by a horse controlled by a foolish woman.'

Rowena's face tightened and she gave him a frigid stare. 'For your information, I have ridden it many times—so many times, in fact, that I could ride it blindfold. I value my freedom, Mr Searle—the freedom to do as I please—a desire which is sufficiently met up here on the high ground.'

'Be that as it may, but you should have more concern for your own safety. Have you no sense at all?'

'Apparently not, and as I have told you before, it is no concern of yours—and I cannot for the life of me think why you make it so. Nor can I imagine what you are doing hanging about up here, unless it is to waylay unsuspecting females. I am neither fragile nor defenceless,' she told him sharply.

'Is there a reason that brings *you* up here today?'

'You have a nerve, Mr Searle,' she snapped, casting an indignant glare at him. 'What I do—'

He raised a hand to silence her. 'Is not my concern.' His gaze went beyond her to Tregowan Hall. 'Tregowan Hall is close by.' He fixed her with a direct stare. 'Hoping to catch a glimpse of your new neighbour, Rowena? I've heard he's come to take up residence, though whether there is enough interest to keep him here is a matter for conjecture.'

'Are you acquainted with Lord Tregowan?' she asked, reluctant to fall into conversation with him, but she was curious about her suitor and felt it was important to glean any information she could about him.

'As a matter of fact, he is well known to me.' His gaze softened. 'Why the sudden interest in Lord Tregowan, Rowena?'

She gave a casual shrug. 'I suppose you'll find out soon so I might as well tell you. I am to marry Lord Tregowan. He—offered for me…I have accepted.'

Tobias looked at her long and hard for several moments, and then his lips curved slowly, his eyes, filled with some secret amusement, raking her. 'Ah, now I see. I really do. So, you have given your father his way, and by accepting Lord Tregowan's proposal he will not have sold you for a mere pittance. My own wealth does not compare with that of Lord Tregowan's—so I must accept that any hope I may have had that you might succumb to my offer and marry me is a lost cause. It appeals to you to be Lady Tregowan, does it, Rowena?'

Rowena stared at him dispassionately. Her longing to sneer was overwhelming. It was his smug, conceited expression she hated most. How she yearned to set him in his place. 'I am sure Lord Tregowan is kind and polite—'

'And hardly the sort a beautiful young woman would want to be married to, to spend the rest of her life with, in a draughty old house. But if you are to marry him, then may your union be long and fruitful.' His chuckle sounded low and deep when Rowena's colour heightened on being reminded of the intimacies she would have to endure to bring about this fruitful result. 'Married to you, Lord Tregowan might never wish to leave Cornwall again.' He saw the flash of fire in the blue-green depths, but went on undeterred. 'Despite our unfortunate encounters, Rowena, would you not find my company more to your liking than that of a stranger?'

'He won't always be a stranger to me—and will you please stop trying to proposition me.'

'I'm only trying to convince you of my merits, Rowena.'

She tossed her head haughtily. 'Then don't try. It would be a complete waste of time. How conceited of you to think you are better than Lord Tregowan— although I would expect nothing less from you.'

'One thing I will say to you, Rowena, is that you would never be bored with me.'

'And what exactly would you want from me?' she queried with icy sarcasm, gentling her mare as it shifted restlessly beneath her.

Tobias disregarded the sardonic edge to her voice, his expression almost leering as his eyes ran appreciatively over the soft swell of her breasts inside its green velvet, and the long column of her slender neck, the bright flame of her lips.

'That question could be settled with no discussion at all,' he murmured softly, 'and conversation is not what I have in mind.'

Rowena gasped and felt a scalding heat creeping over her. His words, though spoken in hushed tones, tore through her with more force than all her father's blustering demands could ever do. 'How dare you?' she hissed, lifting her slim nose to a lofty angle, her eyes dark and dangerous. 'You are insolent, Mr Searle, and you have a propensity to say things that go beyond the bounds of proper behaviour.'

His eyes glowed in the warm light of the sun as he gave her a lazy smile. 'Your endearments intrigue me, Rowena—but why so hostile towards me? What is it in me that arouses this anger, this dislike you have of me? Your father owes me, that I freely admit, but I am no black-hearted villain.'

'I would hardly expect you to admit it if you were,' she retorted crisply.

'I am a fairly honest man in my dealings with others. I have offered you no injury, not ever, and nor will I. Rather the opposite. I admire a woman who knows what she wants and goes directly for it, whatever the consequences, and you really are a lovely woman, Rowena. We could be splendid together, you and I, well matched, if you take my meaning, so I am at a loss as to why you seem to find me so objectionable.' He was still smiling, nudging his horse forward until it was alongside her own.

Rowena drew herself up to her full height and pulled her horse back, as though to ward him off, as though he was about to make some physical attack of her, and the look she gave Tobias Searle was one of icy disdain. 'I want nothing from you in any way. I would sooner starve and see my family homeless than have anything to do with the likes of you.'

He laughed low in his throat and in one effortless motion he reached out and, finding her waist, drew her close, their horses coming together as though in collusion. 'Shall I show you how thinly veiled your insults are, Rowena? Shall I show you what it is like to be kissed by a real man?'

His taunting grin and the strength of his arms made her realise the folly of baiting him. 'Kindly let go of me,' she demanded, struggling to free herself, but she was held in an unyielding vice and there was no getting away.

In the next instant his head had descended to hers and his lips had found their target. Rowena's world careened crazily. His mouth was insistent, demanding, relentless. She drew a sharp breath to scream her outrage, but his mouth smothered her outcry. Her head whirled and she struggled against the intoxication of his kiss.

Tobias's lips moved warmly, strongly, until he felt hers soften beneath his own and she ceased to struggle, her mouth forced to open beneath his mounting ardour. When it, did his tongue slipped between her lips and within to taste leisurely the full sweetness of her mouth. She had never experienced anything quite like that first kiss, feeling a hot sweetness flow through her body, and her mouth clung desperately, honey sweet and swollen He was devouring her lips in a searing flame that shot through her like a rocket.

Tobias dragged his mouth from hers, feeling her breath warm on his cheek as he found the tender place beneath her ear, and the hot desire that almost had her toppling from her horse, and which might have been stopped, flowed madly through her. Again he found her lips and her senses erupted in a ball of flame that almost consumed her. The warmth spread until her skin seemed to glow and her sanity argued against the madness. She should have found his kiss repulsive, but in truth it was wildly exciting. Then his hand rose and caressed the swell of her breast, and her breath caught as she felt him bring her nipple to a taut peak.

With outraged modesty she surfaced from the pleasurable state into which he had sent her and pushed him away, gasping for breath. Holding a hand over her throbbing breast, she could only glare at him, but she could say nothing that could wipe the look of wonder from her face, nor stop the wild, chaotic beating of her heart.

With a soft chuckle Tobias urged his horse away. 'Don't look so indignant, Rowena. You were made for kissing, and I doubt after that you will be satisfied with your ancient suitor. Face the truth of what I've said.'

'A pox on you,' she hissed. 'If you try anything like that again I swear I'll kill you. Go away. I want nothing to do with you. Just as soon as I am wed to Lord Tregowan I shall see my father's debt to you is paid in full, and then you can go to the devil for all I care.'

Tobias's grin broadened to reveal his strong white teeth. He bowed his head. 'As you wish, Rowena. I will be on my way. But you will not be rid of me entirely.'

'Oh, I shall, Mr Searle. You can be assured of that.' The words could scarcely get beyond her gritted teeth, so tightly was her jaw clenched. With a toss of her head she urged her horse on, galloping away without a backward glance.

Tobias watched her go, the smile melting from his lips and being replaced by a serious frown. Rowena's voice had been steady but beneath it was a splinter of steel. Tobias felt his heart move with a mixture of pity and admiration for her. He did not doubt for one minute that she was aware of every one of her father's failings, but on their previous encounter, to her credit, she had defended him. She had become everything her family needed to sustain their tenuous hold on what they had left. Most would have thought that it was enough for any woman, but, judging by her steely manner, she was not one to shirk her duties.

He could not believe that one naïve Cornish girl could possess so much spirit, so much courage, so much grit. He tried to tell himself that it was just lust she had stirred in him when he had first seen her at the ball, that being too long at sea and deprived of the company of a beautiful woman meant any would do. But that did not explain this growing fascination—this obsession—that held him in thrall to Rowena Golding.

When news of the attack by corsairs on the *Petrel* and the capture of everyone on board reached Falmouth, it caused outrage and horror. Yet the seizure of these people was neither unique nor unusual. For more than a century these attacks had been rife, and the trade in white slaves from across Europe destroyed families and wrecked innocent lives.

When Rowena was told, the messenger had to repeat it twice before it sank in and she could only stand there, staring at him in horror and disbelief, and then she understood, and what he said made everything else seem insignificant.

Jane, her beautiful sister, was gone. Dear God, she could not bear to lose her. She could not face a world without her sister's special blend of gentleness and loving and wisdom that calmed her own wild and impulsive nature. She was in the clutches of the Barbary pirates. They would take her beyond the maps of her English mind to some horrible stronghold where she would be sold as a slave.

When the initial shock had worn off, Rowena's natural resilience returned and with it a fierce anger. She was determined that whatever it took, Jane must be found. When her father agonizingly asked what was to be done, she said, 'Pursuit, Father. That is the only way. Somehow she must be rescued. I won't rest until we have her safe back here—where she belongs.' Rowena took his hand and squeezed it hard. 'I will find her, if I have to rake the sea from here to North Africa myself.'

A broken man, he nodded. 'Whatever it takes. Jane should never have left Falmouth on such a perilous journey. It is difficult to see how pursuit can be made until we have precise information about where they have taken her.'

Rowena faced the truth of this. Jane could be anywhere. There were hundreds of miles of sea out there, many islands and coastlines swarming with those wretched pirates.

Chapter Three

In desperation Rowena went down to the harbour to talk to some fishermen she knew, not knowing what she would achieve by this, but desperately hoping to find someone who would help her in her dilemma. The information she was given by one fisherman was unexpected. It would seem there was only one man who could help her—Tobias Searle.

Rowena felt her hopes rise. It would seem the whole of Cornwall had heard of the exploits of Tobias Searle. By all accounts he was the scourge of every pirate and brigand between Europe and the Caribbean. He had feelers everywhere and knew the seas and the North African coast like the pirates themselves.

Rowena stood looking at the *Cymbeline* in silence for a long time. Until yesterday it had been riding at anchor out in the bay, but now it was moored further along the quay. If what she had been told was true, then could she humbly go to Tobias Searle and beg his help? Plead with him to help her, bargain with him? But she had nothing to bargain with. Slowly her gaze shifted from the majestic vessel to the smaller *Rowena Jane,* and she realised she had something to offer him after all.

Rowena hated the thought of humbling herself before her father's sworn enemy, but her desperation to find Jane was the stronger force. If it meant he would help her, she would crawl and grovel to Old Nick himself. He represented her one chance of finding Jane.

She observed the vessel was taking on provisions, as though it was preparing to leave, which she considered strange, since she truly believed Mr Searle would not leave Falmouth until her father had paid him what he owed him.

Walking towards the vessel, she paused at the bottom of the broad plank connecting the ship to the quay, along which members of the crew were carrying casks of water and salt meat and other provisions.

'I wish to see Mr Searle,' she said to the first man she encountered. 'He—is on board?'

'Aye, miss—in 'is cabin with Mr Dexter. Follow me and I'll take you to him.'

The cabin, with dark wood panelling and polished chairs, was quite splendid. Tobias was at a table, poring over a chart spread out over its surface, his finger on a particular spot. Another man stood beside him. Tobias looked up.

'Rowena?' Though he was clearly surprised, it in no way shattered his cool disdain.

'I'm sorry to intrude, but I would be grateful if you could spare me a little of your time.'

He grinned. 'Forgive me. I thought you were the new cabin boy.'

Her eyebrows rose. 'Do I look like a cabin boy?'

His gaze flicked over her in her sky blue muslin sprigged with tiny violet flowers and a violet velvet sash about her waist. Grinning, he had a wicked twinkle in his eye, as though her arrival on board was an amusing diversion. He shook his head. 'Not in the slightest. This is Mr Dexter, captain of the *Cymbeline*. Mark, allow me to present to you Miss Golding.'

Mark Dexter stepped towards her, smiling broadly. About forty years of age, he was a splendidly built man, broad shouldered and bearded, with a lined and cheerful countenance.

'Welcome aboard, Miss Golding. If you will excuse me, I am needed on the quarterdeck.'

When they were alone, Tobias stood still across the cabin, his eyes running over her swiftly, and there was something in their depths Rowena could not fathom.

'And what brings you into the camp of the enemy with such urgency, Rowena?'

She stared at him, the rush of familiar excitement causing her to become tongue tied, affected strongly as she was by the force of his presence. He was dressed in a brown leather sleeveless jerkin over his loose white shirt. Studying him, she was acutely aware of the strong arms where the shirt had been rolled up to the elbows, of the small area of chest exposed by the open neck of his shirt.

Calming herself, she said, 'I have come here on a matter of the greatest importance to me and my father.'

The startling blue eyes rested on her ironically. 'You have come to settle his debt?'

She coloured hotly and shook her head. 'No, I'm afraid not. I am here because I believe you are the only person who might be able to help us.'

'Us?'

Rowena could sense that he was wary, that his guard had been dropped just a little, but his steady gaze told her he was not going to make it easy for her.

'Of what help could I possibly be to you and your father? Did he send you here to plead for him, to use your petty wiles?' His voice was instantly terse.

Rowena controlled her temper as he rested his hips on the edge of the table and folded his arms across his broad chest. He had not invited her to sit down, and she knew he was deliberately keeping her on tenterhooks until she told him the reason for her visit.

'My father knows nothing of this visit. If he ever found out, he would flay me to within an inch of my life for sure.'

A muscle twitched in his cheek. 'Then what is it that only I can do to help you? My curiosity is aroused as to why you have sought me out on my ship without your father's knowledge.'

Confident that he would not turn her away without a hearing, Rowena moved towards him and looked at him directly to allow him to see the velvet softness of her long-lashed eyes. She meant to make use of every advantage she possessed.

'What is it, Rowena?'

She stopped just three feet from him. He was telling

her he had no time to waste on pleasantries. He was busy with his own concerns, his manner said. She would be better served to state her case and be on her way.

'You will know about the *Petrel,* the passenger vessel that was bound for the Scilly Isles and was attacked by pirates?'

His jaw tightened. 'I have heard. What of it?'

'Are you not concerned?'

He shrugged. 'Not unduly. It happens all the time.'

She drew a breath, steeling herself against his reaction. Her face was flushed as she realised she had never felt so unsure of herself. 'This—is difficult for me.'

He eyed her keenly, his brow puckered. 'Really? In what way? I must ask you to state your business—I've not got all day.'

'No, indeed,' she said icily, finding it difficult to keep her temper under control, but knowing she must if she was to win him over. 'You are a man of some importance and a reputation that most seamen must envy.'

His eyes narrowed. 'Let's get to the point. I'm not a man who needs to be buttered up before he can be asked to do anything. Speak plain, Rowena. You want something from me and you must want it badly for you to seek me out like this.'

'I do. The devil drives where the devil must,' she said, feeling that the devil was certainly driving her when she must grovel to this man. 'You will not have heard that my sister was on the *Petrel*, and that she was taken captive.'

At last she had his interest.

'No, I had no idea. I'm sorry. It can't be easy for any of you, but I still don't see why you are here.'

'To ask you to help me find her.'

He looked at her in genuine astonishment. 'Rowena, there really is no other woman who would have the damned impudence to come here, after all that has happened between us, and ask me to find her sister.'

'I know what it looks like, but I—I thought...'

'What? That I would up anchor and sail into some of the most hostile waters in the world to search for one young woman? Did it not occur to you that I have my own ship, my own business, to attend to, and that I would not be languishing in Falmouth harbour if I were not waiting for your father to settle his debt to me?'

'There is nothing I can do about that.'

He looked at her hard and then after a pause, he said, 'You want me to do the impossible. You are asking me to go behind your father's back and take my crew into a hornets' nest, where there is every chance they might not survive.'

Fire sprang into her eyes. She clenched her hands tightly in the folds of her skirt. 'I would not have thought the task so impossible for a man such as yourself. I have been told you know the coast and the sea around North Africa well, and that you are acquainted with some of the Barbarians personally. I have no wish to know the whys and wherefores of this—that is your business—but with all this to your favour you are better qualified to find my sister than anyone else.'

For a moment he looked at her in silence. There was

a glint in his eyes. 'I cannot believe you have come here to ask this mad, impossible thing.'

Rowena felt a wave of desperation as she strove for control. 'Do you think I don't know that? It is mad and perhaps it is impossible,' she exploded, her eyes bright with anger, 'but I have to try. If you will not help me, perhaps you can tell me someone who will, because I swear that if there is the slightest chance of finding Jane I will row all the way to North Africa myself.' Behind her words lay the shadow of a struggle. When she had entered the cabin her objective had looked close within her reach; now it seemed as remote as ever.

'Don't be a fool, Rowena. Look at the facts before you do anything rash. The fanatical, tyrannical network of Islamic slave traders have declared war on the whole of Christendom, and the whole of Europe has been hit by repeated raids, including England's coastal villages. Thousands have been snatched from their homes and taken to Algiers and Sale in chains. The corsairs are highly disciplined. They are ruthless and make a formidable fighting force. No one knows what happens to the captives seized by the corsairs. Once sold, many disappear without trace and are never heard of again. That is a fact, and cruel, as it may seem, you must accept it.'

'Never. I will never accept it. What would you do, if it were your sister who had been captured? Would you not want to go after her, to get her back?'

Rubbing the back of his neck, he nodded slowly. 'If I am honest, yes, I would.'

'Then, please, I beg of you to give it some thought.

If it were within my power, I would pay you anything you asked.'

Tobias cocked a brow. 'Anything, Rowena? I cannot think of any amount of money that might tempt me.'

'You have to help us, for without your help Jane is doomed. Will you please think it over?' Her voice cracked painfully and she was looking at him with eyes that had turned a brilliant and quite incredible green in her despair.

'I have no wish to think it over and no need. I am sorry for your loss, but I cannot help you.'

A great wave of disappointment and anger filled her heart. 'So, you refuse,' she said with a rush of emotion. 'You really don't care, do you? You don't care for anyone but yourself. My sister can rot in some Arab prison and be murdered for all you care and you won't lift a finger to help.'

'Spare me your temper, Rowena,' he said, his voice clipped. 'No one can help her. It would be useless to try.'

'But you must,' she blurted out. 'There is no one else.'

'Rowena,' he said, sighing deeply, 'you never cease to amaze me.'

She bristled at his light, mocking tone.

'The debt your father owes me stands between us. Does that not bother you?'

'Of course it does, and I hate myself for having to come to you of all people for help, which must show you the extent of my desperation. I am quite helpless at going after my sister myself.'

'The hell you are. Helpless be damned. A woman who can approach her father's enemy and beg for favours, and still lift her head with fire in her eyes, is not helpless.' He shook his head, his thick hair falling over his wide brow, unmistakable laughter bubbling in his chest, rich and infectious. 'No helpless female would dare to board my ship alone and with nothing on her person for protection. You deserve a commendation for sheer guts, Rowena. I salute your courage and your boldness. You are undeniably brave—as well as beautiful. But your father is in debt to me up to his ears. Would you compound that debt by adding to it?'

'There—there is something I could give in payment.' With surprise she was conscious that he was now studying her with a different interest. She returned his look. His expression did not alter, and yet she felt the air between them charged with emotion.

'Could you indeed? You mean that you and I could have—a very delightful arrangement?'

His voice was like silk and his eyes had become a warm and very appreciative blue, and Rowena knew immediately what price he was asking her to pay. She felt fury rise up inside her—not just with him, but with herself and the excitement that stirred at the very idea.

'When I spoke of payment, I was talking about the *Rowena Jane.*'

'And why would I want another ship? I have any amount of vessels and no need of another.' He frowned. 'The *Rowena Jane* belongs to your father. What right have you to offer it to me?'

'Father—is quite beside himself with worry about Jane. He would do anything to have her home safely.'

His eyes gleamed, an intense, speculative gleam that Rowena did not care for and she felt a *frisson* of alarm. His contemplation was steady, for he had already set the price in his mind and only waited the moment. 'If your cause is so important, I will bargain with you, but the price will be high.'

'Oh?'

'I prefer payment of a different kind. In short, Rowena, you.'

Her breath came out in a rush and her eyes flared with anger. She gasped with stunning rage at the affront. Never had she been so insulted, felt such humiliation, she told herself, her temper whipping up her colour until her cheeks glowed a poppy red. Deep down she was outraged and if she hadn't been so desperate for his help she would have lashed out at that supercilious mouth and seen the flesh shatter. She despised him more than ever for this, but not so much as she despised herself, for she could not deny that she was deeply attracted by him.

'What are you suggesting?'

He smiled slowly and raised a dark brow as he considered her flushed cheeks and the soft, trembling mouth. 'Don't play the innocent, Rowena. You are a woman—a very beautiful woman any man would desire to have in his bed. You know exactly what I am saying.'

She stared at him, aware of the trap that closed slowly around her. There was a quiet alertness in his manner, like that of a wolf, its strength ready to explode, but docile for the moment. 'Yes,' she said tersely, 'I think I do, Mr Searle.'

'Tobias. My name is Tobias. So, shall we strike a bargain?' His lips curved slightly, and then, with all the time in the world, he shoved himself away from the table and turned to consider the map.

'And my future husband? How do you suggest I explain such an arrangement to him?'

A secretive gleam shone in his eyes. 'That, my dear Rowena, is a matter for you and your conscience.'

Rowena looked at him hard, knowing that, if she wanted his help to get Jane back, she really had no choice but to do as he asked. 'I came prepared to plead Jane's case, to pay in any way possible.' Her voice was low and husky. 'I did not come to pay the price you ask—the highest price of all—but pay it I will, even though I shall despise you for it.'

Tobias looked amazed for barely an instant. He had not expected her to comply so easily. He was well satisfied. It would almost be worth sailing into North Africa's barbarian-infested waters in search of Rowena's sister. 'So, is it a bargain?'

Convinced he had no morals if he could ask her into his bed, knowing she was promised to another, Rowena raised her chin haughtily. 'Yes, we have a bargain—but it will be for one night only.'

He nodded slowly and his eyes glowed intently. 'For one night you promise to belong to me?'

'My need is great,' she said, never more aware of the truth of it as she was then, 'so, yes, if you will help me find Jane?'

'I will do my best. I will not rest until she is safe.'

'And I shall insist on going with you.'

Tobias's eyebrows rose in unison and he stared at her for one long, incredible moment before shaking his head. He moved close to her to lend weight to his words. 'I don't think so. It would not help your sister if you were killed in your impulse to rush after her.'

'I am under no illusions about the nature of the Barbarians who have taken her.'

'And this does not deter you?'

'No,' she said, determined not to be outdone by Tobias Searle. Her eyes had turned from the usual soft velvety blue-green to the spark and fire of emerald. 'It makes me even more determined.'

Tobias's expression warned her that her intention was not only ridiculous, laughingly so, but beset with more perils than she could possibly imagine. 'If you don't mind, Rowena, you will abandon the idea.' He said it reasonably enough, but he was watching her, waiting for her response.

'But I do mind,' she answered, her own voice quiet. Her temper was beginning to rise, for she had an aversion to being told what to do by anyone. 'When Jane is found, she will need her sister. I can see no harm in sailing with you.'

'Can you not?' Tobias's face was hard eyed and keen, and the atmosphere charged with tension. 'The answer is still no. The *Cymbeline* is not a passenger ship and has no facilities for females—besides, the crew will refuse to sail with a woman on board. They're a superstitious lot and consider women on board a working ship unlucky.'

'But I must.'

He heard the desperation behind her plea, but ignored it. 'No, and unless you want me to call the whole thing off you will do as I say. Have you ever been to sea?'

'I've been out—in a fishing boat.'

'That was not what I meant. You are a woman, and too delicate to sail aboard a sailing ship with no one but men for company.'

Taking his remark as an affront, she stared at him. 'Me? Delicate? Do you really believe that?'

'Of course.'

'If you let me sail with you, I will prove you wrong.'

'No. You would be seasick and beg me to put you ashore at the nearest port.'

Antagonistic and angry, Rowena scowled at him. 'I would not.' Seeing that he would not relent, she was about to turn away in frustration, when she casually glanced down at the chart he had been studying with such intensity earlier, giving particular interest to the place where his finger had been.

'Where is that?' she asked curiously. When he didn't reply she looked at him sharply. 'Tell me.'

'Algiers.'

'I see, and so that must be the North African coast.' In the space of seconds she comprehended, bringing her whirling around on him in a tempestuous fury. 'Why, you intend going after the *Petrel*, don't you? When I came in, that was what you were discussing.'

'It was,' he confirmed with a grim smile.

'Why, of all the despicable, underhand... And you let

me beg—plead with you to help me. No doubt you enjoyed that you—you…'

He chuckled low. 'Every minute. I did know about the attack on the *Petrel,* but I was not aware your sister was on it until you told me.'

'Why were you studying the chart?'

'Studying charts is something I do all the time. I know the corsair who attacked the *Petrel.* Let's just say we had a run-in once, and he owes me.'

'So my father isn't the only one,' she retorted, not without a hint of bitterness. 'And you thought you'd go after him?'

He nodded. 'Such is the reputation of this particular corsair that many a determined attempt has been made to send both him and his ship to the bottom of the sea.'

'Not while he has my sister on board, I hope.'

'No, I wouldn't wish that.'

'So, you have your own reasons for going after the corsair captain. Who is he, this man who commands your attention?'

Tobias fixed her with a steady gaze. 'He's an English turncoat who now sails as a Muslim. His name is Jack Mason.'

A coldness shivered down Rowena's spine. 'Not the same Jack Mason who set fire to your ship—the same Jack Mason employed by my father?'

He nodded. 'The same. Mason is a seafarer with piratical habits, who has turned out to be an unusually successful corsair. The *Dolphin* was intercepted by Barbary pirates when it was returning to England from Antigua.

The crew and Mason were taken as captives to Morocco, but Mason found a soulmate in the captain and it didn't take him long to take the turban and join him on his nefarious ventures, stealing a vessel he plundered and making it his own.'

'What does it mean, "to take the turban"?'

'Some call it "turning Turk"—which means converting to Islam. Mason then became known as Hassan Kasem. He is calculating, ruthless, self-seeking and dangerous, and will do anything to wrest what he wants from life. It was unfortunate for the *Petrel* to be in his path. I am sure your father will be interested to learn that his former captain has turned his hand to the unsavoury business of slavery.'

'Yes, he will, extremely interested. When do you sail?'

'Tomorrow. With the tide.'

'And what of my father—and his debt?'

'It can wait for now.'

'Since you were already prepared to track down those who attacked the *Petrel*, I don't know why I bothered to visit you.'

A dazzling smile creased his face. 'Perhaps because I am a confusing and fascinating character,' he murmured disarmingly, his eyes teasing. 'And because I seem some kind of gift to sort out trouble with a rare understanding, as you have rightly been told, of the corsairs.'

There was enough truth behind his words to cause a flush to creep up her neck and tinge her cheeks. 'You do not fascinate me in the slightest—although I do find you somewhat confusing.' Tobias led the way out of the cabin and on to the deck. 'Will I see you again?'

'No. I promise I'll do my best to have your sister brought home—and if you should see the lad who I'm expecting aboard—I believe he's called Tom Ashton—hurry him along.'

'And what does this cabin boy look like?'

He shrugged, turning to Mr Dexter who had come to stand beside him. 'You hired the lad, Mark. Tell Miss Golding what he looks like.'

'I arranged it with his mother, a decent enough sort. Her lad was out looking for work so I didn't get to speak to him, but several could vouch for him. I expect he'll be glad of the work and will be along shortly.'

Tobias watched Rowena trip down the gang plank. Resting his hands on the rail, he smiled his appreciation as his eyes caressed her trim back, leisurely enjoying watching her. Ever since he had met her he had been for ever conscious of her closeness. The memory of her scent lingered in his mind. She was a fire glowing in his blood, and no other woman but Rowena could quench it.

Rowena did see the youth Tobias was expecting on board as his new cabin boy. He stood on the quay with his bundle of clothes at his feet, staring at the *Cymbeline*. His eyes were large in his pale face and he looked thoroughly apprehensive, clearly reluctant to board the ship. He had no taste for adventure or the sea, but with too many mouths to feed and unable to find work locally, he had been pushed into becoming Mr Searle's cabin boy by his mother.

Rowena smiled her understanding and in no time at all came up with a perfect solution to his dilemma and her own.

Tom Ashton couldn't believe his good fortune, and as he hurried home Rowena turned and looked back at the ship, a smug smile curving her lips.

'So, Tobias Searle, you didn't want to take me along. Well, we shall see about that.'

With a floppy brimmed hat on her newly shorn head and carrying her bundle, Rowena quietly left the house, excited, her stomach feeling as though it were tied in knots. After spending a night agonising over her decision about her course of action and trying to bolster the courage to carry out the wild plan she had conceived, as she hurried to the ship she now had no qualms about what she was doing, or about its success.

It was just breaking daylight as she reached the quayside. A number of the *Cymbeline's* crew were hard at work as the ship was got ready to put to sea. Mr Dexter stood on the quayside, concisely and with clarity giving orders as last-minute provisions were being taken on board.

Trying not to appear nervous, she strode confidently to the gangway, but before she had time to place a foot on it she was halted by Mr Dexter. Keeping her head down, when he had ascertained her business, she was allowed on board. Halfway up the gang way she froze when he called out,

'Boy! Wait a minute.'

Slowly she turned. A light swinging aloft touched on her face. He squinted a curious eye at her.

'Your face seems familiar, lad. Don't I know you from somewhere?'

She shook her head, deliberately lowering her voice when she answered him. 'Nowhere I can think of.'

He looked at her a moment longer. 'Aye, well, maybe not. Go below. You'll be bunking next to Mr Searle's cabin.' Turning away, he dismissed her with a shake of his head.

Rowena breathed a sigh of relief. Despite her disguise, had he taken a closer look at her face he might have recognised her and taken her directly to Tobias, who would have put her ashore. Somehow she would have to make herself scarce until the ship was well out to sea, and then, if Tobias recognised her, she would have to face the consequences.

Tobias stood at the port rail. She could not help but admire the fine figure he made in his coat of claret velvet, his dark hair drawn back and bound in a queue. He was standing with his hands behind his back, legs a little apart, relaxed and at ease, but Rowena sensed that he was aware of everything that transpired around him. His handsome profile was bold and there was a lean, rangy look about him. Even his hands emerging from the broad, gold-braided wide cuffs of his coat were long and slender, and she felt a strong thrill of excitement when she remembered how unnervingly blue and intense his eyes were.

Thankfully everyone was so preoccupied with getting ready to sail that no one paid her any attention. She paused to stand beneath what appeared to be a seemingly confusion of ropes and cables and spars, while far above the great masts swayed.

Tobias's cabin was filled with a golden glow shining through the large stern window. Entering the one next to it, she saw it was small and cramped, but having her own cabin would make her deception possible. She heard commands being issued for the sails to be unfurled and the anchor raised. The cable rattled in the hawser and there was a grinding of the capstan. Gradually the ship began to move and there was the creak of timber and the snapping of sails.

When Falmouth was a distant speck and Mr Dexter banged on her door, instructing her to fetch some coffee for Mr Searle, solemnly she left her cabin and prepared to take up her duties.

Tobias did not glance up when she came nervously into the cabin. With Mr Dexter looking on, he sat totting up some figures in a ledger. Rowena placed the coffee in front of him and he proceeded to stir it, taking a drink and signalling for her to fill it up. She carried the pot and poured the liquid into his cup. He was engrossed and she found herself watching him. But in the next instant, he was torn painfully from his preoccupation when she spilled the scalding liquid into his lap.

Rowena started in surprise. Her heart gave a frantic leap and lodged in her throat as, with a growl, he came to his feet. His shout brought a quick grimace from her, but she had no time to pause in consideration of his injury before he roared,

'You bumbling idiot! What the hell are you trying to do? Make a eunuch out of me?'

The stuff of his breeches was steaming, and he was in considerable discomfort. Unable to think of anything better, Rowena grabbed a jug of cold water and threw it where the coffee had spilled. It was a full moment before Tobias released his breath.

'I'm sorry,' she mumbled, shrugging lamely, careful to keep her head down.

'Sorry isn't good enough.' His bark came with the sharp edge of fury as he glowered at the hunched figure of his cabin boy. 'Get out and fetch some water here and now.' Tearing off his shirt, he winced as he picked the wet fabric off his groin. 'And some salve.'

Rowena's cheeks had taken on a vivid red. She fled the cabin; when she returned with a pitcher of hot water, he had only a towel wrapped about his hips, casually unconcerned with his state of undress. Her face flamed. The sight of that broad, furred chest and brown shoulders increased her discomfiture, and she did not dare look lower than that. Nervously she put the pitcher on the table and without looking at her he poured the water into a bowl.

He soaped and rinsed his face, missing his cabin boy's look of embarrassment. Rowena could hardly keep her eyes from that wide, lean, muscular expanse of naked flesh as she held the towel. Emotions raged through her so turbulently she feared he would see them in her face, but he carried on washing, heedless of her unease.

Picking up his razor and strap he began to shave, all the while talking of things to Mr Dexter that meant nothing to her. When he splashed water on to the back of his neck she kept her face averted and fidgeted with the towel. How was she to live with him in the confined space of the ship's quarters and him not see through her disguise? Placing it within his reach, she decided to leave him to it and return to empty the bowl later.

Mark Dexter gave the youth a frown of bemusement as he turned to leave, thinking his behaviour strange, and the harder he looked the more he could not tear his eyes off him.

Rowena suddenly caught his eye and her heart fell. He knew who she was. She looked at him, her eyes wide and displaying worry as she gazed into his eyes and silently pleaded her case. Under his close scrutiny she blushed and went out quickly.

The deck was quiet, save for the murmur of the helmsman and bosun at the wheel and the odd sailor taking a moment's respite now the ship was underway. Rowena went to the rail and waited, knowing Mr Dexter would follow. She didn't have long to wait.

Coming to stand beside her, he coughed. 'You were clumsy back there.'

'I'm sorry. It's my first time as a cabin boy. I—have much to learn.'

'That is not the reason I sought you out. There is something I must say to you.'

Rowena felt a sudden chill creep through her. She waited, lacing her fingers together behind her back, trying to keep them from trembling.

Mark took her arm and drew her closer to his side so they would not be overheard from inquisitive crewmen. They stood facing the sea. 'Forgive me, but I find it difficult to form the right words.'

Rowena raised her chin and turned her head and looked straight at him. 'Throw away convention, Mr Dexter, and simply tell me what you have to say.'

His lips twitched. 'Ah, youth—to be so impatient again.' Sighing, he gripped the rail with both hands and looked into the distance. 'I will say this, though you will not like my words.' He took a deep breath. 'I know who you are. I recognise you—Miss Golding.'

Inwardly she groaned, but she did not lose all hope, for perhaps she could brazen it out. Oh, what a clumsy fool she had been to drop the scalding coffee into Tobias's lap.

'So, the cat is out.'

He chuckled softly. 'It's obvious to any who has two eyes and a wit in his head. I cannot overlook it. I know that you are a young lady masquerading as a youth. Your reasons are your concern. I have no wish to know. Suffice it to say that is your business, not mine.'

'You will not tell Mr Searle, will you?' She looked beseechingly into his face.

He lifted his hat and scratched his head. 'As captain of this vessel, it is my duty. I cannot keep a matter as serious as this from him—nor would I anything else that happens on board his ship.'

'Please—do not. I beg of you—at least, not yet—not until it's too late for him to put me ashore.'

'Do you fear him?'

'No, only what he might do. I have my reasons for the disguise. Good reasons. Please, do not tell him. Besides, what can it avail you to uncover me?'

All Mark saw was a youthful girl. Much against his will he felt his heart warm to the pleas of the plaintive girl. She was right. Tobias would not tolerate her aboard his ship and while they were still in sight of land there was every possibility he would put her ashore.

'Very well—although I'm a fool to agree. Your secret will remain safe with me, for the time being, but it will not be long before Tobias sees for himself—and then all hell will break loose.'

'Thank you. You will have no occasion to regret your decision.'

'I hope not. Should he discover I have been party to your deception, you will not be the only one he puts ashore. But as soon as we lose sight of land your deception cannot continue. If you do not tell him, I shall—unless he opens his eyes and sees for himself.'

One of the galley boys, who gave her the name Boy, showed Rowena her duties. He also painted a picture of their master that shocked her to the core. Apparently Tobias Searle was a terrible rake, a womaniser, and behind that handsome man there was a trail of young women's broken hearts and shattered aspirations that would make any respectable female shudder. She remembered how he had kissed her and flushed with outraged shame. She was terribly attracted to him, this she could not deny, but she was determined to keep tight rein on her heart. He was the last man in the entire world she wanted to show any interest in her.

Tobias spent most of his time on deck, and when he came to his cabin he was always in the company of Mr Dexter or another senior member of the crew and took little notice of his cabin boy. She was relieved enough to be left to her thoughts, her mind ranging free while her body dealt with the daily round of duties. She was anxious about Jane—wondering how her father had reacted when he had read her note—and Lord Tregowan. Dear Lord, let him understand why she had done this and not withdraw his offer of marriage.

And then there was Tobias! She had promised him one night if he found Jane. One night! Those two simple words held a whole world of meaning. His reputation as an arch seducer of women made her feel uncomfortable—and slightly jealous, which both surprised and annoyed her, and served as a reminder never to lose her heart to him.

Chapter Four

When the ship entered the turbulent waters of the Bay of Biscay a huge gale descended and the high seas turned into a fury. With the stomach-churning pitch and roll of the vessel, the world around Rowena was swaying and undulating and she had to hold on to whatever was at hand to remain upright. Her stomach lurched.

Staggering to her bunk, stretched out and suffering tortures every time the ship rolled, she lay feebly cursing as she battled nausea, living in the hideous nightmare of seasickness.

Returning to his cabin and hearing a feeble sound as he passed his cabin-boy's door, Tobias stepped through it and found the wretched boy collapsed on his bunk, tossing fretfully.

'Good Lord, boy. How long have you been like this?'

'It came over me all of a sudden,' Rowena mumbled wretchedly into the pillow, convinced she was going to die.

Tobias lit the lamp, which cast a dim orange glow around the small cabin. Reaching out, he grasped her shoulder and turned her over. Her face was still facing to the wall. Cupping her chin with his hand, he turned her towards him. He could only stare in amazement.

'By God! Rowena! What the hell... I should have known.'

The pressure of his touch was light, but to Rowena it felt like a steel trap. She opened her eyes and a face swam into view, seeming to descend from the wooden boards above her head.

'Go away,' she grumbled wretchedly, afraid to move her head, for movement of any kind only made her nausea worse.

'You'd better explain what you're doing on my ship when I strictly told you I would not allow it. How dare you disobey me? Explain, Rowena,' he demanded harshly.

Rowena actually made herself smile at him, though it was a sarcastic smile. 'If you knew me, you would know better than to command me to do anything—and that includes giving you an explanation for my own business. You know why I am here, so go away and leave me alone.'

Seeing her wretchedness and how she was trying to hold on to her defiance, to brave the sea and his wrath in her desperation to find her sister, touched a hidden spot in Tobias and his manner softened. In the dim light his eyes shone gently as he gazed down at her. The features were unmistakably Rowena's. Her face was drawn and there were dark shadows beneath her eyes—but what in

God's name had she done to her hair? Had she been so desperate to get aboard his ship in the guise of his cabin boy that she'd had to resort to cutting her hair?

'Your hair!' he exclaimed, horrified. 'Damnation, Rowena, who cut your hair?'

'Me,' she gasped. 'It certainly wasn't for the hell of it. Now go away,' she hissed, shoving his hand away. 'Go away and leave me alone. I feel so ill I think I'm going to die.'

'No, you won't.'

'Yes, I will. I will never be well again. Not ever. I will never recover.'

'Yes, you will—although I did tell you you weren't cut out for life on the ocean wave. You aren't the first to suffer seasickness. You'll soon get your sea legs,' he said, gentling his voice to what he hoped was a soothing tone.

She looked up at him narrowly, finding it particularly disgusting that having spent a large part of his life at sea—as had the majority of the men on the ship—Tobias Searle could stand up to any weather. 'No, I won't. I suppose you're going to berate me some more now you know who I am.'

'I'll have plenty to say to you later. When I do, I want you to be in full possession of your wits.'

'It came over me all of a sudden—when I went to the galley to fetch your meal. It must have been the smell of the meat…oh…'

The mere mention of cooking meat was enough to bring on another spasm. Tobias thrust a basin at her and held her head while she vomited. Then, exhausted, she fell back on to the bunk. Her body was trembling and she was breathing quickly.

Seeing how damp her shirt was, Tobias pulled it out of her trousers and began to raise it. In alarm she shoved his hands away.

'Don't touch me. Do you mean to torture me some more?'

'You are ill and unable to look after yourself,' he said in a no-nonsense voice. 'Since there is no other woman on board ship, there is only me, so you will have to make the best of it.'

When his hands paused in their unbuttoning of her shirt, she peered up at him, wiping the hair from her eyes. With sudden realisation of where his eyes roamed, she glowered at him. He was looking at the binding wrapped about her chest to flatten her breasts. There was a strange, disbelieving look on his face.

'Is this part of your disguise, Rowena—binding yourself tightly to conceal your sex?'

She coloured hotly, and, too ill to get up, turned away in sudden confusion.

'Such severe restriction cannot help your cause. I think you will fare better without these bindings.'

His deep voice seemed to reverberate within Rowena's very soul as his fingers began to pull at the offending cloth. She made a feeble attempt to shove them away but he would have none of it. He laughed softly, adding to her unease.

'You're in no condition to fight me, so be still.'

In that moment Rowena's thoughts were far from the

predicament she had got herself into and more on the tempest raging within herself. A sudden explosion of doubt blasted her confidence as her soft breasts were exposed to his bold eyes, and she was suddenly unsure of her own ability to deal with Tobias Searle.

Casting the binding aside, pulling down her shirt and straightening up, Tobias cursed when he banged his head on a low beam; looking around the cabin, he realised it was little more than a cupboard. Without more ado he picked her up and carried her to his own more spacious cabin and laid her on the bed. She moaned in her misery and again retched into the bowl he held beneath her chin, before falling on to the pillows, exhausted, to await the next bout of nausea.

Tobias wiped her face with a cool, damp cloth, and soothed her as best he could. She started to vomit and tried to sit up.

'Lie back and close your eyes,' a soothing voice said.

'Yes—yes, I will.' Her eyelids felt like lead weights as they fluttered closed and she collapsed on to the pillows, already half-unconscious. Cursing her own helplessness and the sickness that left her wholly dependent on Tobias, she sank into a dark void that was tugging at her and pulling her down. As weak and helpless as a kitten, she submitted herself to his ministrations.

Each time she vomited it weakened her some more. Each time the ship rushed up a particularly huge wave she held her breath, then as it plunged into a seemingly bottomless trough she felt as though she were leaving her insides behind. Her groans were smothered by the noise of the storm. The wind screamed through the rigging and the timbers creaked.

All at once she gave a convulsive shudder and suddenly the cabin seemed cold and she began to shiver, and when she did someone covered her with a warm blanket and she became warm.

Throughout the night Tobias sat in the chair beside the bed, watching her. He tended her as he would a child—holding the bowl while she wretched, sponging her face with a cool, damp cloth and doing what he could to take care of her—much to Mark Dexter's amusement and his own chagrin, who said he had always known his talents were many, but he had never taken him for a nursemaid.

'You know who she is,' Tobias argued. 'What the hell am I supposed to do? Hand her over to a member of the crew to look after her? Good Lord, man, they'd ravish her as soon as look at her.' He narrowed his eyes at his captain. 'Of course there is yourself, Mark. I know you can be quite a charmer when you have a mind, and that you are a dab hand when it comes to dealing with the female sex.'

In laughing good humour, Mark put his hands up, palms outwards, and backed away. 'Oh, no. This is your problem, Tobias. You can look after your own cabin boy, while I look after your ship. Although it may raise a few eyebrows among the crew when they find their master is neglecting his ship to nurse his cabin boy. I told you when we left Falmouth that you were risking it, sailing without a ship's surgeon.'

'And I recall telling you that there was no time to find a replacement for the one who left.'

'Then you will have to do your best. Don't worry, Tobias. I'll make sure you don't starve. I'll have one of the galley lads bring you your meals.'

And so Tobias continued to nurse Rowena. His heart went out to her in her misery.

On the second night she lay quite still. Her muscles were perfectly relaxed and she had no consciousness of him or her surroundings. Tobias wasn't unduly worried—having seen people struck down with seasickness many times, he knew Rowena was over the worst of it and when she woke the nausea would have left her.

Bright sunlight was shining through the small window when Rowena opened her eyes. The first thing she became aware of was that the ship was no longer pitching and tossing. She wasn't surprised to see Tobias seated in a chair beside the bed, fast asleep. He seemed to have been with her constantly since she'd become ill, and there were times when she had been floating on the edge of darkness when she had heard his voice—deep, confident and incredibly soothing. Her mind could not grasp the image of the Tobias Searle she knew doing all the amazing things for her he had. It was just too incredible for words.

Some time in the night he'd removed his coat and neck linen. His face was towards her, and she cautiously turned her head further round on the pillow so she could see him better, breathing a sigh of relief when the slight movement didn't set her stomach churning and unleash the dizziness that had so beset her from the start.

With nothing to hear but the creaking of the ship's timbers and the gentle splash of the sea against the hull, in a peaceful doze she studied the man who had given up so much of his time to look after her, sleeping in that dreadfully uncomfortable position. There was something endearingly boyish about the way his swarthy, handsome face was relaxed in sleep, his spiky lashes resting against his cheeks and with the shadowy beginning of a dark beard. There was nothing boyish about the rest of him, however, which stirred a mixture of fascination and unease within her. The slash of his dark brows were drawn together in a scowl that boded ill for someone, even in his dreams.

The fine white linen of his shirt hung loosely over powerful shoulders and the sleeves were rolled back to reveal his tanned forearms. Buff-coloured knee breeches encased his muscular thighs and he wore white silk stockings above black buckled shoes. Her gaze wandered back to his face and rested on his chiselled jaw—stern and uncompromising, she decided—and he was handsome.

Yes, he was handsome, the most handsome man she had ever seen.

She turned her face to the light, and when she turned it back again his eyes were open and he was calmly watching her. He smiled when he met her gaze.

'Good morning, Rowena. Welcome back. How do you feel?'

'Apart from a slight headache I feel much better,' she admitted, returning his smile. 'But I am so thirsty.'

'I know,' he said, reaching over and passing her a cup to drink some cold water.

Feeling better, she rested back on the pillows. 'I realise what a nuisance I must have been, that I have put you to a lot of trouble, but I'll be all right now—better than I look, I think, but that doesn't concern me unduly.'

Her voice was soft and yet her expression was open and direct, and Tobias wondered that she showed no feminine concern about her appearance as other females would have done and calmly accepted that she did not look her best. Most of the women he knew were obsessed with their appearance and to cut off their hair would be tantamount to a death sentence. But Rowena Golding, whose hair was her crowning glory, had thought nothing of cutting it off, simply because it was in the way of things.

This came as no surprise to Tobias, for he was already aware that pretence and pretensions were completely alien to Rowena, and that made her refreshingly unique.

He smiled and said on a light note, 'After all you have been through, you look refreshingly lovely, Rowena. After you've washed and had something to eat— because eat you must to regain your strength—you will start to feel more human. I have no female clothes on board, so you will have to make do with those you brought with you.'

'My trousers are very practical.'

'And your hair?'

'That too. It saves me the bother of fussing with brushes and combs and the like. Male attire is much more sensible. I realise my sickness must have presented you with problems and questions being asked. Does—everyone know about me—about me being a woman, I mean?'

He shook his head, getting up and rotating his shoulders to ease out the kinks in them. 'No.'

'Apart from Mr Dexter. There was no fooling him. I was afraid you would see through my disguise at once.'

'I didn't look.'

Her lips twitched in a smile. 'No, you didn't. Not even when I scalded you with the coffee.'

'I was in too much pain.'

'I'm sorry. You would make an excellent nurse and lady's maid, by the way. You are much better at it than I am at being a cabin boy.'

'As a new cabin boy, you must be broken in gently.'

'Will you tell everyone—that I'm a woman?'

'No. It is important that you continue with the deception. I would prefer the crew to go on thinking you are a youth for the time being.' He frowned at her, his expression suddenly sombre. 'Have you any idea of the seriousness of your escapade? Every man aboard this ship knows what happened in Kingston harbour—some of them were aboard the vessel when it went up in flames—and lost comrades with families back home. They know who was responsible. Mason may have lit the torch, but they believe Matthew Golding to have been behind it.'

'But he wasn't. He is incapable of such wanton cruelty.'

'Maybe not, but if the crew should discover we are carrying a member of Golding's family on board, then being a woman will not save you. They would as soon toss you into the sea as have you on board.'

'Then I promise to make myself as inconspicuous as possible and give them no reason to think of me as anything other than I appear to be.'

'I hope not. I run an orderly ship and the men who sail on her are the cream of their profession, hard-bitten and courageous, but men will be men. Attired as a woman, you would test them to the brink and I doubt they would hold themselves in check. There will be the devil of a commotion if they should tumble to the fact that my cabin boy is in fact a woman.'

'So what am I to do?'

With laughter twinkling in his eyes, he said, 'When you are well enough you will resume your duties as cabin boy. You will be called Rowan, I think.' He chuckled low, his eyes narrowing when he considered just how pleasurable this might turn out to be. 'I like having you at my beck and call, Rowena.'

When she raised her eyebrows in questioning surprise, he smiled, a smile that told her he would chastise her in his own way for having the audacity to deceive him. 'I sincerely hope you have no objections to this,' he murmured smoothly. 'You boarded my ship with the intention of being my cabin boy, and cabin boy you will be, performing all the duties of a cabin boy, until the time I decide to relieve you of those duties. Is that understood?'

'So, you intend to punish me,' Rowena said, not in the least put out, for she really could not blame him for his firm stance.

'Don't doubt it for a minute.'

'Now you know who I am you can't make me be your cabin boy.'

'Oh, yes, I can. As master of this ship I could have you clapped in irons for insubordination.'

Her gasp was one of mock horror. 'You wouldn't.'

His eyes narrowed on her. 'Try me. While you are on board my ship you will have to behave—to obey my every command.' He paused, considering. 'I shall be an extremely hard taskmaster and afford you no special favours. You do not look too bad in your get-up, but you will not be comfortably accepted by the crew if they know you are a female in disguise.' He grinned wickedly. 'If you do not improve as my cabin boy, there may be times when you have to share their quarters.'

'I sincerely hope not,' Rowena gasped again. 'I can't think of anything worse.'

He laughed softly. 'I'll go and get you something to eat.'

'Some bacon would be nice,' she suggested, surprised to find that she felt hungry, ravenously so.

'Your wish is my command, my lady,' Tobias said with a mocking inclination of his dark head. 'We might even stretch to an egg—or even two if cook's in a good mood. But don't get too comfortable in my bed, Rowena, otherwise I may find other duties for my cabin boy to perform to keep me happy.'

His implication, spoken softly and with more

meaning behind the words that she cared for, hit Rowena and she inhaled sharply. Taking hold of a pillow she hurled it across the cabin at him. 'You can dream if you wish, Mr Searle, but that is all you will do.' Laughing softly, he caught the pillow and threw it back, hitting his target on the head, before he turned to the door. Rowena stretched her arms above her head, smiling to herself because she no longer felt seasick. 'Thank you,' she said quietly to his back. He turned and looked at her.

'For what?'

Those candid eyes locked on his. 'For looking after me and staying with me all night.'

Tobias was touched by her gratitude. Inclining his head in the mockery of a bow, he gave her a bold, wicked grin. 'That is the first time I've been thanked by a beautiful woman for spending the night with her. The next time, Rowena, I will make sure it's more pleasurable,' he said quietly, gently reminding her of their bargain.

As Tobias headed to the galley, he felt elated for the first time in days. Rowena was on the way to recovery. Strangely, her transparent machinations didn't surprise or upset him. He couldn't help it. The girl amused him, intrigued him, even though he knew he was letting himself in for a whole heap of trouble by becoming party to her subterfuge.

With all sails set the ship buffeted its way south, the grey white-capped sea suffused with a deep blue. The horizon was clearly visible and there were no ships to either the larboard or starboard sides. Rowena leaned against the rail, inhaling deeply. A fair, warm wind was blowing and the *Cymbeline* was an eager, happy ship.

Feeling much better now she had got over her sickness and acquired her sea legs, she settled down to the shipboard routine, relieved that no undue attention was directed at her, for everyone became used to Rowan the cabin boy in his floppy hat and shapeless garb going about his duties. Her days were regulated by the watch bell. When it sounded, seamen exchanged places. Those who had done their watch went to their hammocks. Others were posted fore and aft, while the young apprentices on the morning watch scrubbed the decks.

The seamen were kept hard at it. As they climbed the rigging their sea shanties rang out, and when darkness fell and they drank their rations of rum, the ship's fiddler scraped away vigorously at a jaunty tune, to which several sailors danced whilst others played dice or sat about telling tales.

Rowena's duties were confined to Mr Searle—mopping and polishing and seeing to the general tidiness of his cabin and making sure his meals were brought on time. It was with some amusement that Tobias would watch her perform her duties, and on several occasions she was sorely tempted to wipe the mocking grin from his lips with her wet mop.

The sun was high and the noon hour was near, the heat of the day having increased. It was almost three weeks since they had left Falmouth; having finished her chores, Rowena perched on a stool at the window in Tobias's cabin, looking out at the vast sea, calm as the *Cymbeline* sailed down the Portuguese coast, getting ever closer to North Africa. One knee was raised and she hugged it to her chest. She had removed her sandals and her feet were bare, as were her shapely calves exposed beneath her short cropped trews.

Tobias was seated in a high-backed leather chair, facing her, content to sit and look. Lazily she stretched her back like a sleek, contented feline, and put her foot to the floor. Reaching behind her, she massaged her waist, letting it sooth her aches and pains.

'So, Rowena,' he murmured at length, 'your disguise seems to be holding out.'

She turned her head and looked at him. 'It's not as difficult as I thought it would be to pass myself off as a youth. Although I take care not to converse too much with the crew in case they begin to suspect I'm not what I seem. As a result they probably think I'm quite brainless.'

Tobias grinned. 'They're easily fooled—unlike you, for I imagine you're not fooled by anyone.'

There was a teasing, secret light in his eyes, which made Rowena think he was laughing at some inner joke at her expense.

'I hope not, and I hope that's a compliment to my good sense.'

'Of course. I do not mistake you for being brainless. Far from it. In fact, I find you to be a proud young woman of remarkable intelligence.'

'Why, that's compliment indeed, coming from you.'

'That was not a compliment,' Tobias corrected.

Rowena shot him a disgruntled look. 'No?'

'No. Were you a woman of ordinary intelligence, you would not be on this ship with me and all the possible consequences of being so. You'd be at home concerning yourself with your forthcoming marriage and thinking about matters of interest to a woman—running a house, children, fashion—instead of torturing yourself about your sister.'

Rowena stared at him with angry disbelief. 'Jane's disappearance is paramount to everything else. It is a situation I cannot—will not—accept. It's all well and good for you to sit there looking all smug and self-important and recommend that I should be at home concerning myself with matters that have never interested me, such as children and keeping house, you can keep such advice for your own wife—'

'Rowena,' Tobias interrupted, biting back a smile, thinking she looked so damned lovely perched on the stool by the window, with her liquid bright eyes and soft, desirable mouth, 'I do not have a wife.'

'You may not have a wife now,' she argued, 'but you will, one day.'

'Yes, I will. I cannot argue with that.'

'Where do the Barbary corsairs land their captives? Where do you think they have taken Jane?'

'It could be to any of a dozen or more places.'

'As long as it's not Sale,' she murmured, more to herself than to Tobias.

'And what do you know about that?'

'One of the apprentices was telling me that Sale is the worst place of all where captives are taken, where slaves are shackled with chains so heavy they can hardly walk, and put in filthy underground pens where they remain until they are sold.'

'I told you your sister could have been taken anywhere,' Tobias said gently in an attempt to alleviate her worry. 'And I have already told you that women captives are treated differently from the men. We'll go to Algiers and I'll make enquiries.'

'Have you been there before?'

'Several times. I trade there with cargoes of timber, which the Algerians need to build their ships.'

Rowena's expression was one of scorn. 'Ships that prey on our own. It is difficult to agree with what you do. Do you consider that a noble occupation, Tobias?'

He shrugged. 'It's a vicious circle. If I don't supply the timber, then some other trader will, and the Arsenal at Algiers is always short of timber. Besides, trading with the Algerians offers some degree of safety to my ships in whichever country they ply their trade. My pennant is well known and attacks on them by the corsairs are rare.'

'Then I suppose we must be thankful for that. Anything that could obstruct our progress would be a hindrance.'

'I agree. The *Cymbeline* is a sailing vessel built for speed, not a merchantman. In these waters we often encounters corsairs, but when the ship's lines are recognised—its long menacing hull, its broadside of cannon and its long platform of fighting men, so not a vessel filled with merchandise—we are left unmolested.'

'Then, taking this into account, we will get to North Africa sooner. I only hope that if we find Jane we can obtain her release.'

'If we find her, there is always the possibility of a ransom. The Algerians demand high ransoms and when an envoy arrives from England to negotiate their release on behalf of their families, he often has insufficient funds to meet their demands. You must understand that the Algerians love to barter. Fresh negotiations take place until an agreement is reached and the captive is freed.

'Sometimes if the captive is important in his own country or holds a title, the ransom money can be enormous and may take several years to raise. The families of these people will advance what they can in a down payment, which will be followed by annual payments until the full amount has been paid.'

'And what happens to the captive while all this is going on?'

'He will be confined, but treated well—until the payments dry up. Then his imprisonment will worsen— although it is in the gaoler's interest that his prisoner is kept alive. This is when the captive is encouraged to write to his family informing them of his sufferings, and the payments begin again.'

'What a dreadful, cruel business slavery is. I'm ashamed to say I have given little thought to the capture of my fellow countrymen until now.'

'Slavery, in many guises, flourishes all around the

Mediterranean, with places in the Muslim world where unfortunate Christian captives are either set to work or held for ransom. Yet there are thriving slave markets in Malta and Livorno where Muslims are bought and sold— the Knights of St John being at the forefront of the trade in much the same way as the corsairs provide white Christian merchandise for the markets in North Africa.'

'And is there no condemnation of this hideous trade from the rest of the world?'

Tobias shook his head. 'The turbulence of politics in the Mediterranean encourages the state of affairs to continue.'

'Rather like the cross versus the crescent,' Rowena murmured with a hint of irony.

'Exactly. And among such disarray the Barbary corsairs thrive.'

Deflated, Rowena looked at him. 'You spoke of male captives, but what about the women? What do you think a woman as young as Jane will be worth?'

'I recall your sister as being fair. Blondes with pale skins bring high prices in the slave marts of Algiers. The Muslims treat their women with respect, so you need have no fear for her safety. As I have just explained, for those who come from wealthy families, their demands for large sums for their release are great. Generally it is the same for both men and women.'

'And what will happen to Jane if the ransom is not paid?'

'She will remain a prisoner.'

'And—what else?'

'A servant in her owner's house—or...'

'What?' He looked at her. 'Tell me.'

'It is likely that she will become her master's concubine.'

'Concubine? You mean—like a paramour?'

'Yes, something like that.'

Tears filled Rowena's eyes and she turned away so he would not see them. 'My poor sister,' she whispered. 'How frightened she must be. She is not strong and she might even die from this. More than ever, I have to find her.' When she looked again at Tobias, her eyes were large and pleading. Slipping off her seat, she went and knelt on the floor before him, placing her hand on his knee, unaware as she did so how the lean, hard muscles of his thighs flexed beneath the tight-fitting breeches at her touch.

'Will you pay her ransom fee if we find her? Please, Tobias. You said I was proud, and I say, yes, I am proud—proud and difficult and reckless and the most wilful female you could ever meet. But if you will do this I will do anything you ask of me—even to humbling myself to any task you give me to do. I'll mop your cabin as often as you wish, polish the woodwork until my fingers bleed, and wait on you like the humblest of servants. I swear that I will repay you a thousandfold.'

Tobias glanced at her lovely face framed by her short cropped hair. She was in earnest, and all the more desirable in her vulnerability. He could feel the heat seeping into him from the small, yet long-fingered hand resting on his knee. Desire was already tightening his loins—and she only had her hand on his knee. He didn't understand why she had such a volatile effect on him, but he understood that he wanted her. He wanted her warm and willing in his arms, and for that he would give her the earth if he possibly could.

With her huge, fear-widened eyes riveted on his face, Rowena saw indecision flicker across his hard features. 'Please,' she whispered, mistaking his silence for refusal. 'You know I cannot possibly afford to pay the ransom, Tobias.' She looked at him pleadingly. 'Will you loan me the money?'

He finally spoke and Rowena tensed with hope. 'Is there to be no end to your demands, Rowena?'

'I have no one else I can ask.'

'What of your husband-to-be? He is rich.'

'Yes, but he isn't here and you are. So, will you loan me the money if a ransom becomes necessary?'

He looked at her through narrowed eyes, and she was too overwrought to notice the odd, meaningful note in his voice as he said, 'It will cost you. That will be two nights you owe me, Miss Golding, instead of the one.'

She swallowed hard. 'I thought you might say something like that,' she retorted, turning a heated glower on him and snatching her hand from his knee. The fact that she was betrothed to another man meant nothing to him. In willingly surrendering her honour to him—not once, but twice—she would become a whore, a disgrace to herself, her family and her future husband, and no matter how she told herself she despised him, she knew it was possible for an arch player like Tobias to break her heart.

'Do we have a bargain, Rowena?'

She lifted her small chin, looking like a proud young queen who'd just been betrayed by someone she trusted. Although her resentment remained, she had to fight against falling under the spell of his deep voice and those compelling blue eyes.

'You know, you really can be quite obnoxious.'

Tobias smiled lazily. 'I know. But I am still rich, and you still need me.'

'I wish I didn't.'

The smile did not waver. 'I know. I will ask you again. Do we have a bargain?'

Rowena hesitated an endless moment, knowing she had no alternative, before nodding imperceptibly.

His smile was one of immense satisfaction. 'If you're worried that I mean to extract payment on our bargain immediately, then you may put your mind at ease. It is my aim to secure Jane's release first, and besides, I have duties enough to occupy me for the present.'

'Such as tracking down Jack Mason.'

'Exactly.'

He averted his gaze, and for a space he stared beyond the delightful young woman at his feet, through the window at the sparkling blue-green sea, deep in his own thoughts. All his life he had believed he was a man who could get what he wanted if he tried hard enough. He was a man who was sure of himself and his own abilities, strong in himself and in his position, and yet weakened by what Mason had done to him and those he employed, and he could not tolerate his own inability to make him pay.

Hoisting himself out of his chair, he stretched and donned his jacket to go on deck. 'One thing has been puzzling me since I became aware of your deception, Rowena. What happened to my cabin boy?'

'I sent him with a letter to Tregowan Hall, asking Lord Tregowan to find him work.'

'And what did you tell your father?'

'I didn't. I left him a note. When will we reach Algiers?'

'If the winds are favourable, about three days. We will put in for water south of Lisbon before we pass through the Straits of Gibraltar. It's the corsairs' hunting ground and the most dangerous part of any voyage, where they target vulnerable merchant vessels passing through. Hopefully we'll sail through unhindered.'

Chapter Five

A panorama of rich green vegetation rose to tree-covered hills that stood out sharply against a sky of cloudless blue. Unable to resist the white surf creaming on the golden sand, as several members of the crew carrying empty casks left the ship, which was anchored close in shore, Rowena turned to Mark Dexter.

'How long do you intend being here?'

'Three hours or little more. Why? Would you like to go ashore?'

'If I may—for a while.'

'Then don't stray too far.'

With bare feet and wearing her floppy hat, Rowena was soon clambering down the rope ladder hung over the ship's side and walking along the seemingly deserted palm-fringed beach. Strolling round a headland, she found herself in a small cove. Looking back, she found that she could no longer see the ship. Unconcerned, she looked at the sea lapping at the shore, prisms of light dancing on the surface. The sun was hot and she longed to wade into the crystal-clear water.

She sauntered unhurriedly down the sandy slope to the water's edge, where tiny crabs scuttled away. Confident that she was quite alone and with the sea exercising a magnetic pull, to allow herself more freedom she removed her bindings, taking the first deep breath since applying them earlier.

Wading into the shallows, she found the water was warm and welcoming. She plunged forward in a gentle arc, immersing her entire body, the gentle swell billowing out her loose shirt. It was an exhilarating feeling as the blessed coolness enveloped her, caressing her skin like silk, and as she swam beneath the surface her body seemed to liquefy. It was wonderful. When she remembered swimming in the Cornish waters, even in the middle of summer, it had been much colder than this.

Breaking the surface, she set out to swim across the small bay, her arms and legs falling into the remembered rhythm, and she moved effortlessly through the water, pausing now and then to float on her back, rising and falling with the gentle swell, her face turned up to the sun, her eyes half-closed.

It was during one of these periods of respite that she became aware of a soft, regular splashing close by of someone swimming. She reared up out of the water just in time to see someone swimming fast and powerfully towards her, cutting the water in a clean, graceful line before diving beneath the water and disappearing from sight. Realising the foolishness of swimming alone like this in a place totally unknown to her, in sudden panic she trod water, looking around frantically for the swimmer to surface—but where?

To her horror a hard arm threaded around her waist, jerking her back against a hard chest. She opened her mouth to scream, her voice dying in a gurgle as she was pulled down and she swallowed a mouthful of sea water. Mercifully her assailant lifted her up and she heard him laugh.

As first she was amazed, outraged and furious. 'Tobias Searle!' she gasped, indignant. 'I would have thought you'd have more to do aboard your ship than to follow me. How long have you been watching me?'

A slow appreciative smile touched his lips. 'Long enough.'

'Long enough for what?'

His smouldering gaze passed over her face. 'Long enough to realise you swim like a fish.' His arm still holding her waist; time was suspended as, trying to ignore her mixed emotions, Rowena stared at him. A lazy, devastating grin swept across his tanned face. 'I was curious to see what my cabin boy was up to. You seemed to be enjoying yourself so much I thought I would join you. You really do swim very well—not at all bad for a cabin boy.'

'I live in Cornwall, by the sea,' she replied, glad she hadn't removed her shirt and trews when she'd decided to take a swim, for she had been sorely tempted to feel the cool water caress her flesh without the hindrance of clothes. 'There's no shortage of water in which to swim.'

'I know of no other woman who would want to. I came to find you to make sure you were all right.'

'I suppose I should be grateful—but, as you see I am not properly dressed to receive you.'

'You could be dressed in sackcloth and ashes for all I care. I assure you, Rowena, that shirt and those trousers are most provocative at all times.'

Rowena thought that after almost three weeks on board ship with just his crew for company, any woman would probably appeal to him. 'The last thing I want to do is look nice for you.'

She was unaware that the dark brown hair, soaked and clinging to her head, was many different shades and dazzling lights, as her eyes flared into life. Tobias's expression was unreadable, smiling, watchful, a knowing look in his eyes. *What kind of man are you, Tobias Searle?* she wondered, and realised she had no idea at all. She gave him a speculative look, deeply conscious that his easy, mocking exterior hid the inner man.

Brought abruptly from her ponderous thoughts, she let out a startled shriek as his hands again jerked her down beneath the surface, gasping for air. 'That,' she cried with laughing severity when she resurfaced as Tobias raked his wet hair back and grinned at her, 'was a very silly and childish thing to do. Almost as childish as this,' she said, sliding her hand over the surface of the water and sending a spray of water into his face before ducking for cover under the water to avoid reprisal and swimming round him.

There followed a laughing, carefree ducking,

swimming and racing session that left Rowena breathless and exhausted. Swimming to the shore with Tobias close behind, she padded up the beach before flopping down on to her back, her chest heaving from her exertions.

'You play too rough,' she reprimanded good naturedly.

Hands on hips, Tobias stood looking down at her, dripping water, and quietly, he said, 'I would be as gentle as you wish me to be, Rowena.'

Rowena melted inside at the meaning she read in his words and his eyes, when she half-opened her own and squinted up at him. Through the veil of her eyelashes she could see the rugged planes of his face. The breath froze in her throat. His only article of clothing was his white sodden breeches, rolled up over his muscular calves. He was well over six feet of splendid masculinity, firm muscled and broad shouldered and narrow hipped. His chest was covered with a furring of black hair that narrowed as it reached his flat abdomen and dipped below the waistband of his breeches.

Disconcerted and embarrassed by the way the sight of his bronzed, shining wet body was affecting her, she closed her eyes. From the moment he had taken charge of her in her seasickness, a subtle change of power had taken place. Until then she had been confident and in control of their relationship. Now, she felt confused and extremely vulnerable.

He sat down beside her, bending his knee on which he rested his arm. 'Your clothes are wet,' he remarked, a slow grin spreading across his lips. He seemed casually unconcerned with his state of undress.

'They usually are when one's been swimming,' she replied, her tone lightly sarcastic. 'It doesn't matter. They'll soon dry in this heat, and I can change when I get back to the ship.' She sighed contentedly. 'It's a beautiful day, don't you agree?'

He gazed at her for a moment, excruciatingly aware of the luscious shape concealed beneath her loose shirt and trews. Her calves and ankles above her well-shaped feet gleamed pale in the sand. His wide, sensual mouth turned upward in the faintest of cynical smiles. 'It's still too early to tell.'

As his gaze swept down the length of her and back again, Rowena abruptly realised how very alone they were. 'Don't you have things to do while the ship is at anchor?'

'Such as?'

'Oh, I don't know—counting water barrels—making sure you don't leave any of the crew behind.'

'I have others to do that. I'd much rather be here with you.'

She glowered up at him. 'Trying to seduce me, you mean.'

He trailed his fingers lightly down her bare lower arm. Her face, young, vulnerable and defenceless and already turning a lovely golden colour, was naked beneath the heavy crop of her hair.

'What do you think I am doing right now?' he murmured, sliding his fingers under the loose wet sleeve of her shirt.

Rowena gasped and wrenched backward. 'I shudder to think. Stop that!' She snatched her arm away.

Frustration crossed Tobias's face for just a moment, as though he'd forgotten he was teasing. If he had been teasing. 'One day very soon, Rowena,' he murmured in a low drawl, 'you will not draw away from me. You'll beg me to continue.'

'I assume you are referring to our bargain. If you must know, I get little sleep just thinking about it,' she said in a vein of honesty, fretting over it. 'But if you don't mind, for the time being I will enjoy what is left of my pride.'

Tobias's eyes gleamed with devilish humour, and his lips drew into a slow smile. 'Very sensible, my love.'

Rowena lifted her chin. 'I am not your love. You are a scoundrel, Tobias Searle, and I am certain I am just one in a long line of women.'

'That I cannot deny. But had you been the first, you might well have been the last.' His eyes had become serious and seemed to probe her being.

Confused by the gentle warmth of his gaze and the directness of his words, Rowena could not determine whether he mocked her or told the truth. She had never known a man with such persistence and single-minded-ness.

'And you have a silken tongue. No doubt you found the tavern girls accommodating in Falmouth during your stay. I believe a pretty young girl called Molly who works at the White Hart is rather free with her favours.'

'I know the wench you speak of. She often sat at my table—even invited me to her room,' he told her casually.

Rowena turned her head and looked at him in

shocked disbelief, unable to quell the sudden rush of jealousy. 'She did? And you went? Just like that?'

Tobias frowned and considered her question before answering. 'No. She recognised I had coin in my purse and might be—generous.'

'Do tell. I'm curious.'

Leaning over her, Tobias shook his head and laughed. He was too much of a gentleman to admit that willing bed partners had always been available to him, but that he preferred discreet, exclusive liaisons with sophisticated women. He looked into her expectant gaze. 'Suffice to say I am not one to dally with tavern wenches. There were many appealing young women in Falmouth who were prepared to be more than accommodating. But not one of them appealed to me.'

Rowena conjured a scowl, which wasn't very difficult considering that she was torn between getting up and running away and demanding to know what he would do next. 'Do you always get what you want?'

'Usually,' he answered. 'Perhaps because I am arrogant or inconsiderate—or selfish.'

'Or all three,' she was quick to bite back, careful to avoid looking at his naked chest.

'Am I bothering you, Rowena?' he asked softly.

'You know you are. Suddenly I feel less like your cabin boy and more like a tasty morsel you are about to devour,' she murmured lethargically before she could stop herself.

He gave a satisfied chuckle. 'A very delectable morsel, Rowena. You should not have come here alone.'

'Am I allowed no freedom? I told Mr Dexter I was going to take a stroll. He didn't object.'

'Which was why he told me.'

'The place is deserted.'

'It might seem that way, but it is not always the case. This place is part of the mainland and not uninhabited. Your presence might attract a group of locals—and very possibly a herd of goats. Mine is not the only ship to put in hereabouts. Stray too far and you might have more company than you wish for.'

Sitting up, she tossed back her gleaming hair with a flick of her head. 'I have. You.'

He rose to his feet and stepped back apace, staring down at her. Her soaked shirt clung to her body, outlining the shapely peaks of her breasts that were high and firm, fuller than her wraith-like slenderness indicated.

Seeing where his gaze was directed, Rowena quelled the instinctive urge to draw her arms across her chest. She felt indecently exposed without the bindings and could feel her nipples tightening.

'Please don't look at me like that.'

'It's hard not to, when you're wearing so little. Might I suggest that before you return to the ship you bind yourself, otherwise my crew will see you for what you are and your life on board won't be worth living.'

Tobias could feel himself responding to her closeness. Maybe it was an indefinable impression, an illusion, a trick of the sun's bright light reflecting off the water, but she seemed changed somehow. What was it? What was in her eyes, and what was in the soft turn of her lips as though she smiled at some private thought? Her soft young face was turned to his and she was gazing at him strangely too, assessing him in some way, her gaze reflective, a glow of something in her eyes, which were a soft green velvet now, the bright gleam gone all of a sudden.

Rowena sat up abruptly, brushing the sand off her shins, feeling the sun beginning to burn the tender flesh. 'We should be getting back to the ship. We were like children in the water—too busy playing games to notice the time.'

'Which we still have plenty of. The ship will not sail without its master. But first I have something to show you. Come, there's a fresh-water pond close by. Sea water dries clothes heavy and stiff.'

'I suppose the answer to that is that one should remove them before swimming in the sea. Although I'm glad you kept yours on.'

His eyes gleamed wickedly. 'They are easily removed—and so are yours.' Taking her hand, he hoisted her to her feet before going to pick up his shirt and sword where he had left them.

'Where are you taking me?' she asked warily, eying his powerful shoulders and feeling a strange fluttering in her stomach.

'Somewhere where you can wash yourself off.'

They left the beach and went into the interior—a thick green plantation of tall wild grass and shrubs and palm trees. Eventually they came to a small clearing, well hidden from the casual eye, and a pond, fed by a seeping spring. The clear water spilled over into a narrow rift to the sea. The air hung motionless, and insects flitted lazily in the air.

There was a strange silence about the place and Rowena looked up at the sunlight filtering through the palms and reflecting off the water. 'How did you know about this place?' she asked, dangling her foot in the pool and feeling the water's coolness.

'We often put in here for water before going through the Straits. I came across it quite by chance.'

'Do you intend to swim?'

'Most certainly.' His eyes met hers in the shadowy light, and, suddenly wary, she stepped back. He looked at her in half-challenging amusement. 'You're not afraid of being here alone with me, are you, Rowena?'

'No, of course not,' she answered, struggling impatiently for the last vestiges of her thin control, feeling it crack under the strain as he studied her. He moved closer, his eyes looking at her for a long moment, and Rowena had the strange sensation of falling.

He was too close and as she put up her hands to push him away, at that moment a slight gust of chill air broke into their solitary world, bringing cold reality with it. She both hated and desired this man who held her own and her sister's future in the palm of his hand.

She had begun to look at him with fresh eyes, noting his authority on deck, the strength held in check as he handled the wheel. She had cleaned his cabin, fetched his meals, waited on him as a cabin boy should, hoping that being with him so much would make him seem less attractive, but so many conflicting emotions tumbled around inside her, fighting for ascendance. And now, as he stood so close to her, he was more attractive than ever, more desirable.

With a low laugh Tobias turned from her and dove into the cool waters of the pool, propelling himself with steady strokes from one bank to the other and back again, his body a dark, sleek mass skimming just below the surface of the water. After a while he paused and looked to where she stood watching him.

'Come on in. The water feels good.'

Unable to resist the pull of the water, in a clean dive she cleaved the water, and with long, flowing strokes swam across the pool, watching him surreptitiously as he sought out the opposite side. Of all the baths she had ever taken, this one struck her as the most wonderful. She really would have loved to have a piece of the scented soap she used at home, but it didn't prevent her making the most of the water.

With a slow, leisurely motion Tobias swam to her side and peered at her expectantly. 'Well?' He came to his feet and stood, the water playing in widening circles about his chest. Wiping wet hair from his eyes, he peered down at her. 'Are you glad you came?'

Her heartbeat quickened and she felt a mixture of fear and joy. She breathed deeply, disturbingly affected by his nearness. Droplets of water clung to his bronze skin, and tinier beads sparkled in the dark furring of his chest. His hair was a dark halo in the forest light, and his gaze was fixed deliberately on her—assessing, lingering and seducing. His smile broadened as his eyes searched her face, then his smile faded and he grew serious. She looked away and colour warmed her cheeks. He was devouring her with his eyes. There was a fire in the blue depths, a blaze of passion and remembrance of the kiss he had give her once before, and longing.

'Tobias, please don't. You really are the most exasperating man.'

'I agree. But you are a woman and I am a man—and…here we are, with no one to see us.'

'Will you be serious?' She bridled. 'Control your lust. I did not come here for this—and please don't paw me,' she complained, brushing his hand away as he reached out to caress her cheek.

His face was in shadow, but his eyes seemed to glow, laughing at her, mocking her. Taking her upper arms, he drew her to his naked chest. 'I told you, I am a man, Rowena,' he assured her, the laughter gone from his voice, 'with all the needs and desires of a man. And you, my love, are so desirable it tortures me to have you near me day after day and not to be able to touch you.'

Deeply affected by the feel of his body pressed to her own, Rowena felt his eyes resting heavily upon her. Her reply was barely audible. 'I struggle with myself at times. It is not easy trying to act as a youth day in and day out surrounded by men who believe that is what I am.'

'The disguise was of your own choosing, but I do not think of you as a youth—more a beautiful woman.'

Rowena knew she should make an effort to extricate herself from this perilous moment, for she knew that this should not be happening, but before she could escape his arms he lowered his mouth to hers. At the first touch of his lips she went rigidly still, her breath indrawn, and Tobias hadn't any idea if it was fear or surprise that made her react so. At that moment he didn't care, bent as he was in conquering the last shreds of resistance in her.

His arms went round her, his only desire to hold her, to kiss her, for her to respond so that he could savour as he had once before the sweetness of her. When he felt her lips quiver and her mouth opened beneath his, he almost groaned aloud with the pleasure of it, as desire, primitive and potent, poured through his veins.

She leaned into him and he kissed her with all the persuasive force at his disposal, his mouth slanting over hers, his hands sliding beneath her shirt, stroking her midriff, her back, sliding lower, splaying against her spine to force her body into intimate, thorough contact with his rigid thighs. Her skin was like silk, and when he touched her breast, sending a white-hot heat searing through her, touching her where no other had dared, he moaned and moulded her body to the hard lean contours of his. It was almost his undoing.

To Rowena, what he was doing to her was something way beyond anything she had experienced before. It was dangerous and exciting, and terrifyingly sensual, and beneath the bold exploration of his fingers, her breasts were beginning to ache and the nipples to harden like tight hard buds. His mouth plundered hers in a devouring kiss that sent her spiralling into a deep chasm where nothing mattered except his seductive, urgent mouth and knowledgeable hands.

Overwhelmed by her own inexperience and his raw, potent sexuality, Rowena fed his hunger, her parted lips welcoming the invasion of his tongue. When he finally dragged his mouth from hers and travelled down the slender column of her throat to where a pulse beat softly beneath her flesh, reality began to return. An image of Jane, her face tortured with suffering, followed by thoughts of Lord Tregowan, perhaps waiting for her to return so they could be wed, and her father, pining over the loss of his two daughters. How could she forget so soon?

Placing the flat of her hands gently against Tobias's chest, she pushed him away. Raising his head he looked at her upturned face.

'Please don't do this, Tobias. I am not so easily persuaded. You have caught me unawares— in a moment of weakness. It must be the heat—or this magical place. But whatever it is, this must end now. I cannot allow you to distract me from my purpose, nor can I forget I am promised to someone else.'

He lifted a quizzical brow. 'And are you so certain he will still want you now, Rowena?'

'My father has told him that I will be his wife, and even though nothing was signed I am bound by my word.'

'Your loyalty is both touching and commendable. But we made a bargain also. Have you forgotten?'

She shook her head. 'No. If Jane is found, one way or another I will see the bargain well met.'

Tobias was studying her carefully. 'Even if it means betraying your betrothed?'

She swallowed painfully. 'Yes.'

He nodded slowly. 'Yes, you will. I shall insist on it.' He seemed to measure his words carefully. 'Until then I shall try to restrain myself, difficult as that will be over the coming weeks, since we are together for much of the time. But you will be mine before we return to England, Rowena. That I promise you.'

Rowena stared at him, realising he meant every word he said. He would have no pity on her, and he would damn anyone who stood in his way. Anger flamed in her eyes and she drew back further.

'I told you, Tobias, I will keep my side of the bargain—but it will be in my own time. Now, I think we should be getting back before Mr Dexter sends out a search party to look for us.' Turning from him, she swam to the edge of the pond and climbed out.

Despite the stubborn lift to her chin and her rebellious tone, there was a tremor of fear in her voice, and when Tobias heard it he became still. Since coming aboard his ship, Rowena had shown so much courage, such indefatigable spirit, that he'd actually believed nothing could shake her. Now, however, as he looked at her hovering on the side of the pool, observing the faint blue smudges beneath her glorious eyes, he saw that the ordeal of her sister's abduction had affected her deeply.

She was amazing, he thought—extremely brave and determined as hell. Perhaps if he wasn't attracted to her, drawn to her, it wouldn't have mattered that she was watching him as if he were a dangerous animal. Hoisting himself on to the bank, with rivulets of water running down his flesh, he stood looking down at her, towering over her, his broad shoulders blocking out her view of anything but him.

'You are right. We should be getting back.'

On the beach Rowena picked up her bindings. Needing more privacy than Tobias seemed concerned about, determinedly she strode to the protection of the trees. When she emerged she found him sitting on the sand, his arms looped around his drawn-up knees and looking out to sea. She paused, her gaze settling on his relaxed, darkly tanned profile. He looked so handsome it nearly took her breath away.

Sensing her presence, he turned and looked at her, his gaze never wavering from her face. 'You go on ahead. I'll give you time to get back to the ship and then I'll follow.'

Without a word, in a daze of suspended yearning, she left him sitting there and did not see the sombre look that hardened his features as he watched her go. Sanity slowly began to return when she realised what she had done. Shame raged through her. It would have been bad enough had he forced her to yield to him, but he hadn't. As if some spell had been cast over her she had wantonly, willingly, participated in her own seduction, and given his reputation as a womaniser, her dilemma where he was concerned increased, and once again she reminded herself that she must not fall under his spell.

How long would it take for him to wear her down, for he knew the effect that moment of intimacy in the pool had had on her? His touch, his lips on hers, had been her downfall, and her pride had toppled beneath his deliberate attack on her senses.

* * *

Returning to her cabin, the fear was still with her. After changing her clothes, she curled up on the narrow bunk. Eventually she drifted into a light slumber, and then to her surprise, aware that someone had entered the cabin, she opened her eyes.

Sitting up, she eyed Tobias warily, searching his implacable features, her sleep-drugged mind registering that he intended to continue the seduction. Pushing her hair from her eyes, she peered blearily up at him.

'Tobias? What…?'

'It was a mistake,' he said flatly. 'You need have no fear that I will repeat what happened between us. While we are aboard ship for us to indulge in any kind of intimacy will only complicate matters for both of us and could well lead to disaster. It won't happen again.'

Rowena gaped as she watched him go out. That was not what she had expected to hear.

True to his word, Tobias made no further advances towards her—in fact, he seemed to go out of his way to avoid her, to forget she existed, and even though Rowena told herself this was how she wanted it to be between them, she found herself watching for him.

Tobias had not forgotten she existed, but his intelligent mind knew it must be like this while they were on board.

Rowena's first sight of Algiers was unforgettable. It seemed to rise up from the sea in a shimmering heat. A massive, formidable fortress commanded the view, its parapet bristling with cannon, and a copper dome sparkled in the Mediterranean sunshine. The town of tightly packed houses spread out and upwards, crowned by what she would later discover to be the Kasbah, or citadel, part-fort, part-palace. Slender, colourful minarets soared into the blue sky next to the green-and-golden domes of the mosques, and even out in the roads the piercing wail of the muezzins in the minarets could be heard calling the believers to prayer.

Rowena's heart was beating with hope and fear. She could not take her eyes off the astonishing scene. Algiers! This then was the object of her reckless journey south to find her sister. It had a kind of beauty that was completely foreign to her, and the joy and relief she experienced in being in Algiers at last were so immense that at first she forgot the dangers which awaited her here.

The *Cymbeline* dropped anchor in the roadstead. It was full of vessels of every description, with boats plying between ships and shore. There were a few merchant vessels and several Barbary ships—ships of prey used for hunting and killing, lean and deadly as leopards, crouched low amid the bulky commercial vessels—but what caught Rowena's gaze was a vessel skimming over the smooth water, low and sleek and dangerous, with a full complement of rowers who knew their work. She thought this must be one of the galleys she had heard about, where Christian slaves were shackled to the oars for the greater part each day. The sight sent a cold shiver down her spine.

Tobias came to stand beside her at the rail. In the heat

of the day he was clad in simple white shirt with full sleeves, black breeches and boots. His hair dipped over his brow and his eyes shone a brilliant blue in his bronze face.

'Quite a sight, is it not, Rowena, this corsair base?' He saw what held her gaze. 'The galley will be returning from cruising the Mediterranean. In the old days there would have been prisoners on board—more than likely Spaniards, Genoese or Greeks, poor devils.'

'And what would have happened to them?'

'They would have been sold in the slave market. As I have told you, the fate of all slaves depends upon if you have money or influence—preferably both. They are the lucky ones. The majority who are taken captive are poor peasants with nothing. At one time some would have been sent to the galleys, others to the quarries for stone cutting and hauling, which still goes on. Escape or rescue is practically impossible. Some masters are not without humanity, but under a harsh master they are quite literally worked to death.'

'Then if it is as cruel as you say it is, death must come as a welcome release.'

'The oared vessels, which have been the preferred warships for centuries, are obsolete. They are too costly to maintain and cannot carry the heavy cannon of the sailing vessels. Do not dwell on what it must be like to be a Christian slave in North Africa, Rowena. It is a fact of this wretched Barbary coast. It goes on. Tell me. What is your first impression of Algiers?'

Rowena tore her eyes from the galley as she shipped her oars, and looked again at the town with its white, flat-roofed buildings climbing the hillside. 'I've never seen anything quite like it. It's both beautiful and savage, the colour and glorious sunshine masking its underlying corruption and depravity. It's hard to believe that Jane is out there somewhere.'

'You must face the fact that she may not be in Algiers. It is highly probable that she will already have been sold on and that she is in a rich man's household—whether as a servant or…'

'A concubine,' Rowena finished sorrowfully, turning away to hide a grimace of pain. 'If that is what she is, then it is something I must accept.' She faced him squarely. 'Please don't spare my sensibilities, Tobias. Be honest and open with me. Whatever has happened to Jane, no matter how terrible, I can take it. I want to know. Do you promise to tell me everything?'

He nodded. 'If she is here, you must realise that she will be well guarded.'

'Well guarded, yes—but not too well guarded, I hope, that I won't be able to make contact with her. I pray no harm has come to her.'

'Jane is probably a lot stronger than you suppose, and though she may be a child in some ways, I suspect she's her father's daughter in a good many others.'

'Yes—yes, she is. How can we find her? I know it will not be easy, but find her I will,' she said determinedly. 'I have not come all this way to be defeated by walls and battlements—not even a sultan, if that is where she is.' She looked at Tobias, who was scanning the ships at anchor in the roads. 'Are you looking for

Jack Mason?' He nodded. 'And do you mean to devote your life to chasing this particular pirate?'

His lips curled contemptuously. 'Not my entire life. I wouldn't waste my time. If he's here, I'll find him.'

'And then what? Will you have him thrown in prison?'

His jaw tightened. 'That will not happen. I will deal with Mason in my own way.' He glanced at Rowena. 'What he's doing is not considered a crime here. Pirates in the Barbary States are not criminals in our sense. Piracy is a profession on the Barbary Coast—just as trading is to Englishmen involved in commercial enterprise.'

'Who is in control in Algiers?'

'Formally it was part of the Ottoman Empire, but now it is essentially free from Ottoman control. The power belongs with the Dey and his cabinet of advisers, the *divan*, but the real power belongs to the Janissaries, who are professional warriors. They appoint the Deys and get rid of them when they don't suit—usually by assassination. This is a shockingly barbaric place, a place where such horrors happen on a daily basis that you cannot begin to imagine.'

'Yes, I'm beginning to realise that. How soon can we go ashore?'

Tobias noted the eagerness in her eyes as she squinted up at him from between dark lashes, and grinned. 'What an impatient nature you have! Later we'll go and visit a friend of mine—when the sun is no longer at its hottest. Maybe he can give us the information we're looking for.'

'And who is this friend?'

'A shipwright who buys my timber.'

'To build ships for pirates who prey on British vessels?'

'Perhaps you will feel easier when I tell you that my friend does not build his ships for pirates. He builds sailing vessels for merchants. The pirates can only acquire vessels that come their way, so to speak—vessels they are strong enough to overcome and capture. If one of them happens to be one of Ahmed's, built with the timber supplied by me, then there is nothing to be done about that. It could just as easily be a vessel built by one of the shipwrights in England, to whom I also provide timber. You will like my friend. He is a good man and we have known one another for many years. If Mason came to Algiers to sell his captives, he will know.'

'And if he didn't come here? What will you do?'

'Keep looking until I find him.'

Tobias had misgivings about taking Rowena with him. In her cut-off trews and baggy shirt she went unnoticed, but if anyone took the time to look closer they would see a fair-skinned, pretty youth beneath that floppy hat she had taken to wearing all the time. There were men who prowled the narrow streets of Algiers on the look out for such pretty youths. They would watch and wait until they were unguarded and then take them captive, for they always fetched a good price in the thriving slave-markets.

Preoccupied by these sobering thoughts, Tobias instinctively moved to stand closer to Rowena without appearing too familiar to those who might be watching.

'I am trying to prevent you doing anything that might

place you in danger, but I have no illusions about what you would do the minute I left the ship if I ordered you to stay on board.'

Her head spun round and her ferocious glare showed Tobias the futility of such a thing. 'Don't you dare!'

He chuckled softly. 'Short of clapping you in irons, there is nothing I can do to prevent you leaving the ship. Of course I could instruct the crew not to row you ashore, but that would draw unnecessary attention to you, and you, you wily minx, are capable of jumping overboard and swimming ashore if you have a mind— if just to thwart me.'

Tobias saw a quick flash of white teeth in a happy grin. 'I see you've got the measure of me at last, Mr Searle, so don't even consider leaving me behind.'

Chapter Six

A small skiff was lowered into the water and two of the crew rowed them to the quay, where a crowd of turbaned functionaries and sightseers had gathered to observe their landing. The skiff sped back to the ship, from whence it would return to collect them later. Hit by the heat and the noise, Rowena followed close behind Tobias as he forced a way through the crowd on the busy harbour, with its countless fish stalls and vendors of fruit, vegetables and brightly coloured unknown spices sitting cross-legged on the ground beside their wares.

They went through a maze of crooked streets and sultry alleys, dusty and swarming with flies, before beginning the climb up the interminable steep hill of Algiers, so steep in places that the climb was broken occasionally by short flights of steps. The street also acted as the main bazaar, where every sort of marvel seemed to spill in profusion from the stalls on either side, and this, along with a multitude of beggars—marked by running sores, some blind and with horribly misshapen bodies—goats and donkeys, made it difficult in places to progress speedily.

Eventually they came to the terraces of houses. The house of Ahmed al Rashid was a white three-storey mansion set high on the outskirts that commanded magnificent views of the harbour and the sea beyond. A manservant opened the door and invited them to enter. Rowena stared in amazement at the great Negro who was grinning from ear to ear as he stood aside to let them pass, before going to summon his master.

She looked about her, struck by the size and luxury of the house. In the centre of the room in which they waited, whose slender colonnades were entirely covered with light blue, silver and pink filigree decoration, was a circular marble pool into which a trickle of water splashed endlessly from between the jaws of a stone lion. She made her way towards it over the glittering mosaic floor, gazing into the crystal-clear water, tempted to reach out and let its coolness spill over her hands.

Her eyes were alight with pleasure as she turned to look at Tobias, who was watching her with the amusement of an adult watching a happy child. 'What a wondrous place this is,' she murmured. 'I've never seen a house with such splendid views—and certainly not a house with an indoor fountain before. It's like a fairy-tale palace. I did not imagine your friend owned such a place as this.'

'Ahmed has amassed a large enough fortune from his shipbuilding to ensure he and his family can live in luxury for the rest of their lives.'

'The—servants in his house—are they slaves?' she asked tentatively.

He nodded. 'Some of them, but Ahmed is not a cruel master. He uses slave labour to build his ships. Some of them are skilled men, having been trained well in the countries they came from. Skilled shipwrights are a bonus in the busy Arsenal and speed things up. You will like Ahmed—and I must warn you to beware, for not only is he a successful builder of some of the finest vessels ever to sail out of Algiers, he is also a great charmer,' he teased, grinning, and Rowena could tell he was inordinately pleased that she appreciated the splendour of the house and the beauty of its setting.

Rowena's preoccupation with the fountain was abruptly cut off when a man suddenly appeared, his eyes going directly to Tobias.

'Tobias!' the good shipwright cried in amazement. 'It can't be.'

Tobias laughed and went to embrace his friend. 'Yes, my friend, it is I, and I am happy to see you again.'

'It must be heaven itself which has brought you here. It's wonderful. But come in, come in, and tell me about yourself. It has been too long. You have brought me some timber?'

'Not this time, Ahmed—but one of my vessels will be putting in at Algiers with a cargo within the month. My reason for coming to Algiers now is not to trade.'

'Then we shall talk of it as we eat.'

Rowena could not tear her eyes away from Ahmed al Rashid. Never had she seen the like. She was surprised that he spoke in perfect English. His richly embroidered robe, which fell straight from his shoulders, was made of silk dyed deep blue, extremely beautiful, like the sea at twilight. He must have been between thirty-five and forty years old and his unturbaned head was covered with a thick crop of black hair. His skin was dark, Moorish, his features fine cut and haughty, his beard black and well trimmed, and his eyes were dark and glowing.

He sat at ease on a low divan spread with bright rugs and surrounded by a heap of brightly coloured silk cushions, in an atmosphere thick with the scent of sandalwood and flowers. A superb parrot preened its long crimson feathers and strutted on its silver perch, cooing like a dove and watching the visitors with its great round eyes. As Ahmed regarded his visitor, a smile curved his full mouth and exposed his strong white teeth.

'So, my friend, how long are you to remain here?'

'Until I have information on where I can find someone.'

'And might I ask the name of this someone?'

'I know him as Jack Mason. Here he is known as Hassan Kasem. He uses Algiers as his base to sell captives. I was hoping you could tell me if he's been here recently.'

'Hassan Kasem,' murmured Ahmed as though considering the name and nodding slowly. 'The renegade— the Christian turned Moor for greed and gain.'

'That's Mason. Have you heard something?'

'Nothing good. He is not liked, nor is he trusted.'

'So you do know him.'

'I know of him. He is called evil names—snake, scorpion, among others not so flattering.' He laughed. 'What is your interest in Hassan Kasem?'

'It is personal, Ahmed. I have been a long time trailing him.'

A light dawned in Ahmed's eyes. 'Ah, now I know. It is about what happened on Jamaica. You have still not resolved that.'

'No, and nor will I until I find Mason. He has a habit of slipping neatly through my fingers. But I dare say I'll catch up with him. He's clever, though, and cunning, but he will not escape me for ever. I have a score to settle with him, a heavy score, Ahmed, and one I mean to make him pay in full.'

'Then I wish you luck, my friend, and I pray to Allah that the day of reckoning will be soon—which may well be, since his ship's consort was taken out by a British man of war in the Atlantic not so long ago. The English captain, Captain Ryan, is making quite a name for himself by successfully attacking vessels belonging to the Barbary corsairs—and I believe he has singled out the *Seadog,* Kasem's ship, which sails alone and is well past her prime.'

'Then I would dearly like to meet this captain. Perhaps I will, but until then I must go on seeking Mason—or Kasem.' Tobias reclined opposite his friend. His handsome face with its strong features and imperious profile was as lean and fine drawn, and almost as tanned, as that of the shipwright. 'This is Rowan, my cabin boy, Ahmed.' He looked to where Rowena sat cross legged on a mat, amazed that she had remained silent for so long. 'He too has a special reason for knowing if Kasem has put into Algiers recently. His sister was among some captives he brought to sell.'

Ahmed looked at the youth who was watching them with a keen eye. 'Then rest assured that if she was brought to Algiers for sale you will know. The Dey's scribes enter every new intake of captives in the city register. Everything about her will have been recorded—her attributes and defects written down. Find it and you will find your sister—but I must tell you that the most beautiful women are snapped up by private buyers. If a ransom can be agreed, then you must realise that whoever bought her will probably demand double the amount he gave for her.'

'I'll make some enquiries tomorrow,' Tobias said. 'Maybe I will be able to see the register.'

'How much start did Kasem have on you?'

'A week, no more.'

'Then there is every chance that you will find her.'

The meal was served by an army of servants in white robes and blue silk turbans. The food was carried on big silver trays—fish and meats and sweetmeats dripping honey. It was spicy and delicious and washed down with hot spiced wines. Rowena was quick to compliment their host as she chewed on something that set her taste buds tingling.

The talk went on more slowly now, for, comfortably settled with good food and the wine's sweetness, Tobias was in no haste to go. In fact, it might have gone on all night long had not a woman entered to speak to Ahmed. She seemed to appear from nowhere, gliding across the floor, her bare feet making no sound on the black marble floor and, but for the silvery tinkle that accompanied her movement, Rowena might have imagined her an apparition.

The woman looked at the dark-haired handsome visitor, blinking, and then she loosed a shout of laughter, her lips stretching wide in her broad face.

'Mr Searle! I give you greetings,' she said, her voice dark toned and rich.

Rowena stared at her. She was a woman with the proportions of an erotic statuette, plump to the point where another pound or so would have been a disaster, but she had kept her curvaceousness, and she walked with grace and was light of foot. Her skin was dark, but she was not as dark as their host, and the attractive curves of her lip and nostril were slightly thickened. She brought to mind those sensual pictures Rowena had seen in books of Delilah and Jezebel, which religious artists paint so enthusiastically.

Tobias got up and bowed to her with respect. 'Fatima! It does my heart good to see you again.'

'You honour us with your presence.' The woman's eyes slipped to Rowena. 'And your companion. But who is this?'

'Rowan—my cabin boy.' He cocked an eye at Rowena, a secret smile playing on his lips. 'Rowan, may I introduce Fatima—she is Ahmed's senior wife,' he said, with slight emphasis on 'senior'.

Rowena's eyes opened wide with confusion and they flew to Ahmed's in disbelief. '*Senior* wife?' she gasped before she could stop herself, two spots of dark colour appearing high on her cheeks. 'You have more than one wife?'

Ahmed was quite undaunted as a dazzling smile broke the line of his mouth. He was obviously amused by her reaction. 'Clearly your cabin boy is not acquainted with our ways and customs, Tobias. Fatima is my first wife,' he explained to Rowena, and on a proud note he announced, 'I have two more wives, Shilla and Zidana, but they are not as clever as my first wife. Their English is not so good, but they were surely designed by Lord Satan's hand—two enchantresses, to turn a man's heart away from pious thoughts.'

As if on cue, two more females appeared from behind a flimsy curtain, each carrying platters of more food, and came to stand with Fatima. One, Shilla, was tall and as black as ebony with almond-shaped eyes. Zidana was smaller and olive skinned. She wore kohl to darken her lashes and thus brighten and enlarge her great brown eyes.

Both were slender hipped beneath loose silk trousers and well-filled short bodices, their midriffs bare. Delicate gold necklaces glittering with gems adorned their chests, and a multiplicity of gold bangles circled their arms. They both wore half-veils from just below their eyes to their chins, but those veils were so transparent as to make a mockery of the Prophet's command for female modesty. Their eyes were most eloquent when they rested on Tobias.

Rowena managed to retain a cool and unruffled expression as they placed the platters of juicy fruits in front of them, their jewellery clinking and jingling as they moved. There was a gorgeous selection of dates and figs, melons, sliced oranges swimming in rose water, mingled with shredded coconut and grapes and sweetened with crystalline sugar. Rowena had never tasted anything like it in her life.

As she ate, she listened to the girlish laughter and voices speaking in Arabic ring out as the three wives sprawled on cushions, and she listened to Tobias reply to their excited chattering fluently.

He was relaxed and smiled with twinkling eyes at Shilla and Zidana, but he sobered as he met Rowena's eyes. She stared at him with a quizzical quirk playing about her lips and a wondering dip to her brow, before looking away, because for one terrible moment she was seized with passionate jealousy and resentment for these two women, so terrible and so unexpected that the glow of the feelings Tobias aroused in her of late began to fade.

Ahmed glanced at Tobias where he sat contentedly, listening to something Fatima said. He had made Shilla and Zidana blush more than once already, with his compliments on their beauty. His charming smile and words had been all for Fatima, but the glint in his eyes had searched for and found his cabin boy.

Ahmed looked across at the graceful, pretty youth and then at his friend. He well knew Tobias and suspected that some mischief was afoot. Fixing his gaze once more on the youth, who was studying him in turn, with awakened interest he did not speak for several moments, but simply sat there, looking at him, and then said, 'I have a surprise for you, Tobias.'

'Oh?' he asked, one dark eyebrow raised in enquiry.

Ahmed smiled, his eyes gleaming wickedly. 'It will be a revelation, I've no doubt, for your companion as well.'

Rowena looked at him with interest. She had indeed always enjoyed surprises and could not imagine the nature of this one.

Ahmed picked a fig from the platter and, holding it up, scrutinised it as though he'd never seen one before.

'Well, Ahmed?' Tobias asked impatiently.

He chuckled and turned to face Rowena. 'It concerns your young friend.'

Despite Ahmed's good humour, Rowena felt the first tentative fingers of fear trail along her spine. She gulped at her wine and waited, her heart hammering against her rib cage.

'Rowan, my friend, is no youth.'

'What?' Fatima exclaimed, staring wide-eyed at first at her husband, then at Rowena.

For the shortest time, too, Rowena sat wide-eyed, astonishment overpowering her vocal capacity. Then, her mind working quickly, she resolved to attempt to brazen herself out of this awkward, embarrassing, and potentially dangerous, position, for if others found out her secret, the foundations of her safe and secure position on board ship would crumble and cause all kinds of complications.

'I must object,' she burst out in her most outraged tone and jumped to her feet. 'You are sorely mistaken...'

Instead of seriously considering this denouncement, as Rowena had expected, Tobias simply began laughing, Ahmed joining him, his two younger wives smiling sublimely in their ignorance as they looked in bewilderment from one face to the other.

'Ahmed, what are you saying?' Fatima demanded, wondering why her husband should make this seemingly inappropriate comment and impatient that he should explain himself.

At last Ahmed recovered his control. 'I am saying that our young guest is not what he seems. Rowan is a girl. It is a good disguise that she has adopted, and no doubt it has fooled most—you, too, my dearest heart.'

Fatima turned to Rowena, who was looking beseechingly to Tobias for deliverance. 'It is true, what my husband alleges?'

Rowena reluctantly met her eyes and sighed deeply. 'It is true,' she finally admitted. 'I am female.'

Fatima looked at Tobias. 'You know?'

He nodded, still laughing, though softer now. 'Aye, Fatima. I have known all along.'

'Of course he knows,' Ahmed was quick to say. 'Either that or his eyes have grown dim. But I was not fooled.'

'But—that is delightful,' Fatima cried, clapping her hands together. She laughed with real amusement, a rich, merry sound, at the astonished look on the young girl's face, for Rowena was staring at her as though she had taken leave of her senses, totally confused, for she certainly hadn't expected this reaction from Ahmed's senior wife.

'I do believe I have upset the young lady,' Ahmed said, chuckling softly. 'Is this so?' he asked kindly, gazing at Rowena's distraught face. She nodded mutely. 'It was not done to tease you, child.'

'You must excuse Ahmed, Rowena,' Tobias remarked, coming to her rescue at last. 'There is no fooling him.'

'Rest assured that we shall say nothing of your true nature—Rowena,' Ahmed said, 'but won't you explain what has prompted you to adopt such a mode of attire?'

'When Rowena's sister was captured by Kasem,' Tobias explained, 'she was determined to find out where he had taken her and to try to get her back. She could not do that as a woman, so she disguised herself as a youth and smuggled herself aboard my ship, which, for reasons I have already explained, was about to leave for North Africa. I did not find out myself until we had put to sea and it was too late to take her back.'

Fatima listened with interest. She could sense the suppressed agitation in the girl, noted her clenched hands, the nervous movement of the brilliant green eyes that were fastened on Tobias, and she perceived that it would be good for Rowena to spend some time with someone of the same sex.

'Your disguise has been successful?' she asked.

'Very,' Tobias provided, gazing with a warm intensity at his cabin boy-girl. 'Although she passes as a somewhat pretty boy, let me assure you that she makes more than a passable girl.'

'I can see that is so now,' Fatima agreed, leaning

back on the mound of silken cushions to study the girl, making a quick appraisal of her heart-shaped face and wing-swept eyebrows above beautiful blue-green eyes. 'It is a terrible shame that you had to cut your hair to compound your disguise, but it does not detract from your looks. I can see you are very beautiful. Oh, child, if you were to dress as a woman, all the men would be in love with you at a glance.'

'But I am not interested in such things. All I want is to find my sister, and to do that I must maintain my disguise—even though I am beginning to tire of it.'

Fatima thought for a moment, her face undergoing various transformations. At last it settled into a most cunning and pleased expression. Her gaze went from her husband to Tobias and her dark eyes gleamed. 'I have an idea.'

'You usually do, my love,' Ahmed said, wary of the machinations of his senior wife's mind. He had no doubt that he would soon discover the source of her sly look.

'Rowena says she has to maintain her disguise—this I understand, since she has to live with all those men on the ship—but nothing prevents her from staying here while you are in Algiers, Tobias. I am sure you could come up with something that would explain her absence—and,' she said, her eyes dancing wickedly, 'I am sure you could find someone else to perform her duties as your cabin boy.'

Rowena saw Tobias and realised in one giddy instant of silent laughter that Fatima might well believe she was Tobias's woman.

Fatima smiled encouragingly at Rowena. 'Do say you will stay with us. It would give us great pleasure to have you as our guest—and to spoil you for a little while.'

Looking at the tall exotic woman and seeing gentleness and kindness in the depths of her dark eyes, Rowena found her friendliness contagious and could not help smiling. She felt the breath of madness touch her face. In an instant her heart had decided. 'I would love to stay,' she exclaimed, a happy look on her face. She looked at Tobias, certain he would have no reason to object, but when she saw the look on his face she was not so sure. She saw indecision flicker across his hard features; thinking he was about to refuse, she tried to soften him by going to him and placing her hand on his arm.

Tobias glanced down at the slender fingers. Heat was seeping through his flesh, desire already stirring inside him—and that with only her hand upon his arm. He didn't understand why she had such a volatile effect on him, but he understood that he wanted her—willing and warm in his arms. He'd got used to having her close to him, day after day, knowing she was sleeping in her cabin next to his own night after night, and he would miss her like hell when she wasn't there.

'Please, Tobias,' she said, mistaking his silence for refusal, 'I would like to stay here—if just for tonight. What harm can it do?'

Seeing his friend's dilemma, Ahmed came to her rescue. 'Come, Tobias, she will enjoy staying in my house with my wives to pamper her.' He saw how the girl's eyes lit up, hopeful and expectant. 'Think, my friend. Does she not yearn for the company of women after being incarcerated for Allah knows how long on a ship full of men?'

'Ahmed,' Rowena said softly, 'you are very kind.'

'Kindness has nothing to do with it,' said Ahmed. 'Tobias knows that I am an aesthete in love with beauty and harmony. When I think of a woman like you having to travel wearing the clothes of a youth on board a vessel with a motley crew, my skin shivers. So, if you do not want to condemn me to a lifetime's remorse, you will honour my house by remaining for a few days.' He laughed loudly, slapping Tobias good naturedly on the back. 'I might even take her unto me to be my fourth wife—to even things up a little among my other wives, you understand.' His white teeth flashed in the black mass of his beard. 'I think she would serve me well.'

'Forget it,' Tobias told him sternly, but with a slow grin. 'Do not strain the bonds of friendship beyond what you already have, Ahmed.'

'Ah, I see that would not please you, my friend. It is heartily sorry I am if my suggestion causes you dismay.'

A trace of humour played across Tobias's lips as he looked directly at Rowena, who was watching him expectantly, although his words when he spoke brought a dangerous blaze to her eyes. 'More like absolute terror at the thought.'

'You think I would do her harm?'

'Not for a minute, Ahmed. It is you I'm thinking of. I am only trying to save you from a dire fate. Rowena happens to be the most mercurial, wilful firebrand you could ever wish to meet, and she has a tongue that could flay the skin off a man's back. I would not wish her on my worst enemy, let alone a trusted friend.'

'Then she is a rare jewel.' Ahmed laughed, a great booming sound. 'A woman after my own heart.'

Tobias gave him a mocking grin. 'So are most women, Ahmed. I knew Rowena would be no exception, and wondered how long it would take you to see through her disguise—although I have to say I was surprised it took you so long.'

Ahmed winked knowingly and leaned towards Tobias, his words meant for his ears alone. 'You want her for yourself, that I can see, and it's not right that her beauty inflame other eyes than yours, eh?' He laughed into his friend's glower. 'Don't be a fool. See what you have, my friend. Her beauty is a treasure beyond all price.' He winked again into the blue eyes as they rose to meet his. 'Should your business tomorrow take longer than you expect, I—and my beautiful wives—will do our utmost to entertain her.'

'Then I will simply have to make sure it doesn't.'

Ahmed gave him a hearty slap on the back. 'Go back to your ship, Tobias, and sleep easy. Rest assured that your young charge will be safe in my house. Besides,' he retorted, seeing where his two young wives' gazes were directed. 'I like not the way my three strumpets devour you with their eyes, for it bodes ill for me.'

When Tobias had left to return to the ship, Rowena went with Ahmed's wives along a passage to a gold-and-blue mosaic chamber that she soon discovered was a bath-house. The ceiling was domed, and in the centre of the floor, surrounded by slender pillars, was a tiled, large sunken bath in which water was steaming.

Rowena gasped, her eyes alight with excitement, never having imagined there could be so much luxury in one house. Towels were to hand, while all around were vials of oils and soaps.

'Why, this is very fine,' she exclaimed, delighted. 'We have nothing like this at home in England—not even in the best houses. It looks so tempting and pleasurable.'

'With enough luxury for a person to wallow in for as long as they wish.' Fatima led her to the edge of the tub.

Shilla and Zidana were chattering excitedly in Arabic, and before Rowena could protest they were undressing her as if it were the most natural thing to do. There was a great deal of giggling as her bindings were unwound, and when they tried to remove them, alarmed, Rowena put up her hands to stop them, trying to hold on to her modesty, but the more she protested the louder they laughed. Standing back they began to undress themselves to show it was quite natural in the world they inhabited to bathe together in the nude.

They slipped into the scented water, beckoning for her to join them, their slender gleaming bodies as supple as snakes as they writhed in the pool. Deciding to throw caution and all her inhibitions to the wind and to give herself up the slow tempo of this life, Rowena began to relax and finished undressing swiftly. Squeals and gasps of admiration were drawn from the three wives when her pale slender body was revealed.

'You are the loveliest thing,' Fatima enthused. 'Such a face—and such a milky skin. You are quite perfect, Rowena.'

Laughing delightedly, Rowena slipped gracefully into the pool where she readily abandoned herself quite passively to the ministering of the two younger wives' gentle hands.

A smile on her lips, Fatima sat on a low stool at the side of the pool, content to watch as Zidana washed her hair while Shilla soaped her all over.

Wallowing pleasurably, feeling the water about her like a caress, Rowena was astonished at the strange sense of well-being that spread through every part of her body. When she stepped out, Fatima was waiting with a thick cotton towel to dry her, before taking her to a divan where she began to massage her body with hands that were amazingly gentle, rubbing in a strangely pungent oil that relaxed her muscles and gave her skin a soft patina.

She relaxed and, spreading her arms, opened her eyes and gazed at the ceiling, at the colourful designs with a picture in the centre, of stars and a moon representing the heavens, and a golden sun in the middle. Pressing her eyes shut, she held her breath to hold on to the pleasurable sensation. Her body seemed to have broken all its earthly moorings. She was like a puppet now, moving to the strings that pulled her, only her brain functioning slowly as her body was ministered to as never before.

Beneath the massaging boldness of Fatima's hands—Fatima had the air of a priestess carrying out some ancient ritual—she was honest enough to admit her treacherous woman's body was coming breathlessly alive, not even against her will, and what she felt was not unlike what she had felt when she had been with Tobias on the beach. What she was experiencing now was very similar—magical, sensual, erotic—and all that was missing was Tobias.

She sighed with contentment. 'You use such wonderful scents, Fatima. Not only do you educate my palate with delicious food, but my nose also,' she murmured, as Fatima proceeded to apply more oil to her skin. The air in the bathing chamber was warm and thick and redolent of perfume, not flower-like, but compounded of ambergris and musk—intoxicating and languid, artful weapons to entrap a man. That she should think such things just then did not surprise her, for Tobias still occupied her mind.

'Where did you learn to speak English?' she asked as Fatima massaged her calf.

'My mother was Irish from County Cork. She taught me. Like your sister, she was taken by the corsairs when they raided her village. She was just thirteen. She was bought and placed in the harem of a wealthy Moor in Morocco, where I was born.'

'Did she ever return to Ireland?'

'No. She remained a slave until she died, but she had no wish to go home. She came from a poor family, so there was no question of a ransom. She came to like the life in the harem with the other women. The Moor—my father—was good to his women. My mother, who had known nothing but hunger and poverty at home, had never known such luxury as there was in the harem.'

'But she was still a slave, Fatima.' Rowena was tempted to say that in her opinion slavery was brutal and devoid of any moral scruple, that these people had once been masters of their own destinies before they had been taken against their will and put through their paces in the slave markets of Barbary. Not wishing to give offence, she held her tongue and said, 'And you married Ahmed.'

Fatima's full lips stretched in a broad smile. 'My father sold me to him. Ahmed is a good man—not only rich, but an influential man in Algiers and in the towns along the coast, because he builds such fine ships.'

'And you don't mind that he has two more wives?'

She shrugged. 'No. Here it is accepted. One wife or three—what does it matter? I am his first wife so I am the important one, and my eldest son, Ishmael, is Ahmed's heir.'

Bathed, scented and draped in a flowing white tunic and feeling more feminine than she had ever felt in her life before, Rowena stood back for the three wives to inspect their handiwork.

Fatima beamed broadly, well satisfied. 'Tobias will not be able to resist you when he sees you out of those unflattering boy's clothes. He is like Ahmed in many ways, honourable, noble and trustworthy, as well as handsome—all the things I cherish in a man—and I have observed he is protective of you. You are a long way from England and have plenty of time to be together, so it will be interesting to see what happens between the two of you.'

Rowena merely smiled and let the matter rest. She spent the rest of the evening lounging on a divan in conversation with Fatima and nibbling on delicious sweetmeats, before being shown to a room of sumptuous luxury, where she slept the night away like a babe.

Tobias arrived after dark on the second night. Ahmed was at his boat yard down at the docks, so he went into the garden to await Rowena.

Rowena was bathing—her experience in the bathing chamber had had a magnetic effect on her and she couldn't resist repeating the experience whenever the fancy took her. The weather was so hot she welcomed the feel of the cool, heavenly water swirling over her body, soothing away her impatience to see Tobias, which had been growing ever since he had left her.

After two days she found herself transformed. The comfortable, indolent life at Ahmed's house, the rich food, the leisurely strolls in the flower-scented garden, and all the dexterous attention of Ahmed's three wives had worked wonders. Her body felt supple and soft, her skin bloomed, and, as Fatima said, was as fine textured as a flower petal. They dressed her in strange, exotic costumes. Her fingers had never caressed such gorgeous silk, and some of the fabrics were so fine as to be almost shockingly transparent. The costumes were not as restricting as the ones she was used to, and she took pleasure in wearing them.

The air was heavy with perfume and disturbed by the rhythmic sound of cicadas. Drinking in the fragrant tranquillity, Tobias walked slowly along a walkway covered in delicate flower-decked trellis. The night was glorious—an African night, the sky dark blue and rich with stars that glittered softly, pricking the surface of the sea with little phospherent wavelets.

From the house, Rowena took a moment to observe him, admiring the fine figure he made. A white shirt, opened at the throat and ruffled at the cuffs, contrasted sharply with his bronze skin, and his lean, muscular build was accentuated by the close-fitting breeches and white stockings. He was bare headed, and his dark hair was tied back at the nape.

Although he moved with almost sensuous grace, there was a sureness in his stride as he walked, as if he carefully planned where each foot would fall. He appeared relaxed and at ease, but there was a quiet alertness in his manner, and Rowena sensed he was aware of everything that transpired around him. She was impatient to see him, mainly because she wanted to know if he had discovered anything about Jane, but there was a small treacherous part of her that told her she wanted to see him for herself.

Stepping out on to the terrace, she was between Tobias and the light, so that her body was outlined through her thin robe. The many scents of the garden— the sweetness of jasmine and the fragrance of fruiting orange and lemon trees and beneficial herbs—leaped up to meet her, filling her head, as though she had been handed a bouquet of flowers.

'Tobias?'

Her familiar voice rose above the sounds of the night. Tobias did not realise how much he had missed her until he heard it, or how the sight of her warmed his heart— and it had only been forty-eight hours since he had left her. She was coming towards him, her robe drifting and outlining her slender form with her movements, her slippered feet making no sound. His admiring gaze took in her fashionable *toilette,* lingering on the gold and jewels adorning her neck and wrists, and Rowena felt herself grow hot with embarrassment.

For a moment Tobias felt as if she had reached into his chest and squeezed his heart. And then he blinked and shook off his strange abstractions.

'Good Lord!' A slow smile of admiration swept across his face as he beheld the lovely young woman. Her dark glossy hair, reflecting the light, was a cap of shining curls.

The dark liquid of his eyes deepened as he became caught up in the warmth of her presence and she read in his face such evident desire that heat flamed for a moment in her cheeks. 'Yes, Tobias? What is it?'

She moved closer still, and though the light was dim he could perceive her lovely face, more serene than he had ever seen it. 'What was in that wine Fatima has just plied me with? A philtre to rouse the blood?'

'And has it?'

'What?'

'Roused your blood?'

'It's definitely affected.' Taking her hand, he raised her fingers to his lips, enjoying the scent and taste of her. When he looked at her there was a twinkle in her eyes. 'You look like some eastern nymph.'

'I thought you would never come.'

'Does that mean you have missed me, Rowena?'

'I thought you might be otherwise occupied,' she prevaricated. 'That you must be too busy with matters on board your ship to get away to see me.'

'Nothing could ever be as important as coming here to see how you are,' he said blandly, and he meant it.

Perhaps it was the magic of the night, the warmth and subtle floral scents, or her need to be close to him, but whatever the cause, Rowena's heart doubled its pace.

In a voice like rough velvet, he said, 'You are beautiful. Where has my cabin boy gone, I wonder?'

Mesmerised, Rowena stared into his fathomless dark eyes, while his deep, husky voice caressed her, pulling her further under his spell.

'The colour of your robe suits you,' he murmured softly.

'It's sea green. Fatima chose it. She says it is the same colour as my eyes.'

'It is well chosen. How do you like living in a Muslim household?'

'It's so far removed from anything I have ever known or could have imagined. I have been made to feel very welcome—so much so that I have serious doubts I shall ever be able to leave.' Suddenly, mischievously, she smiled and cocked her head sideways as she looked up at him. 'Would you embrace Islam, Tobias?'

He stared at her. 'Why?'

'Because then you, too, could have three wives.'

He laughed. 'One wife is sufficient for any man.'

'So,' she said, falling into step beside him as they strolled along the garden paths, 'has your day been productive?'

'I've spent my time chasing up the Dey's scribes and gaining permission to see the register of captives who have been brought to Algiers recently.'

She looked at him, eyeing him with concern as he frowned distractedly. 'What is it that makes you look so grim? Did you find anything out about Jane?' His expression tightened and a cold shiver of fear travelled down her spine. 'You know where she is, don't you?' Coming to a halt, she took his arm and forced him to look at her, her eyes intense. 'Don't lie to me, Tobias, and don't hold anything back. Was she brought here? Has she been sold.'

'I did find her name in the register—and, yes, Rowena, she has been sold.'

Rowena raised her head and looked at him, her lovely mouth pinched and drawn. 'Then whoever has bought her—will he take her for his wife?'

'Not unless she converts to Islam.'

Rowena stared at him. 'Do you mean she would have to renounce Christianity?'

Tobias nodded. 'That is the only way.'

'Then to get her to comply would have to be under

duress. Jane is a devout Christian. She would never willingly forsake her faith.' She shook her head slowly as realisation of what this would mean to her gentle sister became clear. 'To do so would be a source of shame. She would be despised by Christians, and yet if she doesn't I believe she will be severely punished until she is constrained to submit. That will happen, won't it, Tobias?'

In this instance Tobias would prefer that Rowena did not know the truth of what happened to female captives who were taken into rich men's harems and forcibly converted to Islam, afterwards having the dubious honour of indulging their master's sexual whims.

'Jane will be made to convert. You asked me not to hold anything back from you, Rowena, to be honest, so there you have it.'

'They may force her, but she will never give up the consent of her heart. Where is she? Is she here in Algiers?'

'She is being taken to Meknes. She was bought by one of Sultan Moulay Ismail's agents by the name of Suleiman—a top dealer in white slaves who prides himself on his merchandise. He buys girls of excellent quality for the sultan's large and prestigious harem, where women and children live in cloistered isolation.'

Rowena glanced at him sharply. 'This sultan? Who is he?'

'Ismail Moulay is the Sultan of Morocco—a very powerful man.'

'Tell me about him? He sounds very important. Is he a good man—or a man to be feared?'

'Unfortunately it is the latter. He is a cold-hearted

despot who demands absolute deference from his subjects. He is unpredictable, dangerous and utterly ruthless—a man to be avoided at all costs.'

The clear blue-green eyes anxiously questioned. 'Where is this place he is taking her to?'

'Meknes is the imperial capital—approximately five hundred miles away from Algiers by land. The sultan's palace, which resembles an impregnable fortress, has been constructed on a grand scale, built entirely by Christian slave labour—the like of which you cannot possibly imagine. It is a huge complex of luxury that is said to outshine King Louis's Palace of Versailles, yet designed to withstand the mightiest armies and is protected by the black imperial guard, who are well drilled, vicious and ready to attack anyone.'

'Was there any talk of a ransom?'

'No. Jane was quite outstanding and caused quite a stir among the potential buyers. Some of the other females were plain and lacked grace, but your sister sold for a fine price. She was the central jewel of the whole auction, according to the scribe.'

Rowena's rage came to the fore. 'How dare they treat her like a cow at an auction? How dare they? At least we know where she is being taken, and, now we know, I will follow her and speak to her and hopefully take her home.'

Tobias's face darkened. 'It is not that simple, Rowena. When she reaches Meknes and is installed into the sultan's harem, then to so much as glimpse inside would cost you your life. No one but the sultan himself and his eunuchs are allowed into the inner sanctum.'

What Tobias told her snuffed out the joy Rowena felt on being close to her sister. Despite the heat, she felt the ice move in her veins. Something inside her lurched in terror of what she didn't know, for surely the worst had happened. 'But he cannot keep her locked up for ever. There must be something we can do to reach her.'

'Once she is in the harem, there will be little we can do.'

'But—there has to be. I cannot go back without her. You know I cannot,' she cried in desperation. 'I could not leave Jane.'

'You may have no choice, Rowena.' Tobias knew the pain that was in her heart—he could feel it almost as a tangible thing.

'That is not true.' Her voice rose and she stepped back from him, her eyes filled with horror. 'There has to be some way of getting her out. I will go there and see this place for myself if necessary. I will speak to the sultan and ask for her to be set at ransom and freed.'

'It's impossible. There will be risks I don't want to expose you to.'

'I'm not afraid of danger. Nothing can frighten me.'

Tobias caught the spark that ignited her blue-green eyes and the temper behind them. He combed his fingers through his hair in frustration, knowing that nothing he could say would deter her from seeking out her sister.

'Dear Lord, Rowena, you never cease to amaze me. You are so headstrong, so strong willed and full of your own invincibility that you are willing to put yourself in danger.'

'I will do anything.'

'You're deceiving yourself. What will you do? How

can you imagine going to Meknes to get Jane back? You wouldn't get anywhere near her. Be realistic, Rowena. You are doomed if anyone recognises you as a Christian. Your head would soon be used to decorate the walls of the sultan's imperial palace and your body thrown to the lions.'

Rowena began pacing rapidly up and down; as her thoughts grew wilder, so her steps accelerated. 'I will not go home without her. Even if it means working as a slave, under the lash, even if I have to undergo torture,' she uttered fiercely, loudly, 'I shall go there myself and seek her out.'

'Stop it, Rowena,' Tobias retorted sternly. 'You are being irrational. If you want to go there, it would be as well not to shout it from the roof tops.'

Overwhelmed by the terrible feeling of defeat and helplessness creeping over her, Rowena stared at the sea below. She realised suddenly, from the anguish that clawed at her heart, just how close and yet how far removed she was from Jane, even now—more so, because without Tobias she did not have the strength to go to Meknes alone, and if she did succeed, she did not have the means to negotiate a ransom.

Turning from him, she clenched her hands by her sides and closed her eyes so that he would not see the tears that started into them. How could she bear this, knowing that—that devil would soon have Jane at his mercy, that he would take her good, gentle, innocent, beloved sister to be used for his sordid pleasure? She felt sickened at the thought of Jane in the hands of a monster like that.

When Tobias had brought her to this house, like most English people she had very little understanding about Islam, and she'd felt a strange fascination about the Islamic culture. But now she was beginning to see beneath the surface of the frightening world of Barbary, a cruel, dark and sadistic world, and she longed to see the back of it.

Chapter Seven

'No matter where she is, I shall go to her. I shall go to the den of that evil creature who has her.'

Tobias could see that Rowena's nerves were strung tightly and that any more strain might cause her to snap and send her over the edge into hysteria. She had not for one moment believed that her venture to get Jane back would fail, until now, and she could not accept it. For a moment he hesitated. Then he reached out and grasped her shoulders, pulling her round to face him. The sight of her wet cheeks sent a physical pain through his heart and made him speak with more violence than he had intended.

'Don't be a fool, Rowena. Do you imagine for one moment that you will get through the sultan's guards and come out alive with Jane? It simply is not possible.'

'Are you saying that she might be lost to us?' she cried, shrugging his hands away and stepping back.

'Tragically that is precisely what I am saying.'

'No,' she cried. 'I will not accept that—not ever.'

'For God's sake, Rowena, be realistic.'

'Realistic?' she flared, her eyes wide with anger. 'You dare say that to me? I have been nothing but realistic since the day I learned that Jane was taken from that wretched boat. If that beast harms one hair of my sister's head, I swear by my mother's memory that nothing will keep him from my vengeance. I will kill him with my bare hands even if I die for it. One way or another I will go to Meknes, Tobias, so don't you try to stop me.'

Tobias flinched before the cold fury in those glittering eyes and the pallor on that lovely face, the anguish so clearly marked. But when Suleiman reached the sultan's palace and Jane was installed into the harem, he had to make Rowena see the futility of what she still hoped for. His face hardened with his resolve.

'You will not go to Meknes. I forbid it.'

Recoiling as though he had struck her, she stared at him wide-eyed, as though seeing him for the first time. He was a towering, masculine presence. Never had he looked so tall, so handsome—or so inflexible.

'You forbid it?' she gasped. 'You, of all people, cannot *forbid* me to do anything. Go to hell, Tobias Searle. I would never have set out on this mad journey if I'd thought I would have to admit defeat. You promised you would help me. You promised. I might have known you would renege on your word. I should have known better than to lay my trust in a man who would hound a cripple for an unpaid debt. Have you so little honour that you would do that?'

With a haughty toss of her head, turning on her heel she stalked up the path, away from him. She did not see the way his rigid shoulders bunched, nor the way his hands clenched into fists, for her whole body was rising in revolt against this monstrous place that no longer held any appeal to her, where people were held as slaves, thrashed and worked until they died.

Anger blazed up in Tobias; heedless that there might be watching eyes, he strode after her, and, grasping her shoulders, jerked her round to face him so that he towered above her with all his great strength, his face white and his expression hard and implacable.

Never had Rowena seen so much rage, so much fury, in any man. He had a way of wiping all expression from his face when he wished and, as she looked at him, she had no idea what he was thinking. She soon found out. He had been angry a moment ago, but now he was incandescent and she knew she had gone too far. But it was not in her nature to draw back. She tensed to meet his wrath as his face was thrust into hers.

'Honour, you say? Aye, Rowena, I have it.' His eyes were brittle. 'I have more honour than the man who set fire to my ship and burnt the crew while they slept—the same man who has continued to elude me these past four years. He is the one who must be reckoned with.'

'What are you saying?'

He laughed shortly. 'Mason knows what happened on the night your father was shot. Let him tell you. Or you can ask some of the witnesses who were present that night. I don't need to defend myself to you or anyone else.' His eyes glowed in the dim light and he gave her a lazy smile. 'I never claimed to be an innocent, Rowena, but neither am I your black-hearted villain.'

His words brought Rowena up sharp and for a moment she simply stared at him, before recollecting herself. 'Whatever the truth of what happened on Antigua, that is not what this is about. It is about Jane, and I will not be dictated to by you.' Rigid with fury, turbulent tears streaming down her cheeks, she glared at him. His smile vanished and his eyes narrowed and began to glitter dangerously. She did not flinch beneath the barely concealed menace.

'You dare say that to me?' he flung at her. 'Are you not forgetting something? You should be on your knees in gratitude for my forbearance and mercy. When I found you on my ship I could have turned it around and taken you back to your father at any time. It was never too late.'

'But instead you took me along, intending to abandon me at the first obstacle that arose.'

'Believe me, Rowena, the sultan is not an obstacle. He is much more than that. But enough of this.' His voice was hard, flat and biting. He had his own knowledge of the sultan and the situation and he didn't hold out much hope for getting Jane back once she was in his harem, but somehow he must rebuild Rowena's self-esteem, and relax those vibrating nerves. With an effort he restrained the urge to move closer, and put every ounce of conviction he could muster into his voice as he said, 'You are upset—rightly so—but listen to what I say and try to think about it rationally. I am sorry about

Jane, and I will seriously consider the situation. If there is anything to be done to get her back I will do it, but whatever we do, you must calm yourself. No young girl's wiles will see you safe from Moulay Ismail.'

Rowena stepped back. Fear rose within her, not of him but of herself, for in spite of her cruel, accusing words about her father, she wanted him to help her in this more than anything. But she realised exactly what she was asking of him. To go to Meknes he would be placing not only himself, but others he would have to take with him in danger. Little wonder he was concerned and reluctant to do it. Wrapping her arms round her waist and drawing herself upright, she gulped down her tears and nodded.

'Yes—you are right. Does—does that mean you will not abandon Jane?' she asked hesitantly, hardly daring to hope.

He raised a dark eyebrow. 'Perhaps.' He eyed her blandly. There were lines in the corners of his mouth, but his gaze was steady.

Rowena looked at him, conscious as always of an unwitting excitement. Feeling the heat in her cheeks, she averted her eyes. Then looking back, she met his look with a little frown, her body taut, every muscle stretched against the invisible pull between them.

'I'm sorry, Tobias. I do appreciate everything you have done for me—even though it may not look like it.'

His smile swept for a brief instant across his face, but there was a world of warmth in the blue eyes that had seen so many storms, so many days of gazing in the sun and wind and the sky from a heaving deck. He had told her to be rational and realistic, and yet how could he expect her to be wise at her age?

'Your apology is accepted. To abandon Jane would be to abandon you, Rowena, and I will not do that. I would like to be your friend to my last breath, so I am obliged to help you. If it is in my power, I will free your sister.'

'You will? Thank you,' she whispered, her anger draining from her.

'Besides,' he murmured, his hands closing round her upper arms and drawing her close, his cool manner now ripped away, 'we made a bargain, you and I. You have not forgotten?'

'How can I, when you constantly remind me? It would no longer stand if we do not find Jane.'

His face was in the shadows, but his eyes seemed to glow, laughing at her, gently mocking her. 'Listen well, Rowena. If our mission fails, one way or another I will see it out. I promise you that.'

'I don't work like that, Tobias. No Jane, no deal. That is the arrangement we made.'

He smiled assuredly, bringing her closer to his chest, his arms going around her and tightening. 'We have a long way to go. Whether we succeed in freeing Jane or not, I shall have my night of love. I promise you that.'

In the next instant his lips were on hers and his fiery kiss warmed her to the core of her being. All her restraints broke as she felt again the fierce thrill of being in his arms. He kissed her with ardour and passion and she could think of nothing but the exciting urgency of his mouth and the warmth of his breath and the feel of his strong muscled legs against her own.

When Tobias felt her melt against him, with iron control he released her lips and straightened his body, and through the haze of heated passion, Rowena was aware of his strong, surprisingly gentle hands trailing down her back. Beneath the fine fabric of her clothes, her skin felt the warmth of them. That one kiss had been too much and too little, leaving her hungering and aching for more.

Ever since the day of their interlude on the beach something new and miraculous had sprung up between them, growing like a tender shoot into some as yet unknown and lovely flower. There had been no repeat of the intimacy, but everything between them had changed. Slowly but surely she knew they were both lowering their guard. But she would have to be careful and even though she would like to go on kissing him whenever the opportunity arose, she must not forget that as far as she was aware she was promised to another, a man her father approved of—Tobias Searle he did not.

Recollecting herself, she looked up at him and he chuckled softly, his eyes holding hers in one long, compelling look.

'Don't look so aggrieved, Rowena. Your virtue is safe with me—for the time being.'

'Safe?' Tension rode heavily on her words. 'Already you have taken too many liberties. When you are with me I feel as if there's but one thought in your mind.'

'Because that's exactly how it is.' The whisper came

close to her ear as he smoothed her tumbled hair from her brow. 'Of late, watching you has become my favourite pastime, and you don't know how hard you make it for me to resist you.'

'What do you suggest we do now?'

'Go and change out of those clothes. I will take you back to the ship.'

'And what then?'

'We will go to Sale. Suleiman hopes to purchase more captives from ports along the way. If he has left for Meknes, then we will try to apprehend him. Time is of the essence. We must act quickly.'

Just then they heard a pair of slippers slapping along the tiled walkway and suddenly Ahmed appeared in a white robe, an enormous silver-and-blue turban and crimson Moroccan slippers. A heavy gold chain hung round his neck, and his fingers were adorned with an assortment of rings with different precious stones.

Tobias considered this man a close friend, he had said, and while Rowena didn't understand why—each coming from such different backgrounds and cultures— she had to admit a definite, different quality to the man, a mixture of the savage and civilised world she found altogether disquieting.

Ahmed's black eyes sparkled as he looked from Rowena to Tobias. 'I apologise for not being here when you arrived, Tobias. I've been busy on your account.'

'Oh?' Tobias's eyes lit with interest.

Ahmed's gaze went over Rowena appraisingly and he smiled broadly, his white teeth gleaming in his brown face. 'Do you not think Rowena looks handsome—like a rare pearl—lovelier than an houri in paradise? Her transformation from cabin boy to an exotically beautiful young maiden of Algiers is astonishing.'

'Yes, Ahmed, I agree, but I'm afraid I must take her away.'

'Then that is a shame. When must you go?'

'Tonight. We are to go to Sale.' He looked at his friend with a sombre frown creasing his brow. 'So, what have you been up to on my account?'

'I thought you might be interested in knowing where Mason went when he left Algiers.'

Tobias became alert, his eyes hard, his body taut. 'Where?'

'His intention is to cross the Atlantic to the West Indies. He is heading for Madeira to pick up the northeast trades.'

'How do you know this?'

'Oh, I have my informers. So you are on the point of leaving for Sale—but now you know where Mason is heading, you will follow him into the Atlantic, I think?'

Tobias sighed and his shoulders slumped. 'No, Ahmed. We are to go after Rowena's sister—which could take some considerable time.'

A puzzled expression creased Ahmed's brow. 'But you have been hunting Mason for four years. Are you saying that you will allow him to slip away when at last you have him within your grasp?'

Tobias nodded and when he spoke his voice was tight. 'That is precisely what I am saying, Ahmed.

Suleiman, the sultan's agent, is sailing to Sale. From there he will take his captives overland to Meknes. I am hoping he is in no hurry and that he will languish a while in Sale, in which case there is every chance I can catch up with him before he leaves.'

'Then what will you do? Will you offer ransom?'

'Unless I can spirit her out of Suleiman's clutches then there is nothing else I can do.'

'To the agent, a slave, particularly a pale-skinned beauty, is too valuable a commodity to free. If he agrees, he will demand a high price—double or more what he paid at the market.'

'I am prepared for that.'

Ahmed stared at him in disbelief and then shook his head slowly, fingering his beard. 'Ah, then I wish you luck, my friend. You will have your work cut out. The sultan's palace is a viper's nest. It is dangerous to go there. Better to reach the young lady before she is swallowed into the harem.'

'Which is why we must leave at once.'

'And Mason?'

Avoiding looking at Rowena, Tobias stiffened, his expression grim. 'He will have to wait.'

'But you may not get another chance.' He shook his head slowly. 'You and Mason have been locked in a kind of unscripted duel across the oceans for a long time. I know what apprehending him means to you. He knows you are still after him?'

Tobias nodded. 'He knows.'

He spoke evenly to Ahmed, but Rowena could detect

underlying currents in his tone. He was seething with frustration and anger, and she had a strong suspicion his anger was directed at her. He didn't want to go to Sale. He felt obliged to do so and was simply being chivalrous.

Her conscience awoke. She was relieved that Tobias had agreed to follow Jane and she would be for ever grateful, but there seemed an overwhelming emptiness about it all now. She began to realise the enormity of what she was asking of him, and the disappointment he must be feeling for letting Mason slip through his fingers lay like a dead weight upon her mind. She felt ashamed of badgering him into going to Sale, but she could not go after Jane without him.

Ahmed smiled and wished them well, smiling encouragingly as he turned to go back inside. His head was bowed as he silently invoked the intercession of Allah and his Prophet Mohamed in his friend's safe journey to Sale.

'Tobias, I—I want to thank you for what you're doing for Jane—but I'm—sorry,' she said hesitantly, trying to marshal her scattered thoughts, which had been thrown into disarray by Ahmed's appearance and disclosure about Jack Mason.

Tobias swung his head round to face her and she shrank from the cold look in his eyes. His jaw was set in a hard line and the lean hard plains of his cheeks looked harsh and forbidding in the silver Mediterranean moonlight. 'I don't want your thanks, Rowena. I'm merely doing what my conscience dictates.'

'But—'

'Leave it,' he bit out fiercely. 'We are going to Sale

and that is final. I suggest you go and change and make your goodbyes. We will head back to the ship. The sooner we get under way the better.'

Rowena's mouth went dry and her heart began to beat in heavy, terrifying dread as she sensed that Tobias had seemingly withdrawn from her. Without a word she slipped away to say her farewells to Fatima, Shillah and Zidana, although with the tightness in her throat she found it hard to respond politely to their regret that she was leaving and accept their good wishes. From this point there would be no turning back, and she knew Tobias must have the sense of being caught up in an implacable destiny.

Tobias took Rowena back to the ship, offering no conversation of his own, speaking only when spoken to. There was a remoteness about him. He had withdrawn from her.

Gradually she fell silent and followed him without trying to make him talk. She felt the pain of his frustration, his anger and helplessness as though it had been inflicted on her, though the pain was in a different place. Her heart was beating with a dull and heavy feeling of shame, that being so wrapped up in her blind determination to find Jane, she had not recognised and acknowledged Tobias's own need.

A boat was waiting at the quayside to take them back to the ship. Lanterns lit up the deck and a smiling Mark Dexter was standing at the rail to watch them aboard.

'Nice to have you back on board, Master Rowan,' he said by way of welcome.

'It's nice to be back, Mr Dexter.'

'I trust you've had a pleasant time ashore.'

'Very agreeable, thank you.'

His face tight and grim, Tobias addressed Mark. 'I want to be away at first light, Mark. We are to go to Sale. Inform the crew, will you?'

'Sale?'

Tobias nodded. 'I'll explain it all later.'

Rowena glanced at Mark and wished she hadn't. The sombre expression on his face was too unsettling, almost as if their journey to this other North African port was about to cause some kind of complication.

'And Mason? Since the young lady is being taken to Sale, he must have been here—could still be here.'

'He's gone—heading for the Atlantic. Ahmed believes he is to cross to the Indies.'

'And you don't intend going after him?'

'No,' Tobias answered curtly. 'Not this time. Make ready to sail in good time, Mark.'

Mark shifted uncomfortably, for, like Ahmed, he was astounded by what Tobias was about to do. He shook his head, knowing full well what agonies Tobias must be suffering. What Rowena could not know was Tobias's rage and fury when he had seen his ship on fire, knowing there were men on board unable to escape the flames.

Never had Mark heard such shouts of fury, such vicious promises to make whoever was responsible pay for that cowardly act of murder. And now, when Mason, the perpetrator of the wicked deed, was within his grasp,

Tobias was prepared to let his prey escape while he went chasing after Rowena's sister. Mark could well imagine what that was costing him.

'Sale is a fearful place, is it not, Mr Dexter?' Rowena asked.

He nodded grimly, his own far-from-pleasant memories of his time spent in that rat-infested nest a long time ago coming back to haunt him. Sale was one place he had never hoped to see again.

'The most infamous city on earth. Our voyage will be one of extreme danger.' He looked at Tobias. 'We will be lucky to reach Sale without being captured by the corsairs ourselves. We both know the Sale Rovers are nothing but a bunch of ruthless, fanatical pirates, with whom there is no parleying. What shall I tell the crew?'

'If they think we are going after Mason, there'll be no objections from them. They chafe at the loss of several decent men. They only wait on the proper moment to make him pay for what he did, and he will suffer a far worse fate if their plan comes to an end.'

'You intend to deceive them?'

Rowena was watching Tobias intently as she awaited his reply to Mr Dexter's question, but he avoided looking at her. 'I have to. Suleiman has three or four days' head start on us. He is unaware that he is being pursued, so will see no need for haste. He will lose time if he hopes to pick up more captives, so hopefully he will still be in Sale when we get there. When I have negotiated the release of Miss Golding, there will be nothing to prevent us going after Mason.'

Tobias looked at Rowena, speaking tersely. 'Go and get some sleep while you can.'

Without bothering to so much as glance in her direction, he turned on his heel and headed for the helmsman.

Dawn brushed the sky a deep magenta, melting into a softer rose pink before the sun, rising golden on the horizon, sharply etching the detail of the *Cymbeline* in its gilded light. The morning progressed, the sky fading to a subdued blue, and the translucent turquoise and aquamarine that dipped and rolled in a languid motion became the sea beneath it. Canvas sails billowed, stretched by the wind, and the sloop skimmed the waters like a beautiful white seabird in effortless flight.

Rowena sat on the broad sill, her arm resting on her drawn-up knees, gazing at the African coastline. After a while Tobias walked in. From the corner of her eyes she watched him pour himself a drink, swallowing it down in one gulp. The cabin suddenly seemed too small for his great height. Her heart set up its familiar wild beating as she looked at him. His expression was unreadable, his head a tumble of dark curls. The lines of his face were heavy about his mouth and cheeks, and there were the signs of strain under the blue eyes. Again she experienced the depth to which her mind and body stirred whenever she was in his presence.

As she rose, her breath froze at the coldness she saw in his eyes when he fixed her with a long and thoughtful stare. The remembrance of their parting on deck the night before, of what had been a bitter end to a perfect two days, touched her deeply.

'Excuse me,' she murmured, crossing to the door, somehow managing to hide her disappointment at his icy reserve.

His eyes narrowed. 'Where do you think you're going?'

'I thought you might like some privacy. Besides, I would like to go on deck. It's hot down here. I need some air. You—have no objections?'

Instead of answering, he lifted his brows and regarded her in cold silence. Rowena decided to take his silence for assent and was about to leave when he halted her.

'Wait a moment.' With a deep sigh Tobias shoved his hair from his brow and rested his hips against the table. His shoulders relaxed and he looked at her without animosity. 'You don't have to leave on my account. I'm sorry, Rowena. I was a brute to you last night. It was cruel of me to behave as I did.'

Going to stand in front of him, she smiled softly. 'I am the cruel one. You had to make an impossible choice. I am relieved you chose to help me. I am indeed grateful—although there was a moment, when Ahmed told you where Mason was heading, that I thought you would abandon me. I could not do this on my own.' There was an air of remoteness about him that struck straight at her heart. 'Tobias,' she said hesitantly, 'what about Jack Mason?'

His face hardened and she felt her heart sink. How were they to discuss this terrible dilemma if every time his adversary's name was mentioned he turned away from her, and, if they were not to talk about it, how was she to know what he was thinking?

'What about him?'

'I want to tell you that I am sorry. I am not so insensitive not to know how you must be feeling. You wanted to go after him—and knowing him for the scoundrel he is, I cannot blame you.' A hard gleam flashed into her eyes. 'Like you, I want him caught—to pay for what he did. Perhaps when we find Jane, it may not be too late and you can still go after him.'

'Forget it. It's not important,' he added with a touch of bitterness that betrayed his anger and hurt.

Rowena was stabbed by it to her very soul. 'How can you say that?' she flared, her voice raised with passion. 'What Jack Mason did cannot be passed off as unimportant. Do you think you're the only one to hold a grievance? He did my father a grave wrong too, don't forget. Mason stole his ship and in so doing ruined him. My father is unable to wipe the slate clean of all past memories and he will suffer until his dying day because of it.

'When we reach Sale and Jane is released, you must go after Mason, Tobias. He must be brought to account for what he did to both you and my father. I no longer intend being an encumbrance to you. Perhaps Jane and I can find passage on another ship to take us back to England.'

'No. Do not even think about it. Two English-women—alone in a den of wild beasts? Whatever happens, you will remain with me.' Suddenly his eyes became penetrating. He had not missed how her eyes had burned with a fiery determination when she had been speaking of Mason. 'You speak as though it is you who have more grievance towards Mason, Rowena, and yet, since he was employed by your father and spent most of his time at sea, you cannot have known him very well. You must have been no more than fifteen when you last saw him. Do you have reasons of your own to despise him?'

His voice was harsh, crackling with some emotion Rowena could not even guess at. It was a question she did not want to answer. She averted her gaze. The mere shadow of the memory made her feel dirty, battered, ashamed. What Jack Mason had tried to do to her was something she had put to the back of her mind; she had no wish to resurrect it and air just now.

'You are right. Our paths didn't cross until he was about to leave on that last fateful voyage with my father. I—I didn't like him. He was too arrogant, too sure of himself.'

'And when and where did you last see him, Rowena?' Tobias persisted, folding his arms across his broad chest, refusing to let the matter rest.

She shrugged and turned away from his unrelenting gaze. 'What does it matter now? Like you said, it was a long time ago and not worth bothering about.'

'But it does bother you. I can see that. When and where, Rowena?' he demanded. 'Did Mason threaten you?' His stomach knotted at the thought that this might be so.

'Well—it wasn't—I mean…' She knew she was babbling, but somehow it seemed prudent to keep what had happened the last time she had seen Jack Mason to herself.

'Tell me.'

Suddenly angry, his persistence beginning to annoy her, she turned her head and glowered at him. 'If you really must know, he…' She faltered, not knowing how to go on.

'He attacked you.'

She nodded vehemently. 'Yes, that's what he did.'

'And being the quick-tempered, many-sided vixen that you are, you fought back.'

'It was my natural instinct.' She faced him squarely, her chin tilted upwards as she continued to speak in her own defence. 'I met him when Father brought him to the house. There was something about him I didn't like. It took me all of two seconds to discover how odiously obnoxious he is. Jack Mason, however, took an unfortunate fancy to me and began pursuing me. When he realised I was serious in refusing his advances, his pursuit turned ugly.'

'But you were fifteen years of age.'

'Yes, just. He did attack me, when I was riding in my favourite place—where you came upon me yourself, if you remember. I was alone, very young, very vulnerable and very stupid—I realise that now—which was why I acquired my beautiful, faithful dogs to protect me from monsters like Mason in the future. He was vicious, like a crazed animal. When he saw I was no simpering miss and prepared to put up a fight to stop him attacking me, he forced himself on me and tried to ravish me.' Lifting her head, she looked directly at him. 'But he didn't. I fought and by some miracle managed to get away.'

'Does your father know about this?'

'I didn't tell him. He was on board ship, getting ready to leave Falmouth. Besides, it would have served no purpose. The vessel was about to leave and Mason would be on it. He could do me no further harm and Father wouldn't have to go to the trouble of finding another captain, which would have been virtually impossible at the time—I knew how important the voyage was to him.'

Tobias stared at the tempestuous beauty standing before him, her face both delicate and vivid, her eyes flashing like angry jewels. His face hardened and so did something inside him, something that now felt it would do murder on her behalf.

'I am appalled by what happened to you, Rowena. I would like to kill Mason with my bare hands.'

This was true, and now he knew her he could well explain the violence of his feelings. Anger was boiling up inside him, an anger so great it was like a physical thing. Mason had attacked her—that bully, with the reputation of a prize fighter, a broad-shouldered, swaggering scoundrel—for reasons he didn't want to think of. The images of this lovely girl   fifteen, she had been being pursued, knocked down by that brute who had attempted the worst kind assault on her body a man could inflict on a woman, appalled him and filled him with a savagery that could not be appeased until he had run the perpetrator down and hung him from a yardarm on the pirate's own ship.

Rowena saw the way his jaw had clenched and his

lips were clamped in a thin white line. His hands were clenched in fists by his sides and his eyes were hard, with an expression that was hard to define. The sun shone through the window full on to his face, giving his bronzed flesh a golden glow, and it seemed he could not speak.

At last he did. 'Did you see him again after that?'

'No. He left Falmouth that same day. Tobias, nothing would please me more than to go with you after that beast, but I hope you understand that Jane must be my priority. If she reaches Meknes and is forced to convert to Muslim, she will become lost to her family for ever. That is what you said.'

'I did. There can be no ransom—and nor can a convert expect to be set free by his owner, as many converts wrongly assume—especially when that owner happens to be Moulay Ismail.'

'Will you promise me something?'

'What?'

'When we have freed Jane—because I am determined that we shall—will you go after Mason, find him and make him pay for what he did to you?'

Grimly pressing his lips together, Tobias nodded and left the cabin, more determined that ever to find Mason. He would take care of that monster, not just for the men who had perished on his ship, but for Rowena also.

The *Cymbeline* ran within sight of the North African coast, sailing west. They passed Tangier, an abandoned English outpost, and continued unhindered through the straits, turning south to Sale, regardless of the hopes and fears the *Cymbeline* carried with her.

Rowena could have been forgiven if she lost her nerve on her first sight of Sale, which occupied a commanding position on the north bank of the Bou Regreg river estuary. With its rocky shoreline, this was a dangerous, well-fortified nest of corsairs. Its massive forbidding walls, turreted battlements and towers and green-glazed minarets that sparkled beneath the North African sun were visible from far out to sea. Each side of the river estuary had been enclosed by stout battlements, and two castles bristled with cannon fronting the sea, hinting at the menacing threat within the walls of Sale.

On account of little depth of water, vessels of large burden could not enter the harbour and were obliged to wait for high tide before they could nudge further in shore. The *Cymbeline*'s anchor was dropped outside the shifting sandbar that provided Sale with a defence from the sea.

Tobias came to stand beside Rowena at the rail. 'Were I not aware of what this place is like, I would say Sale looks quite enchanting,' she murmured, without turning to look at him, brushing her hair from her face. It was so windy she had to hold her hat on to stop it blowing off.

'I suppose it does, but the only difference to its counterparts in other North African cities is that the slave markets—which at one time were the largest and most profitable in North Africa—have undergone great changes since Moulay Ismail came to power. One of the first things he did was to close the slave market—not out of kindness, but because he wants to keep all the slaves for himself.'

'When do you intend going ashore?' she asked, gazing at the city beyond the great walls with a great deal of fear and apprehension.

'Shortly.'

'Where will you begin looking for Suleiman?'

'Among the city's merchants. They will tell me if he is still in Sale. If he has left, I shall find out when and follow.'

'Is it a long journey to Meknes?'

'About four days.'

'About the ransom, Tobias. Do you have the kind of money Suleiman will demand?'

He nodded. 'Rest assured that I shall take enough with me to cover the ransom.'

'I can't thank you enough. I will pay you back, I promise.'

He grinned and there was a devilish glint in his eyes. 'I know you will. If not in money, then in kind. Be sure I shall insist on it. I am eager to do well in your service, Rowena, and receive my reward.'

Rowena's breath caught in her throat. The gleam in his eyes made her body turn warm and melting and her cheeks flushed, but she was determined to remain in control. It was too important for her to lose her wits now.

Tobias smiled into her eyes. 'You do remember?' he said softly. 'I want you to enjoy me as much as I will enjoy you.'

The flush on her cheeks deepened. 'Believe me when

I say that if matters had stood otherwise, I would never have dreamed of making such a bargain.'

'Twice,' he reminded her smoothly.

She looked at him askance. 'It's becoming something of a habit,' she retorted drily.

He grinned. 'A habit I approve of. If we go on like this, my sweet,' he murmured softly, 'your prospective bridegroom is going to have to do without you in his bed indefinitely.'

'He probably will anyway. I don't expect him to marry me after what I've done.'

Tobias's eyes narrowed and a strange, almost secretive smile curved his lips. 'You don't know that for certain. He might surprise you.'

Rowena sighed and gazed across the choppy water to the city beyond the high walls. 'I don't have your faith, Tobias. I fully expect him to have withdrawn his offer when I get back to Falmouth. Have you been to Sale before?'

'Once—some years ago,' he told her, the smile vanishing from his lips. 'I exchanged a cargo of woollens and silver for silk and ivory and other commodities brought in by desert caravans from central Africa. I felt the menace of Sale then, and had no wish to return in a hurry.' He pushed himself away from the rail. 'I must speak to Mark before I go ashore. Whatever happens, I want the ship to be ready to leave at a moment's notice.'

'I'll go below and get my sandals.' Rowena had taken to walking about the ship bare footed, but she would find it rough going without her sandals on land.

'Why? Are you going somewhere?'

'With you.'

Undecided, he frowned. 'I'd rather you didn't.'

Her expression was mutinous. 'Don't tell me what to do, Tobias Searle. Jane is my sister and I am coming with you. If you should find her, she's going to need me.'

'Very well, but have no illusions. It's going to be difficult securing Jane's release—if we find her. There are also corsair vessels all around us, and they have a fierce hatred of Christians. What is more to the point, when we have secured Jane's release we have to leave this place without delay.'

'Of course. I understand.'

'And as for leaving me to pursue Mason and trying to acquire passage back to England on another vessel, forget it. Alone, you and your sister would be like lambs in the lion's den. Jane would be recaptured, and you, and then neither I nor anyone else will be able to get you out of the sultan's harem. What I am about to do will be dangerous. I want to know you are safe on the *Cymbeline*.'

'But we can't go into the city by ourselves.'

'I don't intend to. I'll take two of the crew. Even so we may have trouble.'

They were so intent on focusing their sights on the town that they failed to see the vessel appear out of the sun, bearing down on Sale under her full spread of canvas, a tall white billowing pyramid. The captain of the corsair ship, dressed in an immaculate white gown edged with crimson and gold braid, stood at the bow. He placed the spy glass to his eye, playing his sight over every part of the *Cymbeline,* before coming to rest on the pennant fluttering sprightly from its masthead—the bold bright gold S curled round the letter T against a crimson background. Then, with a smile that would have disturbed the *Cymbeline'*s master, he ordered the captives to be made ready to be taken ashore.

Chapter Eight

⁓⁓⁓⁓⁓⁓

Since getting out of the boat, Rowena felt she needed another pair of eyes to take everything in. Sheep, donkeys, mules and a few nonchalant camels carrying all manner of things on their backs wandered about among the crowd. The streets and alleys were hot, dusty and chaotic. They were also filthy and full of rubbish and flies and scavenging dogs. She found it claustrophobic, the stench appalling.

This, then, was Sale, hopefully the end of her crazy journey undertaken against all better judgement, but how was Tobias to find Suleiman in this intricate network of streets and alleys? Sensing a powerful need to stave off the discouragement that had followed hard on the heels of triumph on reaching Sale without mishap, Rowena closed her eyes and whispered a silent prayer to God, fervently beseeching him to take pity on her sister and allow her to be returned to them.

A hand gently touching her shoulder made her open her eyes. She saw Tobias looking at her intently.

'Do not forget where you are,' he murmured, just loud enough for her to hear. 'It is reckless to pray out in the open. This is a country of infidels with not a church or a chapel in sight—nothing but mosques where these miscreants pray to Allah. If anyone were to see you, we would all be doomed.'

'Forgive me. I had forgotten. Do you know where to go?' she asked, finding his nearness reassuring.

The two crew members, like Tobias armed with pistols and sword, stayed close together.

'I know where the merchant lives that I dealt with when I was here last. It isn't far from here.'

Aware of a great commotion, of voices raised, hostile voices, some louder than others, they paused to look behind them. Rowena stared at a procession—a wretched band of Europeans herded together, coming towards them along the street that wound between white-washed houses. She was so appalled at the sight her eyes beheld that she gasped and flattened herself against the wall to let them pass by.

They were being jeered at and cursed by the locals, and stones were thrown, some hitting their targets with accurate, painful precision. There were about fifty of these pitiful captives, bruised and barefoot, a large iron ring riveted to the ankle of each man. A long heavy chain was attached to the rings, which the slaves were obliged to drag behind them. Their heads were bowed, their expression all sad terror, bewilderment and apprehension.

When they had shuffled by, Rowena stayed frozen to the spot. Even Tobias stood staring after them.

'Poor things,' Rowena whispered, her face beneath the floppy brim of her hat shadowed by a deep sorrow. 'To be treated like that. God save them. Those men guarding them are savages—the devil's own. Where are they being taken?'

'To the *matamores*—a worse place you cannot imagine.'

'What are they?'

'Underground cells, subterranean hell holes, where they are kept before being taken to Meknes. But come. Try not to dwell on what you have seen. It will not change anything.'

Tobias went on his way, but feeling a cold sensation on the back of her neck, Rowena turned and looked back. Her eyes beheld a tall man standing in the shadows watching her. He looked austere and stood so still he could have been a stone statue. Dressed in a white robe and black turban, the only part of him she could see was his inscrutable eyes.

Her heart missed a beat and her lips grew dry. The moment was taut with tension. She felt she would suffocate for a moment and recalled a sudden flash of memory—a long-forgotten scene of being dragged off her horse—and a warning shiver seemed to run through the now quiet street like a cat's paw.

Suddenly the man moved and seemed to melt into the shadows, as if he were part of them, and she shivered, feeling a sinister, ill-omened cloud flit over her mind.

Telling herself she was seeing and imagining things, she spun on her heel and hurried after Tobias.

After traversing more streets, Tobias led them into one in which some of the wealthy merchants of the city lived. There were no dung heaps here and flowering creepers trailed over trellising. Tobias stopped in front of a solid door set in a high wall. It opened when he knocked to reveal a servant, a Moor in a white robe and black turban. Tobias spoke to him in Arabic, and the servant ushered them inside an inner courtyard and garden, with exotic blooms everywhere and roses and sweet-scented jasmine climbing the walls.

'Wait here while I speak to the merchant,' Tobias told them, following the servant into the house.

To Rowena the waiting was interminable. When he reappeared his face was drawn and his eyes troubled.

'What is it, Tobias? What is wrong?' she asked, unable to still her fears. 'What did the merchant tell you?'

'Suleiman left for Meknes two days ago.'

Rowena stood motionless, as if turned to stone, her face pale and stricken. 'But—that's terrible,' she gasped, anguish suddenly catching in her throat. 'What should we do?'

'Right now we must get back to the ship.'

'But—you can't mean that. You told me that if Jane had left Sale you would follow—and now you are talking about going back to the ship. This is not the time to give in. We have to do something.'

The pain in her voice cut Tobias as sharply as a knife.

Her words ran on, spilling from her as if only by giving them voice could she exorcise the terror that gripped her. He longed to take her in his arms and soothe her as he would a frightened child, but with two of his crew looking on, he could not.

'We will find her—no matter how long it takes or how large the cost. You must believe that, but if we are to go to Meknes, the journey has to be prepared for. We must have transport—horses or mules—and food.'

Rowena nodded, trying to still her terror and remain calm, though it was nigh impossible. 'When will we be able to leave?'

'If I can have everything arranged, in the morning at first light. I'll take you back to the ship and then I will return. The merchant has offered to help in the way of horses—providing I promise to return to Sale in the future with a cargo of wool and other English goods he has a fancy for,' he added drily. 'So come. We are wasting time.'

Rowena returned to the *Cymbeline* without being aware of anything around her. Her anguished mind quavered inside her and her heart turned over as the fear that she might never see her sister again, that Jane would be condemned to spending the rest of her life as an object of pleasure for a rich and powerful sultan, overtook her.

On reaching the ship and after speaking to Mark, Tobias was rowed back to shore. As Rowena watched him go, Mark came to stand beside her.

'I hope he will be all right,' she whispered. 'He should have taken someone with him.'

'Tobias can take care of himself. Try not to worry. He'll be back before you know it.'

Rowena looked at him, her concern for Tobias there in her eyes for Mark to see. 'I hope so. I really don't want anything to happen to him on my account. I could never forgive myself. He has told you that we are to travel to Meknes.'

Mark nodded, his expression grim. 'It is a journey that may well be fraught with every kind of danger. Tobias is concerned about you and doesn't want to place you in unnecessary danger.'

The absurdity of this was such that Rowena laughed. 'How can that be? He cares nothing for me.'

'Is that so? No man risks life and limb and those of his crew for a woman he cares nothing for,' he murmured with absolute conviction. 'Why not let Tobias go alone and stay with the ship? You will be safer here.'

'No. My mind is made up. I will go with him. But will the ship be safe here in Sale—with all those corsairs and all those cannon breathing fire and shot down your neck? Is there not a strong possibility of you being attacked when attention is drawn to a European vessel in Sale's waters?'

'They know we're here and, no, I doubt there will be trouble. To make sure of this, Tobias has gone to make contact with the ruling divan. Hopefully he will be greeted with courtesy. Merchantmen from all over Europe have suffered at the hands of the corsairs at one time or another and will continue to suffer until something is done to clear them from the seas. Some countries pay the corsairs an agreed amount to leave their ships alone, whilst the British and Dutch East India companies pay a levy and treat it the same as normal shipping insurance.'

'Does Tobias?'

He nodded. 'In the long run it's worth it.'

Rowena's curiosity about Mark Dexter got the better of her. 'You said you have been to Sale before. I sense it was not of your own volition, Mr Dexter.'

His expression hardened and something dark entered his eyes. 'No. Far from it. I was sailing to Genoa when the ship I was on was attacked by corsairs. I was taken captive—along with twenty of my comrades and brought to Sale. It was hell,' he added hoarsely.

'What happened? Did you escape?'

'There is no escape from Sale.'

'The ship—was it one of Tobias's?'

'His father's. I was but a youth at the time. He came and paid the ransom for me and those of his crew who were still alive. He was a fine man. I shall be for ever in his debt.'

Rowena's gaze riveted on the bright blue boat carrying Tobias to shore and, despite everything, an aching lump of tears swelled in her throat. It was disquieting to dwell on the knowledge that she could care for him. 'In his debt,' she whispered. 'If Tobias helps me find my sister that is exactly how I shall feel.'

As she closed the door behind her a gnawing disquiet crept over her. Of late she had begun to think of Tobias far too much and now those illusions were beginning to spill over and consume her. She sat on the bed in dismal meditations, and though she tried to banish him from her thoughts and think of Jane, her mind spun on aimlessly. Suddenly her fear for Jane had shifted to Tobias. Her concern for him was immense and she did not even dare think what she would do if he did not come back.

Later, anxious for his safety, she went into the main cabin and in a woman's way tidied the table and whatever else her eyes lighted on. Tobias's jerkin lay over the back of a chair. Picking it up, she trailed her fingers over the soft leather, savouring the manly smell that filled her head. The barest hint of a smile played across her lips, and her eyes glowed with a warmth she could not explain.

'What is happening to me?' she murmured in some wonder. 'I am like a woman waiting for her man, seizing upon one of his garments to relive past moments.' She sighed, bemused by her mood. She had never felt his presence as much as she missed his absence. *But I will not be drawn,* she assured herself, draping the jerkin back over the chair. She sighed again to ease the lonely ache that sprang up in her heart. *He will come back. He will come back soon.*

Restlessly she went on deck. It was almost dark and the moon lit up the shining surface of the sea. Suddenly her heart leapt when she saw Tobias being rowed back to the ship.

Coming to stand beside her, Mark smiled kindly at her anxious features. 'I told you he would come back safely.'

'Thank God,' she uttered, smothering a cry of joy as Tobias hauled himself on board.

'How did it go?' Mark asked.

'Better than I expected. I was treated with the greatest courtesy by the *divan* and they were most attentive. Being my usual charming self, I enjoyed three hours of their hospitality before bidding them farewell.'

Mark chuckled low in his chest. 'You always did have the devil's own, Tobias. I know of no other as adept at flattery and disarming his enemies with a flow of smooth obsequies as yourself. And the mission to Meknes? What had they to say about that?'

'They saw nothing wrong with it—which is not uncommon, for many European ambassadors come to petition and negotiate ransoms for fellow countrymen. Some are successful, others who do not have sufficient funds are not so successful. You will be relieved to know I have been assured that the *Cymbeline* will be in safe harbour during my absence.'

'They know who you are?'

He nodded. 'My vessels are often seen plying their trade in Portugal and the Mediterranean. The *divan* may be religious fanatics, but they are also pragmatists and are willing to adhere to anything within reason if they stand to benefit.'

'So what is it they want—to trade?'

'Precisely. I told them I would consider it—but I have no intention of sending any of my vessels to Sale in the present climate.'

'And Jane?' Rowena asked, her face dark against the starlit sky.

'Providing I have the means with which to pay the ransom for your sister—and she has not converted to Islam—then they can see no reason why Moulay Ismail will not set her free.'

Rowena's heart soared with relief, only to be brought back down to earth by Tobias's next words.

'It is early days,' he told her gravely, hating to be the one to dampen her enthusiasm. 'The trek to Meknes, for which I have everything arranged, will be long and arduous, and despite what the divan said, the sultan is a cruel despot and not noted for his good humour. He holds most visiting envoys in contempt, and deception and betrayal are second nature to him— and anyone who refuses to defer to him is in danger of losing his head.'

'Then we shall have to be careful. See, the moon has risen. You must be hungry. I'll go below and prepare you a meal.'

She slipped past him and went down to the cabin, and Tobias let her go without making any attempt to follow her. Instead he went to stand at the wheel, looking at the thin line of light on the horizon before coming to rest on the dark silhouette of a ship some considerable distance away. Unable to discern either its name or see the colour of its flag, he turned away.

* * *

Rowena lay down in pursuit of sleep she sorely wanted, but it was a long time coming. Dreadful thoughts and images haunted her mind, and every time she closed her eyes and fell to sleep she was thrown into the grip of a nightmare and tormented by terrible dreams of Jane.

A cry woke Tobias. His first thought was of Rowena. Going to her cabin, by the silvery light of the moon shining in through the small porthole, he could see her lying on the bunk with her arms crossed over her face, as though to blot out some intolerable sight, and she was breathing rapidly. Gently pulling her arms away, he took her hand.

Her eyes flew open. 'Tobias!'

'I didn't want to wake you but I heard you cry out.'

'Did I? I didn't know. I'll be all right.'

'If you're sure.'

'Yes—thank you, Tobias.'

He went out, but, unable to get back to sleep without falling back into the shocking nightmare and not wanting to be alone, half in panic she got up and found her way to Tobias's cabin, needing the reassurance of his strength to see her through the night. Knocking softly, she pushed the door open. Tobias got up from the bed and went to her. She looked defenceless, like he'd never seen her.

'I hope you don't mind,' she whispered, 'but I don't want to be by myself.'

She'd only meant to seek his company, taking strength

from being in his presence, but somehow she found herself moving wordlessly toward his still figure. His hard fingers folded securely around hers, squeezing gently as he drew her towards him, and suddenly his arms went round her. The monstrous fears, which crowded and closed about her, reluctantly retreated. She sagged thankfully in the protective circle of Tobias's arms.

'What is it?'

'I didn't want to be alone. It will be a long night and I'm so…'

'Anxious?'

'Frightened.'

'About the journey?'

She nodded, her cheek against his shirt. 'I'm afraid something will happen—something dreadful. This is a terrible place, Tobias. I hate it.'

'I know you do.'

'Today, when I saw those captives that had just arrived in Sale, I thought I saw Jack Mason. Oh, he was dressed like everyone else in Sale, and his face was covered, but I am certain I saw recognition in his eyes when he looked at me. But—it can't have been him—can it?'

Taking her upper arms and pushing her away slightly, Tobias cupped her face in his hands, his gaze intent. 'Rowena, listen to me. I don't know if it was Jack Mason. If it was, then you need not be afraid while you are with me. He won't hurt you—but you don't have to go with me tomorrow. You will be safe here on board with Mark.'

'I'm going with you, Tobias. Please don't try to stop

me. I want to be there when Jane is released. It's important to me.'

He nodded, understanding. 'Then come. You must rest. We have a long journey ahead of us tomorrow.' Taking her hand, he drew her down beside him on the bed, taking her in his arms and holding her shuddering body close. 'Go to sleep.'

He held her as he would a child that needed comforting. She was content to curl against him and rest her cheek against his chest. He was disturbed by what she had told him about Jack Mason. More than likely she had been mistaken, but if Mason was here in Sale, there wasn't a damn thing he could do about it until he returned from Meknes, and by then he would have flown.

'Tobias.'

'What is it?'

'Do you think we'll get Jane back?'

His arms tightened and he rested his lips on the top of her head. 'I hope so, Rowena. Now go to sleep.'

She snuggled closer and sighed through the drowsiness that engulfed her before she slept.

Tobias stared down at her in the silvery light. Her body was so soft curled against him, and he could feel her unrestrained breasts were hard buds again his chest. Despite the insulating barrier of his trousers and shirt his mind instantly began reminding him of all the delectable female attributes he held within his arms. In slumber her face was naked within the heavy cap of her dark hair. She had the ability to be at one moment a very young, innocent, vulnerable and defenceless girl, and the next a termagant who could snap her temper as easily as he could snap his fingers.

For a moment physical desire that was like a living flame between them blazed in him so fiercely that at that moment he would have done almost anything to take possession of her body and lose himself in forgetfulness of all the problems that pressed down on him. But there was no answering urge in Rowena's body as she slept, her soft breath fanning his chest. He wanted her, all of her, in a way that went beyond lust and desire. He had never felt like this about a woman, which made Rowena all the more special.

One way or another he could not take advantage of her now. If he were to give way to his own desires and rouse a willing response in Rowena, once the barrier had been breached, all his carefully laid plans for the future would be put in jeopardy. Besides, it would bode ill for the journey facing them and complicate matters between them. There would be plenty of time for such things as loving once this nightmare was over.

As Rowena slept, so did Tobias, and he did not wake until she stirred in his arms, aroused by the loud chorus of sea birds greeting the dawn. Looking down at her features softened by sleep, he could not help but wonder at her thoughts. He shifted his head on the pillow to whisper a question. 'Are you comfortable?'

Rowena nodded shyly, remembering where she was, but strangely reluctant to move. 'Are you?' A long sigh escaped her lips.

'Never more so.'

'Thank you for letting me stay,' she murmured, closing her eyes to go back to sleep. She nestled against the warm, hard body beside her, seemingly unaware of what lay ahead of them, and her slumber deepened. Then there was warm breath in her ear, a whisper so soft she could not distinguish it from her dreams.

'Rowena, are you asleep?'

'Mmm, Tobias,' she sighed in a soft, drowsing breath, unable to break the lingering essence of sleep. She snuggled closer, soothed in the security of his presence.

Half-rolling on his side, Tobias rose above her slightly and nuzzled his nose in the soft fragrance of her hair. Her eyes flickered open and her smile was sublime. Gazing down into her slumberous eyes, he saw a kind of gentle beauty and unquenchable spirit that took his breath away.

'Has anyone ever told you,' he murmured, 'that you have the smile of an angel?'

'Don't you think that remark is a little sacrilegious,' she teased, 'when I have just spent the night in your bed?'

He stifled a laugh that rose in his throat. 'No, but it probably is when you consider what we might do if you remain. Unless you wish to fall victim to circumstance, Rowena—which could rapidly get out of control—I suggest you remove yourself from my bed.'

Her eyes flew open as she realised full well his meaning. The heat of his hard, semi-naked body and lust-filled eyes were graphic proof. 'Oh!' Scarlet cheeked, she moved away from him, and, swinging her legs over the side of the bed, stood up, shoving her hair out of her eyes. Now she was fully awake her nerves were stretched taut.

She felt crippled with the knowledge of what faced them. How could it have slipped her mind? Of course, there was the fact that Tobias was a practised seducer and he had taken liberties with her in the past, but when she had sought him out in his bed, wanting nothing more than to feel his arms around her, to banish the nightmares tormenting her, it had been her doing.

But deep inside her she knew it had been more than that. Tobias had become so special to her in every way. He was her strength. She stood greatly in the debt of this man and was glad he had been there at a time when she was in need of help. She could not envisage her life without him at this time. She had never felt like this, not ever. It was as if her body were awash with feeling, alive with need, and despite her determination to keep her heart intact, she was afraid that she might do something wild and completely against her nature.

Looking at him now, she tried unsuccessfully to maintain an expression of cool disdain, for how could she when he looked so outrageously handsome and dissolute, lounging nonchalantly on the bed with his dark ruffled hair and lopsided grin? And with his shirt sagging open to his waist, revealing a mat of dark fussy hair, he was the personification of a rake.

Tobias rolled off the bed, amused by her obvious embarrassment and chuckling softly. An almost lecherous smile tempted his lips as he watched the emotions flitting across her face. Rowena had never been able to hide her feelings—she had never had to.

'I see I have your attention now. I cannot think of anything I would rather do right now than linger with you in my bed, Rowena, but if we are to leave for Meknes it will have to wait for another time.'

She had the grace to look a little ashamed as she backed away to the door, unable to tear her eyes away from his towering presence. 'I'm sorry, Tobias. I really should have known better than to come to you last night. What if…what if someone had come in…?'

'They didn't,' he stated flatly, moving towards her. Placing his hands on her shoulders, he looked down into her intriguing eyes—his so blue, hers an indeterminate shade between blue and green, touching her in hidden places. 'My sweet Rowena, you have nothing to be ashamed of. Nothing happened. Last night you were in the grip of a very unpleasant nightmare and you needed someone. I'm glad I was available. Everything is the same as it was before. Now, go and get ready to leave. The sooner we are on the road to Meknes the better.'

By mid-morning a party of four horsemen took to the main highway that runs between Sale and Meknes, more than one hundred miles inland. To deflect the curious, woollen scarves covered their heads, which partially covered their faces from prying eyes and the dust kicked up by the horses. Dressed in simple white Moorish robes, which concealed their weapons of defence, they looked no different to any other Muslim traveller.

Following other travellers familiar with the terrain, they journeyed through the ancient timbered forest of Sale. Having been told by the merchant who had seen them on their way to beware of dangerous animals— lions, wild hogs and many others—they rode close together, constantly peering into the trees, so dense that those who entered and were unfamiliar with the tracks became lost and were never seen again.

Tobias had seen to it that they had enough food to see them through to Meknes. Being fluent in Arabic and almost as dark as a Moor, Tobias could pass as one of them, but he preferred not to draw unnecessary attention. They had goatskins of water fastened to the horses, for springs and waterholes were few and far between.

There were many travellers going both ways, and the occasional column of European slaves heading for Meknes. The sight of these unfortunates wrenched Rowena's heart, and in helpless frustration, because she could do nothing to ease their torment, she would avert her eyes.

Fortunately the journey was uneventful and despite the sun being hotter than she had every known, it was often tempered by a strong wind. They passed impoverished villages where the inhabitants lived miserably in makeshift dwellings. It was hot and dusty during the day and the nights, when the sun vanished and withdrew its warm rays, were extremely cold. They were thankful for the shelter of the tents they had brought with them.

They pushed on as quickly as possible, stopping around noon during the hottest part of the day to find shelter and to eat and rest the horses. The two men Tobias had chosen to accompany them, were both around thirty years of age and splendidly built, Henry, with a shock of short curly black hair, and Sam, with receding fair hair.

Tobias had chosen well in their protectors because both men were strong, trusted, hard-bitten, sharp-eyed sailors, much superior to the average seamen, who also fell to their tasks with a minimum of talk and efficiency. Tobias had told them the purpose of their mission, and that the young lady he was to offer a ransom for was Master Rowan's sister. Having developed a respect and trust for the man on whose ship they had served and often fought for the best part of ten years, they accepted this without demur.

Rowena went to great pains to give Sam and Henry no cause to suspect her true gender, taking great care to attend to her personal needs when she was sure of absolute privacy, and relying on Tobias to make sure they were otherwise occupied.

Every now and then Tobias would glance at Rowena. She would meet his gaze and smile and her beautiful eyes would shine in her unveiled face, which was flushed and so very young. She was the girl he had met when he had sought her out above Falmouth, the wild girl who would do anything she wanted to. And he had loved her for it and made plans, until Mason had attacked the *Petrel* and forced him to take another direction.

After three nights on the road, as the sun sank towards the horizon in a glory of crimson and gold, they had their first glimpse of Meknes. Silently they paused and contemplated the city overlooking the River Fakran. It was like a fantastic jewel, concocted in the last century by Moulay Ismail, the very sultan who still ruled his massive domain by fear.

The cultivated valley of fields and orchards rose to low houses built in mud and clay. Behind them crenellations like lace festooned the high white wall, glowing pink in the sunset like some delicious sugary confection, which gave an aura of enchantment to the scene. It stretched for miles, curving away out of sight. Beyond could be glimpsed a forest of gleaming, glittering turrets and minarets and gilded domes of the sultan's imperial palace. It was built on a grand scale—an impregnable fortress to withstand the mightiest army on earth.

Rowena could not believe her eyes. Silently she contemplated this gorgeous pink jewel. 'What manner of man could build a place like this?' she breathed, complete awestruck.

'An emperor,' Tobias answered. 'The building never stops. Everything you see—the wall, every column and battlement—has been built by an army of Christian slaves, and they are kept in the most wretched state. Too many have succumbed to the rigors of hard labour. The sultan orders a new building to be built almost every day, and just as quickly has it pulled down if it doesn't suit his taste. What you see is just one of his palaces. In fact, the complex is huge. There are a further fifty palaces at least, where scheming viziers and eunuchs keep their courts. It is all interconnecting, with stables, pleasure gardens, orchards and harems, all housing the sultan's concubines, which runs into hundreds—possibly more. No one knows exactly.'

'But—the children?' Rowena asked, completely overwhelmed by the sheer scale of everything.

'Are well taken care of.'

'What do the women of the harem find to do all day if they are kept in isolation—hundreds of them all cooped up together? I cannot imagine a worse fate. Do they not get bored?'

Amused by her question, Tobias laughed softly. 'All the time, I imagine. You should know better than I what women do—primp and preen and paint themselves in front of their looking glasses, I suppose, spending hours at it, since they have the time and nothing else to do.'

'And only each other to show off to, since the sultan cannot possibly be with them very often, there being so many.' She sighed, her eyes sweeping over the city. 'I wonder where Jane is within all this. If it's as large as you say it is, then we may never find her. It looks pretty impregnable to me.'

'The city has been designed to withstand a possible siege, and with granaries and a reservoir and a massive standing army, it could last for decades.'

To Rowena's surprise Tobias turned his horse around and left the road, indicating that Henry and Sam should do the same.

'What are you doing?' she called after him. 'Can we not enter?'

'Nothing can be achieved tonight. We'll eat and then

bed down outside the city. If we were to ride into Meknes tonight, we would have to find lodgings and draw unnecessary attention to ourselves. Better to begin making our enquiries in the morning.'

Reluctantly seeing the sense of this, Rowena followed. They searched for a place to camp for the night, settling on somewhere they thought would be safe enough in a grove of tall trees set back from the road.

Rowena slid off her horse and began preparing herself for another night in the open.

Early the next morning she was awake and eager to enter the city. Dawn came with a hint of orange and gold. The numerous dogs within the city began their incessant barking. They seemed to be competing with the heavy wooden mallets pounding the clay into shape to be added to the ramparts.

She was surprised to see Sam and Henry squatting in front of their tent, seemingly in no hurry to leave. Tobias was with the horses, where three of them nuzzled at the sparse grass, and he was saddling the other.

'What are you doing?'

'Getting ready to leave.'

She experienced a vague feeling of foreboding. Something she did not quite like about his manner was beginning to take form and she tensed. 'Then I'll go and tell Sam and Henry to get ready.'

'I'm going alone, Rowena. I have decided.'

She stood and faced him squarely, staring at him in disbelief. 'What?'

'I want you to remain here with Sam and Henry. You will be quite safe.'

'I'm sure I shall be, but I am not staying here without you.'

'Yes, you are,' he told her, ignoring her impassioned plea. 'Please don't argue with me.'

'I am going with you, Tobias. Devil take it! I have not come all this way to be left behind at the last minute.' Her voice was vibrant with emotion, that ever-present temper threatening to erupt.

'You will. I've told you, Sam and Henry will protect you.'

'I don't need to be protected.' Rowena was angry and indignant, and his conceit goaded her resolve. The utter helplessness of being a woman totally at the mercy of a man struck her with full force. Then her dominant self-respect flared into life. 'What do you expect me to do? Wait here?'

'Precisely. And I don't expect to have my orders questioned,' Tobias rapped out, tightening the horse's girth.

'And I am not some kind of subordinate who takes orders,' she flared. All the time anguish at the thought of being left behind at the crucial moment was tearing at her insides.

Tobias stopped what he was doing and looked at her. Dear Lord, when she was all fired up and her eyes spitting sparks in her sun-kissed face, she was like a beautiful, vibrant goddess, but his judgement was tempered not with admiration, but with fear. Taking her arm, he dragged her to the other side of the horse where the world seemed to dwindle to just him and herself, where they could not be observed by the other two.

His eyes were glacial when they locked on to hers. 'I expect to be obeyed,' he hissed, 'especially when it comes to taking you inside such a dangerous place as Meknes.'

'And what do you think will happen to me?' she flared, too furious to quail before the murderous look tightening his face and the dangerous spark that entered his eyes. She was instantly alarmed by the hard set to his face, as if her defiance had distanced them. She tried to pry her arm loose from the iron grip of his fingers, but his fear for her and his anger with her made him cruel. 'Beneath these robes, who is to know who or what I am? I look no different to everyone else.' Her eyes were narrowed and mutinous and her jutting chin challenging. 'If you don't take me, then I shall go by myself.'

'Damnation! Don't you dare. Be reasonable. You cannot enter that place alone. You neither know nor understand the language. Open your mouth once and you will find yourself arrested.'

Tobias was white lipped with anger, a fierce, knife-edged anger that made Rowena take a step back. The coldness in his eyes and set to his mouth would have done justice to an executioner, but she would not give up. 'I shall. I don't care.'

'I do, and I would be obliged if you would accept that you have certain obligations, which seem to have slipped your mind.'

'To you, I suppose you mean,' she scoffed. 'Dear God, do you think of nothing else but that—that wretched bargain?' Even as she uttered these words, inside her that treacherous spark ignited and she felt the warmth of it spread throughout her body.

The corner of his mouth quirked and his eyes glittered down at her. 'I do think about it—often, if you must know, but not at the moment, my love—'

'I am not your love,' she hissed, the Rowena temper so rigorously suppressed of late erupting in all its fury.

'No, but you will be. You misunderstood me. It was to your sister I was referring when I spoke of obligations. What good will you be to her if you are captured—which could very well happen in that nest of miscreants? I have never been to Meknes, but I have heard sufficient to be alarmed and afraid of what I will find when I get in there. When I have made my observations and made enquiries as to the whereabouts of Suleiman, I shall return and decide what to do next.'

'But—you don't understand...'

A deadly smile twisted his lips and his voice became dangerously quiet. 'It is you who does not understand, Rowena. Jane is a prisoner, and so she shall remain as long as the sultan demands it. What did you imagine would happen when we got here—that he will be moved by her plight, open the gates of his palace to her and simply let her go free, wishing her every happiness?'

'And if he had an ounce of decency he would do that very thing,' Rowena cried irrationally, unable to conceal her desperation.

The grip on her arms tightened and he thrust his face close to hers. 'Confound it! Stop this nonsense and wait here. Can't you get it into that stubborn head of yours that it is you I am thinking of—your safety? I can't for the life of me think what all this is about.'

Her head came up. 'Can't you?' she said, realising that Tobias was her greatest protection. 'I'm scared, Tobias. I'm scared you won't come back. What shall we do if you don't? It doesn't bear thinking about.'

Tobias stopped what he was doing. Cupping her chin in his hand, he looked deep into her eyes, and when his mouth closed over hers, she was surprised at the tenderness of his kiss. Warm and firm and yet infinitely tender, his lips moved persuasively over hers. She did not resist. There was reverence as well as desire in that passionate demand. The reverence quickened her heart.

When he raised his head she felt much calmer. 'Why did you do that?'

He gave her a slow smile. 'Because I wanted to, and to soothe your fears.'

'I'm sorry I made a fuss,' she murmured, impressed by his knowledge of the situation, her anger vanishing as quickly as it had come. 'I know how difficult this must be for you and that I must seem ungrateful, but I'm not, truly.'

'I do know that. You're in no danger here and I will return just as soon as I have gleaned enough information to know how to proceed next. Sam and Henry are well armed, don't forget. You're a survivor, Rowena. That's what I like about you. Be patient a while longer.'

Ten minutes later, alongside Sam and Henry, Rowena watched him ride towards Meknes. She would remember every detail of that sun-bronzed, strong face, alive with the challenge of what lay ahead. His words and his kiss lived on in her mind, filling her with restlessness of many questions. She was moved by her admiration for him, by what he said and did, and disconcerted by the sudden violence of her feelings. But she must never let herself forget what was in it for him and the bargain they had made. He would go to any lengths to make her his conquest. She was his prey. He intended to seduce her, and nothing was going to deter him from trying.

But that was in the future, when Jane was free and they were back in England. For now she was glad of Tobias's support, his protection and his strength.

Chapter Nine

Rowena spent the day watching the road, her heart beating with fear and hope, jumping at every white-clad figure that emerged from the city mounted on a horse. Many people passed by where they camped under the wayside trees, but Rowena and her companions were all sufficiently dusty and unkempt to attract no more than a perfunctory glance.

The sun was going down in a blaze of red when she saw Tobias riding towards her and her heart leapt. Scrambling to her feet, she waited for him to come closer. His head was bare and the light gleamed on his dark hair. Something in those brilliant blue eyes that settled on her made her catch her breath. Once more she felt her body heat with passion, and for once she did not care. He had not been gone more than half a day and she had missed him and long been denied the intimacy of being close to him, and on board ship, having determinedly kept her mind from such feelings, now she recklessly welcomed them.

Yes, she desperately wanted to see Jane set free from her captivity and had spent a good part of the day thinking about her, but Tobias had occupied the greater part of her thoughts and she could not altogether hide her delight and relief at seeing him return—and he had about him an air of optimism that lifted her spirits.

She went to him, holding his horse while he dismounted. She smiled. 'I'm glad you're back.'

As he wiped the sweat from his eyes, his imposing figure blocked out the trees behind him. Tobias met her gaze, his eyes moving over her easily and familiarly, his lips curved in an answering smile. 'I'm glad to be back. See,' he said, unfastening a sack from his horse, 'I've brought some food.'

Rowena stepped back when Henry and Sam came to relieve him of the provisions, hoping its contents were more appetising than the dried meat and couscous that had been their staple diet since leaving Sale. Opening the sack, they were all delighted to find a collation of dates, melons, figs and sweetmeats and other tasty morsels.

Not until they had eaten and Henry and Sam had drifted away to indulge in a game of cards—their favourite pastime—did Tobias give Rowena his news.

'We're in luck. Certain important developments are happening in the city,' he told his companion, who was sitting cross legged on the ground, avidly listening to everything he had to say. 'A party of Englishmen led by a

Commodore Charles Stewart arrived a few days ago, with a treaty signed by the King. He is to negotiate the release of British and colonial slaves. The treaty also decrees that British ships will not be apprehended or plundered.'

'And will the sultan sign the treaty?'

'Stewart expects a prompt and successful response to all his demands. He is hopeful of meeting with the sultan tomorrow.'

'And were you able to meet Commodore Stewart?'

He nodded. 'I was shown to his lodgings.'

'And Suleiman? Have you managed to find out anything about him—and his captives?'

'I haven't been able to track him down, but there seems little point. The women he brought with him are already in the harem.'

Rowena's heart sank. 'And will Jane be freed do you think?'

'We will have to wait and see what happens between the sultan and Stewart.'

'What kind of man is he?'

'He is exactly the kind of man who might be able to get the sultan to agree to his request. He was a sea captain, with a turbulent career. He is amiable, charming and a master of flattery, with all the airs and graces of an ambassador, and in the court of Moulay Ismail, where sycophancy rules, Stewart will prove himself a master.'

'What shall we do now?'

'Wait and see what happens.'

* * *

Their arrival coincided with the end of Ramadan, which Muslims were obligated to spend in fasting and ritual prayer. It was celebrated with much festivity and feasting. To break the monotony of waiting for things to happen, Tobias asked Rowena if she would like to partake of the pageantry. Her eyes lit up eagerly.

Tobias's face was uncovered and Rowena saw his teeth gleam and was happy to see he was smiling. The smile comforted her and gave her courage. Returning his smile, she met his gaze and nodded. 'We might as well. A bit of fun can't go amiss while we are waiting.'

'That's true.'

'We'll walk to the city. The exercise will do us good. Besides, the streets will be so crowded it will be difficult finding somewhere to leave the horses.'

Reaching for her hat, Rowena scratched her head and grimaced before covering her hair. 'Dear Lord, how I would like to wash my hair. Never in my life have I felt so filthy. I swear that if I go to live at Tregowan Hall I shall have the luxury of a bathing chamber installed and wallow in it every day.'

'You will? So you still intend to marry Lord Tregowan?'

She nodded, falling into step with him as they began walking towards the city. 'If he hasn't withdrawn his offer to marry me—although if he hasn't, he might when he realises I am neither respectable or chaste.'

'Chaste! Now there's a word to play with.' His remark was studied and slow, and his smile was almost salacious. 'You are referring to the fact that you will no longer be chaste when you have met our bargain.'

'What else?'

'And you will?'

She was unable to meet his eyes. 'Yes. I have debts to pay, and the least of them to you. Unless…'

'No.' The blue eyes glinted like hard metal and he grinned confidently. 'A bargain is a bargain, Rowena. Sooner or later you will honour it.'

They joined the close-packed masses, which stirred like a field of corn in a strong breeze. Henry and Sam, having heard nothing about Meknes that made them want to enter, preferred to stay behind with the horses. Rowena was mesmerised by the city. Bronze doors and porphyry columns sparkled in the sun. Moorish stucco was chiselled and fretted into intricate honeycomb, beautiful mosaics were designed in geometric perfection, and slabs of jasper and marble all caught and reflected the African sunlight.

The parade, which began mid-morning, was a magnificent affair, one that surely gratified the vanity of Moulay Ismail. It could be heard long before it came into view. There was much firing of guns as a cavalcade of soldiers on horseback came into view, followed by an even more colourful and flamboyant troop of guardsmen carrying a large red standard with a half-moon in the centre.

They fired indiscriminately and Rowena commented laughingly to Tobias that it was a wonder no one was shot, although there was much singeing of turbans. A magnificent troop of foot soldiers clothed in leopard skins came next and they all filled the parade ground. Rowena wrinkled her nose at the acrid stench of burning powder.

And then came the moment Rowena and Tobias had waited for—the arrival of Moulay Ismail himself. He was a glittering figure, seated on his horse decked with pompoms and streamers, the saddle of beaten gold set with emeralds and other precious gems. Holding a gun he was surrounded by gorgeously dressed fawning attendants and his loyal black guard decked in armour followed by more impressive foot soldiers, bearing standards, battle axes and spears.

Never had Tobias or Rowena seen anything to compare with this magnificent gaudy spectacle, but it was the man on the horse that held their gaze. Tobias felt the hair at the base of his scalp prickle as though it were lifting. The imposing figure managed to convey a disquieting presence, and Rowena was sure the man gave off a special smell, rank and menacing, of power, dangerous and deadly.

Rowena had given little thought to what he would look like, and was surprised to see he was a toothless old man with a withered frame, perhaps in his seventies. His cheeks were hollow, his lips above his forked beard fleshy. His eyes were sunk deep into his head and his aquiline nose was like a bird's beak, and he coughed and spat all the time.

Having no wish to remain any longer, she touched Tobias's arm. 'Let's go back. I've seen enough.'

Each day Tobias rode into the city, hoping for new developments. Commodore Stewart had been in discussions about the release of the British and colonial slaves with the sultan, but the sultan was in no hurry and was anxious that the ambassador be shown the glories of his imperial palace. It took several days for the sultan to sign the treaty.

After many delays and setbacks and Stewart's impatience growing daily concerning the release of the slaves, one of the sultan's favourite wives interceded. She went to the sultan and appealed on Commodore Stewart's behalf, whereby the sultan expressed his willingness to comply.

Tobias arrived back at the camp with grim news for Rowena.

Rowena listened to what he had to say, immensely relieved to learn of the captives' release, but there was something wrong.

'And Jane?' she asked tentatively.

'The sultan has failed to free any of the women in the harem.'

Sick horror froze the air, paralysing the young woman who had waited so long to hear the outcome. She opened her mouth to speak, but her voice failed, and she moved her head in a small, helpless gesture that was more pitiful than words. The sight of her distress sent a physical pain through Tobias's heart.

'I'm sorry, Rowena. I know how much this means to you.'

Her eyes were wide with an effort to hold back the tears of angry despair. At that moment all the hope now lay in ashes at her feet. 'No—by merciful heavens, it can't be true! It can't possibly. It's a disaster,' she cried out, anger fighting with a disappointment more profound than she had ever known.

Tobias knew the pain in Rowena's heart. He could feel it almost as a tangible thing. She was in a different world, far removed from the peace and quiet of her home town of Falmouth. Here she walked in a land of strangers, whose culture and religion were so very different from her own. For all that, he was moved by her frustration and bitterness.

'It doesn't have to be a disaster, Rowena.'

She stared at him, becoming aware of how tired he looked, and how hard he must have tried on her behalf. 'No, you're right. It doesn't. We must go on. We cannot weaken and let go. We have come so far. I cannot abandon Jane to the life that will be forced on her. Her position will be intolerable. What is your answer to the problem, Tobias?'

Needing to have something to do, she began placing pieces of wood on the fire. It flared into rosy sparks, and, placing a can of water in the middle she sat back on her heels.

Tobias looked at her candidly. She seemed more thoughtful than she had earlier and was struggling within herself. He was silent for a long time, then he cleared his throat. 'What you say is right. There is only one important fact as I see it, and that is what we both agree on and what we see is right. I too have made up my mind not to abandon Jane.'

Rowena spread her hands on her knees, her face strained. A small muscle worked in her cheek and her hands trembled slightly. She looked him full in the face, a deep respect in the depths of her eyes. 'Thank you, Tobias. You'll never know how much it means to me to hear you say that.'

She felt the tears gathering in her eyes and kept her head bent as she poured the boiling water over the tea to infuse the leaves. When it was ready, Tobias took the cup she offered.

Making herself more comfortable on the ground, she took a sip of the hot liquid and looked around her. 'The wildness and brutality of this place has changed me,' she murmured at length. 'It has brought out strengths and weaknesses I didn't know I had. And it will go on testing me until I get back home.' Her lips curved in a wobbly smile. 'Probably all spent and worked out.'

'But not defeated,' Tobias said softly.

Her smile widened, but it was a brave, tired smile. 'No, not defeated. Were all the English captives released?'

'Those who have survived the enforced labour and the brutality of their captors—apart from the renegades.'

'The renegades?'

'The apostates—those who renounced their Christian faith.'

'Even though they did so against their will?'

He nodded slowly. 'Even so.'

'Then they have the rest of their lives to regret doing so. What shall we do now?'

'I raised the issue with Commodore Stewart. There

is nothing he can do—in fact, he intends leaving Meknes with his released captives before the sultan changes his mind and prevents him. Stewart is of the impression that Suleiman, who is close to one of the sultan's wives, can be bribed.'

Rowena's eyes flew to his. 'Suleiman? Will you…?'

'We have nothing to lose.'

'Only our lives should the sultan find out,' she pointed out quietly.

'That is true, but we have to think positively, Rowena.'

'I do try,' she whispered, her stomach tightening with the cruelty of it all. She had set her mind not to be frightened, yet her knees were weak and an uncontrollable trembling made holes in her resolve. Her chin quivered and the sting of tears smarted her eyes. She was terribly afraid, not knowing what was in store for them, but convinced the miscreants of Meknes planned some hideous fate for them all.

'I have always thought of myself as strong and able to cope with anything, but nothing has prepared me for this. This place frightens me so much. We can expect no more than slavery here and I soon recognise our plight will scarce be better than that of Jane's if we fail.'

'I won't pretend it will be easy. These people hate the Christians so much, if they find out one has escaped from the harem they will become like untamed beasts. They hate us so much that they are unable to contain their joy at having one in their power. If anyone takes their prey from them, they will probably tear the whole place down.'

'Let them,' Rowena cried. 'I don't care. We don't belong to this country. It is a wicked, evil place and I hate it. The only thing I care about is Jane.'

Tobias flashed her a sidelong glance. 'And that is all?'

She turned her bright, blue-green eyes on his and declared with some arrogance, 'Yes, yes, it is. Jane is very dear to me and I cannot bear the thought of the hands of those infidels touching her, and even if I should lose my life in the attempt, I must try every means of saving her.'

Tobias's mouth curved in a silent smile while a sparkle danced in his eyes. 'And who said anything to the contrary? I merely remarked that it would be difficult and that we run the danger of sparking a revolt, that was all.'

'I know and I'm sorry, Tobias. But I do so want us to succeed and I shan't rest until I see Jane.'

'We won't fail.' It was the thought of Jane being handed over for the sultan's pleasure that made the palms of Tobias's hands go damp and he was conscious of a terrible empty feeling in the pit of his stomach, although he endeavoured to reassure Rowena. 'We have to do it now. Fortunately the sultan has been so preoccupied with Commodore Stewart's visit that as yet he's not looked at the new additions to his harem—although his black guard have eyes and ears where others don't, so I shall take care to avoid them. I have enough gold to make it worth Suleiman's while. Lesser men have attempted to cheat the sultan, when well aware that he would order them to be put to death. They were too greedy or stupid to care, and though Suleiman is not stupid, he is certainly greedy and may be persuaded.'

'Tobias—I know just how much I am asking of you. Yes, I want Jane freed, but not if it means you will come to harm.'

He grinned easily. 'I am deeply touched by your concern, Rowena, but you can rest assured that when it comes to danger I am like the proverbial cat with nine lives.'

'And how many of those lives have you left, Tobias?'

'Maybe one—or two,' he said, getting to his feet. 'We shall have to wait and see.'

Sam and Henry had gone to sleep. Rowena wandered away from camp to where Tobias sat some distance away behind a clump of bushes. He was looking down into the valley, at the twinkling lights coming from the houses outside the city walls. His arms were round his knees and he seemed preoccupied. He had been noticeably quiet all day and Rowena knew he was feeling the strain of waiting.

Tobias heard her approach and turned slightly to acknowledge her, before returning his gaze to the scene below him.

Rowena sat beside him, drawing up her knees in a similar pose. 'You're quiet, Tobias. How are you feeling? You look tired. You're feeling the strain, aren't you? I can tell.'

He turned his head and considered her a moment and then he smiled. 'I didn't realise I was so transparent.'

'Well, you are,' she said, getting to her knees, 'and I would like to do something about that.'

He smiled lazily and stared at her. 'What do you suggest?'

'Well, I could make you feel more relaxed—if you will let me.'

He considered protesting, and then, feeling the heat of her, he decided against it. 'And how do you aim to do that?' he asked in a tone of mild curiosity.

'By massaging your shoulders. Fatima showed me how to do it. She was very good at it, so don't expect too much from me, a mere novice, but it might help.'

'Ah, Fatima,' he breathed. 'And did Fatima teach you anything else by any chance?'

'Such as?' She knelt behind him, unable to resist touching him. Placing the palms of her hands on his shoulders, she casually began kneading the muscles that she felt were taut and all knotted up.

Tobias closed his eyes, savagely aware of her. His whole body quivered when she ran her warm hand up the back of his neck beneath his hair. 'How to please the opposite sex. Now what are you doing?' he asked without giving her chance to reply to his query.

'Trying to relax the muscles at the back of your neck. They really are very tight. Does this help?'

'Mmm,' he admitted as she pressed her thumbs into his flesh and circled in a gentle insistence over his neck muscles until they began to loosen by degrees. Had she no idea how she tempted him, how his whole body was beginning to ache and throb with his need?

Moments passed in which Tobias allowed himself to drift into the pleasure of her touch. Slowly the tension began easing from him. 'You didn't answer my question?'

'What question?'

'About what else Fatima taught you?'

'I didn't want to answer it, that's why. I know Fatima has skills beyond my comprehension—skills I am sure would please you—but she only taught me a little of what she knows, so you will have to be content with that. Now would you kindly stop talking and enjoy your massage—or perhaps you would prefer me to stop?'

Feeling suddenly deprived along with a huge pang of disappointment when she stilled her hands and he thought she had done with him, Tobias tilted his head back and smiled ruefully at her. 'Don't stop. I promise not to say another word. Do as you will, Rowena,' he murmured, closing his eyes in surrender, growing lax and mesmerised by sensation as her fingertips moved with feathered lightness over his back. 'I am completely in your thrall. My body is yours to do with as you wish. I am like clay in your hands.'

With a subdued answering smile and her wide, warmly glowing eyes holding a certain ingenuous naïveté—a slight betrayal of her inexperience—she continued with the massage, pausing just long enough to lean over his shoulder, her soft face almost coming into contact with his and her short hair tickling his cheek as, to his amazement, she unfastened the buttons on his shirt. Pulling it down over his arms she slid her hands inside and over his bare flesh, moulding them over the warm bulk of his shoulders, savouring the maleness of his steely muscles and satiny skin.

Feeling the muscles tauten beneath her fingers, she said softly, 'Don't. I'm trying to get you to relax, not tense up.'

Tobias could not believe his good fortune. He was entranced—he had never been so aroused in his life as, like some pagan worshipper, Rowena continued kneading and caressing his flesh, her hands sliding over his shoulders and down his chest and upper arms. He had not asked for this and she didn't have to do it, and that only meant that she wanted to. He was barely even aware that several moments had passed when she asked,

'Do you mind if I ask you something?'

'I thought you wanted me to be quiet.'

'I've almost finished now, so it doesn't matter.' Pulling his shirt over his shoulders, she went and sat in front of him, hugging her knees to her chest. She peered at him in the gloom, pleased to see the harsh planes of his bronzed face were smooth and the contours of his square jaw softened. Seen like this, he looked much less forbidding. 'Are you feeling better now?'

His heavy-lidded gaze fastened on her soft lips. A huge constricting knot of tenderness and desire tightened his throat and he was tempted to draw her into his arms, but he managed to resist and smiled, a deliciously warm, languid smile. 'No, much worse.'

Rowena was a little wounded by his reaction, a cloud of disappointment sweeping over her face. 'Oh—I'm sorry,' she said, her magnificent eyes searching deeply into his. 'In what way do you feel worse?'

He gave a soft laugh, captivated by her artlessness.

'I feel the way every man always feels when he wants to make love to a woman and he is denied doing so.'

Rowena felt her face flushing. 'Oh! Is that really how you feel?'

'It is, but I can wait,' he murmured, his words meaningful, reminding her of their bargain. 'Why did you do it—the massaging?'

'Because I thought the strain was getting to you. I thought you needed to relax.'

'Then feel free to repeat what you have just done to me whenever you think I'm looking—strained.'

'Did I do it right?' she asked almost shyly. 'You can tell me the truth.'

He started to laugh at the absurdity of the question, but he went motionless when she said,

'I've never done anything like that before.'

He stared at her.

'You didn't like it,' she said, her heart sinking as she read his face.

'Like it? Of course I liked it. Now come here so that I can convey my thanks,' he murmured, taking her hand and pulling her towards him. Taking her face tenderly between his hands, he silenced her fretful worries with a gentle kiss that deepened. Fully expecting her to protest and draw back, when no protest was forthcoming, slowly he parted her lips and tasted her tongue, his mouth caressing and savouring the satiny cushions of her lips.

Still on her knees, Rowena began to melt against him, returning his kiss more urgently. Tobias felt her desire and ended the kiss, breathing heavily. Pulling back, Rowena stared at him, her eyes big and dark and strangely haunted in the pale light of the moon. He trailed a finger down the soft curve of her cheek.

'I want to make love to you—properly—to return the favour.'

Turning her face, Rowena lightly kissed the palm of his hand. 'You will get your wish, Tobias, when Jane is free.'

'Yes—I shall insist on it. I think you said you have something to ask me. Go ahead.'

Her eyes were candid as she asked, 'What really happened on the night my father was shot? He was convinced it was you. He also convinced me, but now I cannot equate the man I have come to know with a villain who would shoot a man in the back in cold blood.'

Apart from a tightening of his expression, his face remained unchanged. 'Contrary to what your father told you, it was true what I said when we first met. I am not guilty of shooting him—although since his back was turned to his assailant and he knew I had come looking for him, I can understand why he would think that I did.'

'Do you know who did it? After all, you were there. My father can't recall what happened exactly, but he remains convinced it was you.'

'One day, hopefully, he will learn the truth—that the man he employed as his captain was a cold-blooded killer.'

'Jack Mason? But why would he shoot him?'

Tobias shrugged. 'Who knows how the mind of a murderer works? But I would say the *Dolphin* and the cargo were an incentive.'

Rowena sighed and let her eyes stray towards the city.

'Poor Father. I think he'll want to kill Mason himself if you don't do it first.' On a sigh she stood up and looked down at him. 'Good night, Tobias. Hopefully it will be the last we will spend in Meknes.'

Tobias watched her go, feeling lonely now. How good it had felt to have her close, the feel of her under his hands, the heat and velvet of her, the taste of her, and the response in her to his kiss. He had set out to make a conquest of her, only to discover the terrible loneliness of his own heart, the emptiness inside him that cried out for her tenderness.

To kiss Rowena, to serve her, to give her so much pleasure until he had her moaning and sighing in his arms, would give him pleasure—at one time such thoughts would have made him step back, for that was a very dangerous situation indeed, but not with Rowena. He wanted to give her the earth, and, if not the earth, then whatever he was capable of.

Commodore Stewart managed to establish contact with Suleiman and sent word to Tobias at their camp. It took sixty minutes and the princely sum of one thousand pounds to overcome Suleiman's scruples. After which Tobias was told to wait outside the Bab Mansoor gate at noon the next day, where the young woman would be brought.

There was more than a trace of uneasiness in Tobias's voice when he told Rowena.

'Then if you are to go, at least let me go with you.'

Tobias looked at her and smiled, shaking his head. 'I would rather you didn't.'

She sighed. 'I can't help worrying.'

'I don't want you in danger.'

Rowena paled, her stomach contracting with foreboding. 'Then you could be in danger?'

At the fear clouding her eyes, Tobias took hold of her hands, surprised to find them trembling. 'If everything goes to plan there should be no danger. But it is wise to be careful. In this garb I shall be quite safe. When I return, you must be ready to leave.'

'Will you ride to the meeting place?'

'No. Mounted I would be more conspicuous.'

Rowena was prey to increasing anxiety all day and throughout the night as she waited for the time when Tobias would have to leave. Fretting that everything would go wrong, she watched and listened to the distant sounds of the city, telling herself that there was no reason why Suleiman couldn't be trusted and why everything shouldn't go well and, given luck, Jane would be riding with them back to Sale.

It was time for Tobias to go. Rowena stood facing him, taking judicious note of the taut set of his jaw and feeling the first tendril of fear coil in the pit of her stomach.

'You will be careful?' she whispered anxiously, placing her hand on his arm, only then noticing the menacing air of excitement that rippled through his big, lean frame.

'I'll be back with Jane before you know it.'

'Go' was all she said.

* * *

Several of the sultan's infamous *bukhari* or black guard were stationed at the Bab Mansoor, greatest of all Meknes's ceremonial gateways. These men were haughty and brutal, highly trained and fiercely loyal to their master. They focused their attention on the noonday traffic that was jostling through the archway. Nothing unusual, just the everyday crowd of people drifting in and out, and the tall man in dusty white robes meeting with a fat man in a blue silk tunic and turban and a woman in a hijab did not merit any more attention than anyone else.

Rowena stood and watched the two figures coming up the hill to the camp, her heart soaring when she recognised Tobias and daring to hope that he had been successful in freeing Jane.

Tobias reached out and drew the figure in the hijab forward. 'Your sister,' he murmured.

The nervous strain of her captivity had been too much for Jane and she burst into tears of relief when she saw Rowena. 'I thought I would be locked away in that awful place for ever,' she sobbed, pushing the veil aside so she could better see her sister. 'I was so afraid I would never see you again.'

The shock of being smuggled out of the harem beneath the noses of the eunuchs guarding her, followed swiftly by being handed over to a man she believed was a stranger to her, since his face was partially concealed by his head covering, and hurried away from the city to she knew not where, only to find herself reunited with her sister, was almost too much and she cried and clung to Rowena, refusing to let her go.

Tobias moved towards them and gently disengaged her clinging fingers. Above her head he gave Rowena a knowing look. 'We have to go.'

Jane's emotionally overwrought state and dark-ringed eyes in her drawn face had a huge effect on Rowena. 'I'm sorry, Jane,' she said, hugging her sister one more time. 'As soon as I heard you had been taken I was determined to follow and get you back.'

Jane was silent for a moment, her eyes searching her rescuer's bronzed features. 'I remember you. You are Mr Searle. I don't know how you come to be here, but I thank you—and yet why should you help me? I am no one to you but the daughter of a man who owes you a debt already. There is no reason why you should endanger your life for mine.'

'All will be revealed later,' he told her. 'Come. There is need for haste. I want to put as much distance between us and this place as possible before nightfall.'

Jane's attention was momentarily diverted to Rowena's clothes. 'Where in the world did you get those dreadful garments?' she exclaimed with shuddering distaste.

'Hush, Jane,' she said quietly, glad that Sam and Henry were out of earshot, for if her disguise was blown open now it would take some explaining. 'I can't explain now, but it's important that I retain my disguise.'

Jane's instinct seemed to tell her what was happening. Tobias heaved her bodily on to the horse.

'God bless you, Rowena,' she whispered softly. 'I'll try not to hold you up.'

'Rowan, Jane. My name is Rowan,' Rowena said, speaking gently as to a child in shock, climbing on to her own horse and taking the reins. 'I'll explain later. It's important that we get away from here, so come, we must look forward now, not back. Are you all right to ride?' She nodded and Rowena smiled. 'I knew you would be.'

Rowena would say that for Jane. Once she understood the urgency of the situation, she didn't take fright, or weep any more, or plague them with further questions, but urged her horse on with the rest. Rowena had known plenty of women who were better at riding than Jane, but none gamer than Jane when the stakes were down.

Mile after mile the country unrolled itself under the pounding hoofs of their horses. They were rough-gaited, short-striding plodders, but their stamina seemed boundless. Rowena felt extraordinarily relaxed and relieved. The joy of having rescued Jane from the sultan's clutches was exhilarating, even if the task would not be complete until they reached home.

When darkness fell and they made camp, Rowena and Jane talked quietly to each other away from the others. Rowena stared in shocked amazement and more than a little curiosity at her sister's attire beneath the robe and hijab that covered her hair. She saw that she wore a short brocade jacket above her bare midriff, and below that harem trousers made of a diaphanous material like mist and air. She was covered, yet appeared almost naked.

'Heavens above, Jane!' Rowena exclaimed, looking at her. 'I shudder to think what Father would say were he to see you dressed like that.'

Jane laughed. 'He would have an apoplexy, that's for sure—as he would were he to see his eldest daughter dressed as a youth and dancing attendance on his worst enemy as his cabin boy. But tell me everything about how this has all come about.'

Rowena gave Jane a detailed account of everything that had happened since the day she had been taken captive, and Jane told Rowena of her capture by Jack Mason and how he had laughed when he had discovered Matthew Golding's daughter was one of his captives. Several women had been taken off the *Petrel*. They had been treated well, so as not to reduce their sale price when they reached Algiers—and Jack Mason had not been disappointed, for young and desirable she had been sold into the sultan's harem.

She had been in the harem at Meknes several days before she had been smuggled out—long enough to realise she would have been forced to renounce her Christian faith and that she could never expect to be released.

'What was it like in the harem, Jane—and—and were you…?'

Jane smiled when Rowena hesitated. 'I was not there long enough to meet the sultan, Rowena. I am still a virgin, thank the Lord,' she told her quietly. 'When we were taken off the *Petrel,* we were very afraid, not knowing what was to happen to us or if we would ever see our families again. Inside the harem—of which there are several housing the sultan's many wives and children—it was luxurious to say the least.'

Rowena smiled at the dreamy look in her sister's eyes as she remembered all she had seen during her short time in captivity. 'I hope you don't regret being rescued, Jane, because we are not so far away that we cannot turn back.'

She laughed softly and gave her a warm hug. 'Of course not. Oh, but it is a truly remarkable place, one you cannot possibly imagine. The sultan has lavished a veritable fortune on beautifying his imperial capital. The result is a palace so exquisite it is unlike anything else on earth, but behind it all there is undeniable cruelty,' she whispered, pain replacing the dreamy, faraway look of a moment before. 'The unfortunate, terrible part of it all is that building is constantly in progress, with thousands of European slaves at work every day. They are so badly treated it is heartbreaking to witness their suffering.'

'I know. I saw some of them myself. But what of the sultan—does he have many wives?'

'Hundreds. The imperial harem is jealously protected. Every one of the sultan's wives is accompanied at all times by a eunuch guard. In fact there are so many guards I am surprised you managed to get me out at all.'

'It is Tobias we have to thank for that. He bribed Suleiman—the man who bought you in Algiers—to arrange your release.'

'He did? Oh, Rowena, how much did he have to give him?'

'A thousand pounds.'

Jane paled. 'That is a large sum of money. How on earth shall we ever be able to repay it? Father can't possibly.'

'It will be sorted out later, Jane.'

'But he will be for ever in his debt. Why, it's not as though they are good friends—quite the opposite, in fact.' Jane gave her sister a long, searching look. 'There's something behind this. Yes, there's more to this than meets the eye, so please don't tell me that Mr Searle has gone to all this trouble out of the goodness of his heart. Why would he risk his life for someone he has only briefly met?'

'I told you. I smuggled myself aboard his ship. He didn't find out until we were too far away from England to turn back. He was going after Jack Mason anyway, and he agreed to help me find you.'

'And that's all?'

'Yes.'

Jane smiled and turned away. If Rowena couldn't see what Tobias Searle felt for her, then she really must be blind. Jane had seen it as clear as day, though he did do his best to hide it.

'I think I like your Mr Searle, Rowena.'

'He's not my Mr Searle, Jane and he never will be. Do not forget that I am supposed to be marrying Lord Tregowan—if he'll still have me, that is.'

'Of course he will, but you are entitled to change your mind.'

Rowena shook her head, a bleak look in her eyes. 'I don't think I will be granted the privilege—not if things are the same at home as when we left.'

Reaching out, Jane took her hand and cradled it in her own. 'Things will work out for you, Rowena, as they have for me. You are truly my dearest sister and I am very happy to have you. Without your determination to find me I am under no illusions about what would have happened to me. My gratitude is so deeply felt that I cannot explain the measure of it.'

'And you don't have to. I'm sure you would have done the same for me.'

They pressed on to Sale. At one point Tobias glanced back at Rowena and saw with amazement that her eyes were sparkling and her teeth gleaming white between eagerly parted lips. He was glad to see she had recovered her sense of determination and spirit that had carried her through the weeks before they had come to Meknes. When they had left Sale she had been tense and sick with worry about her sister, but the woman riding beside him now—the woman Henry and Sam still believed was a pretty youth—was vibrant in health, darker, tawny skinned and clad like a bandit.

Rowena straightened proudly to meet his gaze as he soaked up the sight of her, for he was more thirsty for her than for water. *Dear Lord,* he thought irrelevantly, feeling his blood stir and his loins stiffen, *but she's beautiful.* He knew many women who knew how to please a man, knew exquisitely where and how to touch him, how to move. But such women were for a moment's pleasure and no longer.

The woman he was looking at was one of strength,

of character, as strong as the mountains and rocks themselves. The man who possessed her would have no need for the other kind.

Chapter Ten

The man had been waiting, standing like a shadow on the edge of the crowd on the waterfront. He watched the five figures approach on foot, three men and two women, one garbed in a hijab and the other as an untidy youth. And so he waited.

The crowd was dense and Rowena felt herself being pushed towards a dark alley. With considerable alarm she realised she was becoming separated from the others. As she glanced along a narrow street, shadows seemed to flit around the walls, but even as she looked they retreated and faded from view. Then there was a sound, a footfall. The shapes came back, vague movements on either side, but she had eyes only for the man who stepped out of the shadows and stood calmly watching her.

She would know that face and that arrogant bearing anywhere for, once seen, Jack Mason was hard to forget.

Cold sweat prickled her skin and panic threatened, but she would not let him see she was afraid. Her stomach twisted in a hard knot, but her face remained impassive as she moved towards him.

This surprised Mason and he cocked a quizzical brow. 'So you're not afraid of me—Miss Golding?'

'You are a treacherous, backstabbing villain, Jack Mason. I am not afraid of you.'

'Then you should be.'

He clicked his fingers and Rowena turned to run, but someone came from behind, his powerful arms encircling her and preventing her flight. Even as she drew breath to scream, something hit her on the back of the head. Then everything exploded in a million twinkling lights before she fell into a void as deep and bottomless as a black abyss.

'Where's Rowan?'

Henry and Sam looked up at Tobias from the boat. Jane looked around frantically, and then they all exchanged glances, their faces reflecting their sudden anxiety, for Rowan had been there a moment ago.

'The lad was here when we hailed the boat…' Sam faltered, for the tension on the master's face was palpable.

Tobias looked into the crowd, his eyes searching for the familiar floppy hat, paying no attention to the large covered package being hauled into a neighbouring boat by two robed men.

'Sam, take Jane to the ship. I'll look around. He can't have wandered too far.'

* * *

Climbing on board the *Cymbeline,* Tobias was met by an anxious looking Mark Dexter.

'Well?' Mark asked, searching Tobias's hard features.

Tobias shook his head. 'There was no sign of her. It's as though she's disappeared into thin air.' His eyes scanned the deck. 'Where's her sister?'

'Down below. She's in quite a state.'

'That's not surprising. I'll go and speak to her—although what the hell can I say? I'll return to the waterfront and search again, but I need more men.'

'Before you go, there's something you should see.' Mark handed him a spy glass. 'Take a look at the vessel over there.' He pointed out the ship Tobias recalled seeing and commenting on before he had left for Meknes.

With a terrible foreboding taking shape in his chest, lifting the spy glass, Tobias focused the barrel on the ship with its towering forecastle and stern. The decks were crowded with men. It was a hefty two-masted ship of about one hundred tons—a slaver past her prime by the look of her. She was painted a greenish-yellow colour that would have made her almost unnoticeable had she been lying in a cove with her sails furled.

He focused the spy glass on the blood-red flag with a black death head above two crossed cutlasses. An experienced seaman was able to identify the ships of all seafaring nations by the colours flying from her masthead. Pirates had their own flags, but they also had a variety of other flags. When they wished to hide their identity, they simply flew an appropriate national flag, but this vessel was flying its own. Something about this particular corsair vessel brought a coldness to the pit of his stomach that began to uncurl when he focused on the name emblazoned on its hull.

It was the *Seadog*—Jack Mason's ship.

Tobias took in the situation at once. The cold fire in his eyes bespoke the fury churning within him. Shaken by a cold, killing rage, he held himself in tight rein until the rage cooled. 'Mason. I now know I need look no further for Rowena. On the day we arrived in Sale she told me she thought she'd seen Mason, but she couldn't be sure. The man she saw was with some captives that had just been brought ashore. If it was Mason and he recognised Rowena, then it is no coincidence that he is still here.'

He stiffened, suddenly alert as the *Seadog*'s sails began to unfurl and fill with the wind. 'But look—the bastard's leaving.' A thunderous frown drew his thick black eyebrows into a single line as he watched the corsair vessel. 'This is our chance to capture him— after four years he is within our grasp. Weigh anchor, Mark. The tide is high. We can't wait.'

Tobias was instantly in command, Mark realised, watching as he moved swiftly to the helm. It was the air of authority, unhesitating, exuding confidence and skill, demanding and receiving instant obedience, that had made him such an effective master, the reason his men were willing to follow him without question.

The *Cymbeline* carried a large crew of a hundred men. This would give the vessel an equal fighting force if they were threatened by pirates and, like pirate vessels, when it came to a fight the *Cymbeline* needed a large crew to work the guns.

The pain in Rowena's head made her aware of the slow rolling motion of the ship's floor beneath her—but whose ship? It certainly wasn't the *Cymbeline*. She gingerly opened her eyes and her world expanded. A faint light percolated through an iron grille above. She saw she was in the small hold of a vessel, propped up against a barrel, and there was a painful lump on the back of her head.

It was airless and the stench—a combination of a stale foulness of bilge water and rotting human waste—turned her stomach. She had no way of knowing what time it was or how long she had been unconscious, but one thing she did know was that Tobias would have no idea where to look for her when he realised she was missing.

In her mind's eye she could see his panic when he found her gone, and the horror and the anger and—most undeservedly—the guilt that would show on his face that he had somehow let it happen.

As her eyes became sharper, she saw there were chains and shackles strewn over the floor—grim evidence of the ship's occupation. She peered through a narrow aisle between stacked crates and water casks. The hairs on the back of her neck stood up when something moved in the deep shadows at the end, and she shuddered on seeing a rat.

Struggling to her feet, looking down she saw she was

in a sorry state, and somewhere along the way she had lost her precious hat. Hearing a loud scraping, her heart almost stopped when up above the grille covering the hatch was flung back. Booted legs appeared over the edge and someone climbed down the ladder into the hold, carrying a lamp. Reaching the bottom, he turned. A leering grin displayed uneven rotting teeth, and in that moment of nightmarish terror, it seemed the devil had taken human form.

It was Jack Mason.

The captain of the corsair ship was dressed in Moorish garb. After he set the lamp on a barrel, the yellow light flickered upward, carving his face from the shadows behind him. She stared at him in horrified disgust. His lustful perusal pierced her meagre garments, and she could not hold back a shudder of revulsion.

'Welcome back, my *dear* Rowena. I had almost begun to fear my man might have been over harsh with you. I trust your quarters are to your liking?'

'I've had better,' she managed to utter.

'I also trust you are feeling well enough to be accommodating.'

'To you? Never!' His stare seemed to burn through her linen shirt and bindings as he sauntered closer, having to bend his head slightly to stop it hitting the roof.

'You've changed,' he said flatly.

'It's hardly surprising—in four years.' Brawny, towering, threatening, he stopped inches in front of her. 'Why have you done this?'

'To lure Searle—and I have a score to settle with

you. The two of you have become—close. When Searle finds out where you are, he'll come after you. Then I'll have him.'

Fear licked like a flame around Rowena's heart. 'You mean to kill him?'

'He's become a nuisance. The man's been on my tail for too long and he's beginning to annoy me.' He chuckled low. 'I go a-roving for plunder and slaves. Searle goes a-roving for justice and duty. He needs to be taken care of. And then when he's out of the way, you and I have some unfinished business to take care of, darlin',' he murmured.

Tracing his finger along the soft curve of her defiant chin, he laughed nastily when she backed away. He had long craved to fondle her soft skin while she trembled before him, to look at her nakedness and see the proud, complacent smile turn to a grimace of fear.

'I haven't finished with you yet—but I'll have you out of that ridiculous garb, Rowena Golding.' Reaching out he placed his big, dirty hand on her breast.

Scared of what he might do, Rowena hid her fear and held her ground, biting back the protest that flew into her mouth when he squeezed the tender flesh beneath the bindings until he hurt her. Making no attempt to be gentle, he watched for her reaction, almost as if he wanted to hear her beg for him to stop, but she would not give him the satisfaction of crying out. She merely stared at him, emotionless and defiant.

Smiling thinly, with his other hand Mason clutched her hair and dragged her head back, his foul-smelling breath fanning her face. 'You might have fooled Searle, but I knew who you were when I saw you in Sale.'

Rowena's glaring hatred was there for him to see. 'So—that was you?'

'Aye, Rowena,' he said, dropping his hands, 'with my latest batch of captives—fifty in all.'

'I saw them.'

'I seized them from a merchantman I came upon when I was sailing to Madeira. Aye, well, they'll know slavery—beneath the heavy whip of a less than humane master. The sultan will be delighted with the haul—' his brows lifted and he smiled '—though they were not as delectable as your sister Jane. I saw you got her back.' He shrugged, unconcerned. 'It doesn't matter to me. I got a good price for her.'

Seeing red, Rowena took the lantern and swung it at his head. He ducked and a grip of iron seized her wrist before she could dash the lamp at him again. Wresting it from her, he gave her a violent push. She fell back and stumbled, clutching the bulwark to save herself from hitting the floor.

'You're fast, if not quite so fast as me.' He placed the lamp back on the barrel. 'That's better,' he jeered when she backed away from him, watching him warily. 'Not so haughty, are you—when you fear?'

A cold, terrifying dread of what really lay in store for her began to make itself known. Rowena had no illusions about the fiendish intentions behind the loathsome façade. No one would come if she called. She was all alone, as if she stood exposed on the scaffold. The swaggering brute could hardly have made himself more sickening in her eyes. He was odious, and given her choice between throwing herself overboard and submitting to him, she would choose the former without hesitation.

'I am not afraid of you.'

'You will be,' he mocked. 'I vowed to finish what I started, before you attacked me so viciously for trying to be—' he cocked a mocking brow '—friendly. Yes, I vowed to have my revenge.'

'How could you do that? I was just fifteen years old.'

'Old enough to know what to have a man feels like.'

The colour drained from Rowena's face as his words brought back the memory of that day and what he had tried to do to her. 'You had your revenge, Jack Mason, when you shot my father in the back and left him for dead.'

'Pity he wasn't. So, you know about that.'

'I now know it wasn't Tobias who did that cowardly deed. He has too much honour to do something as despicable as that. I know you used my father to serve your own interests.'

'I needed a vessel and the *Dolphin* would serve until something better came along.'

'Until you could steal one, more like.'

He shrugged. 'If you like. And the crew were in favour.'

'So, you plotted together—to mutiny and overcome my father.'

He nodded. 'And any man loyal to him.'

'Who you no doubt threw overboard before sailing

off to God knows where to embark on an orgy of plunder,' she flared scathingly.

'No harm would have come to your father, had he not interfered with my plans and decided to sail with the *Dolphin* at the last minute.'

'He didn't trust you, that's why.'

'He was right not to.'

'Why did you shoot him?'

'He was in the way. When Searle caught up with us, he held your father, as owner of the *Dolphin,* responsible for what had happened to his own ship in Kingston harbour. After confronting him, Searle went in search of the harbour master to have him arrested.'

'And you crept up behind him and shot him in the back before he could accuse you to the authorities, making off with the *Dolphin* and leaving Tobias to take the blame.'

'I may have been a trifle hasty—I accept that, but I have no regrets.'

'You ruined my father in every way, did you know that?'

'He's lucky,' he sneered. 'I thought I'd killed him, until your delightful sister told me otherwise.'

'You are a spineless coward, Jack Mason.'

'Hassan Kasem. I converted to Islam.'

'A pathetic renegade.'

'Absolutely,' he confirmed without shame. 'When the *Dolphin* was captured by corsairs, it was expedient for me to do so at the time.' He shrugged lazily. 'What does it matter? Either way, I have no opinion on religious matters. One God or prophet is as much like another. It's Jack Mason I care about. I only do what suits me.'

'You are contemptible and a coward.'

'What I did doesn't trouble my conscience. I sleep easy. As for you—' his fleshy lips curved in salacious smile as his eyes travelled over her '—you have courage. I admire you for that. And you are desirable— at least you will be when you look more like a lady and don't stink so much. As yet I haven't made up my mind what to do with you. Whether I keep you for myself— to while away the time in pleasurable companionship when I am at sea—or sell you at the first slave market we arrive at, resign yourself to your fate,' he told her with brutal frankness. 'In fact, you might be worth being carefully preserved intact to bring me a rich price in the slave market in Algiers.'

His face twisted into a malevolent grin as his eyes bored into her. 'No one will come to rescue you.' He laughed wickedly under his breath before he turned and hauled himself up the ladder. Rowena shivered at the sound. 'Don't think I've done with you yet. I'll be back.'

Overcome at the fearful position in which she found herself, Rowena stood there, frozen in space, before sliding to the floor. Her dread was that before help could reach her, this beast, who was dead to propriety, might overpower her. A violent shaking possessed her. She wanted to cry, but knew what greater disaster awaited her if she weakened. She was so thirsty and tired and the evil red rat eyes watched her from the darkness, ready to come closer the second she closed her eyes.

'Oh, God,' she whispered. 'I shall go mad.' In that stinking, suffocating, airless prison, claustrophobia began to set in. 'Help me. Someone help me. Please, Tobias…'

The *Cymbeline* cruised swiftly along the coast while the sun dropped like a blood-red rose in the sky, and with the cooler air of the evening she turned and followed the corsair vessel into the deeper waters of the Atlantic.

The following morning, with the *Cymbeline* crowding on more sail and gathering pace on her prey, they were suddenly presented with another menace. There was a light mist coming down behind them and a great bank of it was rolling in from the sea—a ghostly sight that made one's flesh crawl and one's blood run cold. The sea was dead calm.

Standing at the helm, where he had stood for most of the night, Tobias turned his head this way and that, straining his eyes and ears, cursing the fog that would enable the corsair vessel to slip away. His jaw and mouth were set like stone and like a black shadow came the thought that that bestial savage had Rowena at his mercy—even now might be ravishing her—and that she might be suffering unmentionable agonies.

The fog lost them considerable time, but by mid-morning, to everyone's relief, a stiff breeze rose, thinning the mist. It was good to hear the lines and hawsers singing in the wind once more, the timber creaking with each rise and fall.

Having expected the corsair vessel to have slipped away, they were proved wrong. There could be no mistaking the strangely coloured ship some two miles distant, heading east towards the straits. Knowing that Mason would be hoping to disappear into one of the hundreds of hidden coves along the north African coast, Tobias ordered all sails to be set and heeled far over into the wind under every inch of canvas.

Mason scrutinised the approaching ship. He had hoped to throw off his pursuer when the fog had descended. He was surprised at the speed with which the *Cymbeline* had left Sale. On finding Rowena missing and recognising the *Seadog* in the bay, its captain known to him, Tobias Searle wouldn't have taken long to work out what had happened to her and set off with a sail full of vengeance.

As the morning advanced and the sun blazed down on them, it became evident that the gap was closing. By mid-afternoon the *Cymbeline* was within range of the *Seadog*.

'With Rowena on board, I daren't risk firing on her—unless it's to demast her,' Tobias said to Mark. 'I've seen the carnage a broadside can wreak aboard a ship and know it has no favourites. We must aim at the rigging to spare Rowena. We'll try to halt her by firing the forward gun.'

There was a bright flash of light followed by a puff of white smoke and the timbers shuddered. The shot fell short, but as the day wore on the crew continued to prime and fire their guns at fifteen-minute intervals—indeed, they appeared to be energised by the intensity of the battle and being able to bring the hated, murdering Jack Mason to his knees at last, and fought with gritty determination. The *Seadog* returned fire with deranged fury in a continual wave of assaults, their shots falling wide, but now she had shown her intention to resist.

Hour after hour the *Cymbeline* pressed home her attack, causing such havoc among the masts and sailing gear and tearing rents in the canvas that eventually the corsairs would have no alternative but to hove to and become vulnerable to boarding.

Hard put to maintain its course, in a last desperate attempt the damaged *Seadog* retaliated with a broadside, which Mason had loaded with swan shot—nails, glass and pieces of iron garlanded with lighted fuses. The effect on the crew of the *Cymbeline* was catastrophic— but not as catastrophic as Mason had intended. Two men were killed outright, ten were injured.

Angered but keeping a cool head, Tobias pressed on, ordering the injured to be taken below to be dealt with, and all except four of his men to hide out of sight below decks with their weapons at the ready while the *Cymbeline* made its final approach.

Despite being told to stay below, Jane came on deck, greatly distressed at the scene she came upon, of wounded men being carried below. Thinking of nothing other than helping to relieve their suffering, she went with them.

When the smoke from the blast had cleared, Mason noticed that the *Cymbeline*'s decks were almost empty and assumed most of her crew had been killed or injured. He'd put up a stout resistance, but it had become apparent that with two masts shattered and without rigging, the crippled *Seadog* was unable to repel the enemy. But with the *Cymbeline*'s crew having suffered many casualties and been severely weakened, Mason did not believe that all was lost.

As he sat and waited for the enemy to draw close, Mason hoped to overcome by sheer force, and when the battle was won and Searle and his crew cut to pieces, take off on the *Cymbeline*, which, despite his bombardment, had remained intact. It was a fine vessel, and it would be a prize indeed to steal Searle's flagship.

Down in the hold Rowena listened to the confused sounds on deck, awash in a despondency and a misery so complete she had never known such feelings could exist. When the ship shuddered under the weight of the cannonade, in her terror her thoughts turned to Tobias and Jane. Each time she heard a shot hit the ship, she became convinced it would be holed and sunk at any moment. She was going to die, she knew it, and they would never know.

The lookout on the *Cymbeline* shouted that a ship had appeared on the horizon. Looking through the spy glass and studying the approaching vessel, Tobias didn't take long to recognise a Royal Navy man-of-war flying the British ensign bearing down on them under her full spread of canvas.

When the two vessels were close enough to manoeuvre and the *Seadog* was fastened to the other vessel with grappling irons and ropes, Mason and his fellow pirates vaulted aboard the *Cymbeline*. As they did so, the men he had thought wounded emerged from hiding, fit and ready. To his dismay, Mason immediately realised that he was outnumbered. It was too late to turn back, so he and his men had to stay and fight to the end.

The pirates, wielding muskets, pistols and cutlasses, swarmed across the *Cymbeline*'s decks. They were a fearsome-looking bunch—their faces and tattooed arms were burnt and weathered nut brown. They wore a variety of clothes—canvas trousers, garish-coloured waistcoats and shirts and some with scarves tied round their heads. Others had long hair twisted with ribbons in small tails, and had daggers shoved into their trousers and pistols hanging in holsters.

All on deck waded furiously into the fray. It was a vicious mêlée of swinging cutlasses, hacking and slashing and shooting, but the pirates were outnumbered and dwindling fast as they fell wounded or dead. All the while Tobias had Jack Mason within his sights, and when he saw him leap on to the gunwale and vault across to the *Seadog*, sword in hand, he was hard on his heels, cutting down two pirates who barred his way.

Laughing scathingly into the face of his pursuer, Mason flung back the hatch and pulled his pathetic captive, who was banging on the closed hatch, out. Blinded by the sudden light, Rowena fell to her knees at the pirate captain's feet.

Tobias's manner was almost calm as he paused and

watched Mason's eyes covetously peruse and savour and grab the arm of that which he considered belonged to him. A more observant man than the pirate might have noticed the distinct hardening of Tobias's lean features and the coldness in his gaze—and taken warning.

Rowena fought like a wildcat to get free of the vicious hold, clawing with her nails and kicking her captor with all the strength she could muster, but, weakened as she was by hunger and thirst, she was no match for his brute strength. In a rage Mason cruelly twisted her arm behind her back until she cried out in pain and fell to her knees before him. Drawing a dagger from his boot, he held the blade close to her throat. Her eyes now betrayed her fear.

Suddenly the pirate captain felt a sword's blade at his own throat and he stiffened.

'Drop it, Mason, if you value your life.'

Mason found his wrist seized in a grip of iron. Slowly, against his will, the blade was raised away from Rowena's throat and he stared into Tobias Searle's softly smiling face. He released his hold on Rowena and she dropped to the deck and rolled away, her arm on fire.

'I knew you were rash, Mason, by your murderous actions in Kingston harbour—but not foolishly so.'

Mason's hand dropped to the pistol in his belt, but Tobias caught his arm. Mason struggled and managed to get free, drawing his sword. His eyes sought out his opponent's face and saw in it a strength and will he had never doubted existed, and that in his mind he would not rest until he was made to feed the fishes.

'So, Mason—face to face at last,' Tobias hissed.

'So we are,' he replied, his teeth bared in a snarl.

'You are an outlaw, Mason, and debarred from all communication with the civilised world. When you fired my ship and killed some of my crew, I swore to hunt you down like the dog you are. You dared to strike at me, so now I claim the forfeit. We'll see what the authorities at the naval base in Gibraltar have to say. There is no mercy for pirates.'

Mason's laugh was fiendish and rent the air. 'Ah, my friend, I have a great love for my neck and would not see it stretched on Gibraltar. Never. I will be damned and in hell before I let myself be taken by the British.'

'Then if I can't see you hang, I shall at least be afforded the pleasure of laughing when we feed your foul carcass to the sharks.'

'Then goddamn you,' Mason yelled, leaping towards him, swinging his curved sword.

Tobias laughed and circled his opponent, then lunged towards his chest.

From where she crouched, Rowena watched Tobias fight Jack Mason, who was a nimble, sure-footed opponent, but hampered by his long robe. Tobias seemed like a stranger to her, a man she had never known, darting, thrusting with his sword, his dark hair falling over his brow. As she watched her heart silently wept for him, for she could not bear to consider the almost unimaginable consequences of this fight, but mercifully, as the two men danced and leaped about the deck, avoiding ropes and casks that got in their way, it was apparent that command of the combat was in Tobias's hands.

Suddenly there was a shot and a puff of white smoke from across the water, from the British man-of-war, then another, and white fire struck Mason between his shoulders. Then, with a look of immense surprise on his face, dropping his sword, he fell to his knees before he slumped forward on to his face. Blood spurted from his back, spreading in an immense red stain across his shoulders.

Glancing at the naval vessel that had drawn level, Tobias saw several musketeers on board firing at the pirates. Looking down at Mason, he nudged him with his foot. He did not move. With her eyes wide in her stricken face, Rowena could not believe that the man who had brought so much misery to her family and others was dead. She wanted to go to him and hit him, to slash his vicious face with a knife, to cut out his evil heart and feed it to the gulls screeching and squawking overhead as they circled the three vessels.

But, no, how could she? She had not been raised to be a defiler of the dead. Pain rippled through her. Slowly she rose to her feet, and, looking around, saw the carnage on the decks of the corsair vessel. The fighting had stopped and the crew of the *Cymbeline* were rounding up some of the defeated pirates. Others had fled to their own vessel and taken to the longboats, pulling away from the badly damaged ship with all their strength, their frantic exertions carrying them swiftly towards the north African coast three miles distant.

Trembling uncontrollably, a weariness was in

Rowena like a weight, pressing intolerably upon her heart. She thought her terror must have driven her mad after all, for there, in front of her, was Tobias, and she thanked God with all her being that he wasn't dead.

Tobias fell to one knee and looked at her. Her hair was matted, her skin filthy and encrusted with salt, her face tense and deathly pale. When she raised her eyes and gazed up at him, tears clumped on her long black lashes, her beauty caught him like an unexpected blow to the chest, for never had she looked lovelier than this.

'Rowena?'

She stared dumbly at him, and although she tried to speak her lips made no sound. Tears prickled in her eyes and the sheer weight of what she had been through—the excruciating terror of the hours she had been held captive and then watching Jack Mason die—overwhelmed her and seemed to eat into the deepest recesses of her mind. Tobias's kindness sharpened it almost beyond bearing. She wanted to thank him, but her throat was choked.

'Don't be afraid,' Tobias murmured gently to reassure her. 'Mason cannot harm you now.'

She nodded and began to shiver violently.

Taking her hand, Tobias drew her away from curious eyes. The sun warmed her. She was grateful.

'Rowena… Answer me, I implore you. Are you all right?'

Again she nodded.

'What happened?' Panic stiffened his face as his blue eyes searched hers. 'Dear Christ! Am I too late?'

She fumbled hopelessly for words. Unable to see the suffering in her eyes when she raised them to his, Tobias could not resist doing the thing that seemed most natural—to take hold of her and wrap his arms around her. His heart was emotionally exhausted after the extremes of rage, anguish and guilt that he'd experienced ever since he had found she'd gone—and the vengeance he'd exacted on Mason could not erase any of it. The fear he had felt when he'd discovered her gone, that any harm could come to her, made him enfold her more tightly.

'It's over. I've just had a brush with death and it tends to put everything into perspective. Jane is returned to you and Jack Mason is dead. He cannot hurt you or Jane or your father any more, so let us put all this behind us and concentrate on getting you home.'

At last Rowena found her voice. 'Oh, Tobias. Thank God you came. He'd been waiting for me in Sale, ever since he saw me that day—you remember?—biding his time. He knew why we were there.'

The pain in her voice cut sharp as a knife. He felt a surge of deep compassion as she huddled against him. He held her more tightly, trying to communicate some of his male warmth to her and to still her trembling. Holding her a little away from him, he regarded her closely and she felt her thoughts probed by careful fingers.

'My lovely Rowena,' he whispered. She gazed up at him and his heart clenched at the world of vulnerability behind the blue-green blaze of her eyes. Drawing her back into his arms, he placed his lips against her hair. A dark rage filled him that she should have been made to suffer. 'It doesn't matter. Mason is dead and you are alive. That's the most important thing. I won't let anything bad happen to you. I am here to look after you.'

She buried her face in his chest. 'Tobias—he—he…'

'Don't. Not now,' he said hoarsely. He wanted to soothe away her fears as he would a frightened child. Somehow he must help her to rebuild her self-esteem, but it was hard for him to talk quietly, rationally, when mounting passion was making his own heart beat fast, drawing him to her. 'It's over. You are safe. When I realised you were gone, I did everything I could to find you. It wasn't until I saw the *Seadog*, which I knew was Mason's vessel, that I realised he must have taken you.'

'He—he tried to…but…'

Tobias pulled away and looked down into her face, hope lighting his features. 'He—he didn't—'

'No,' she cried with a shudder, 'but I thought he would.'

'Thank God,' Tobias murmured softly, relieved to see her beginning to relax as the tension left her. 'But you are safe. Take heart. Your ordeal is over.' Placing his fingers under her chin, he tilted her face up to his and smiled, his piercingly blue eyes soft with warmth. 'I hope I don't offend your feminine sensibilities by suggesting you hoped I would come to your rescue?'

A tremulous smile quavered on her lips. 'What kept you?'

'The fact that I didn't know what the hell had happened to you, and a sea fret that almost swallowed us up. But come, I'll help you back on to the *Cymbe-line* and then I must meet with the commander of the naval vessel. Jane has been out of her mind with worry and will be relieved to see you returned unharmed.'

'I can't think of anything I would like more that to see Jane—apart from a bath. I must look awful and smell even worse.'

He grinned. 'That's more like the Rowena I know.'

She looked down at Jack Mason. 'He has got what he deserved. Is revenge sweet, Tobias?'

'Do not be misled, Rowena.' His voice was quiet and subdued. 'There is revenge, then there is justice. Some-times the two must be dealt with as one.'

The cold logic of his statement made her shudder. Almost fearfully she enquired, 'And your revenge—or justice—is it still directed at my father?'

He countered her question with one of his own. 'Has he not done wrong against me?'

'I don't know any more, Tobias. I can only hope that, when we reach England, all will be resolved.'

An official-looking naval officer, Captain Ryan, climbed aboard the *Cymbeline* to speak to Tobias. After making his acquaintance, he looked down at Mason with distaste. 'I've been after this devil for months. He's been cruising the Atlantic and the Mediterranean, preying on legitimate shipping for long enough. Got his consort a while back. And you?'

'Mason and I had—unfinished business.'

'Well—I hope it's done with now. You've been to Sale?'

Tobias nodded. 'And Meknes—to pay ransom for a captive in the sultan's harem.'

'You were successful in getting her out?'

'Aye, thank God. You know about the treaty signed by his Majesty King George?'

Captain Ryan's lips twisted with derision. 'I do. It won't last. Treaties have been drawn up and signed by Moulay Ismail before. This treaty will be no different. He will renege on the agreement. In no time at all he'll tear it up—as he did the treaty he signed with Queen Anne. Where do you go next?'

'Back to England, but I intend to stop at Gibraltar on the way.'

'Then allow me to escort you. We'll have a drink together—toast the demise of another damned corsair. What do you say, Mr Scarle?'

'I'll look forward to it.'

Captain Ryan returned to his ship with a sense of one more victory.

The *Cymbeline* sailed on, leaving the naval vessel to deal with the pirate ship and the prisoners. Most of the *Cymbeline*'s crew were for burning it with the prisoners on board when the booty had been taken off. Captain Ryan had decided to sink the vessel, which had begun listing badly. Some of the sailors spent most of their time nursing wounds, but they were triumphant to have got rid of Jack Mason.

Now their mission was accomplished and all Rowena's concerns about Jane were set aside, her mind turned to the bargain she had made with Tobias. Suddenly everything was changed and she became aware of Tobias as never before. No matter how she tried to keep him at arm's length, spending time with Jane in the cabin Mark had vacated as the ship sailed to Gibraltar, though she kept herself well occupied, it was impossible to ignore him.

Tobias watched her as closely as she did him, and often when she wasn't looking at him she could feel the heat of his eyes boring holes into her back. What manner of man was this who crept into her dreams, who spied upon her very mind? She could not bring herself to face Tobias Searle, who was silently demanding that her side of the bargain must be met.

The cabin was hot. Tobias had eaten his meal and was sitting relaxed at the table. Having cleared everything away, Rowena was about to leave when his hand shot out and took hold of her wrist. Gasping, she spun round. Mocking blue eyes gazed back at her. She tried to pull her wrist free and he laughed.

'Easy, my love.' Now his eyes glinted like hard metal. 'I have a distinct feeling that you have been avoiding me of late. Is there a reason for this?'

'No—of course there isn't.' She sounded sharp and in control, but underneath it panic had set in. He let go of her wrist and she backed away from him.

Tobias's teeth flashed in his bronze skin as he laughed again and Rowena could only remark the resemblance he bore to a swarthy pirate. He rose to his feet and his eyes smiled at her, touching her everywhere. A flush mounted her cheeks as she experienced not for the first time that sensation of being stripped by his bold gaze.

'You and I have unfinished business to discuss, Rowena. I would like to talk to you.'

'Talk?' she repeated. He nodded. She eyed him suspiciously. 'What do you want to talk about?'

'Us. There is the matter of the bargain we made.'

'Bargain?' she said tentatively. The way he was looking at her made her feel like a hen before a wily fox.

'Aye, bargain, Rowena. A promise is a promise. Was it so lightly spoken to be discarded at your will? Will you not see out the bargain we made?' He raised a dark brow and considered her flushed cheeks and the soft trembling mouth.

'I—I—yes,' she stammered.

He surveyed her panicky expression. 'Suppose you tell me why the prospect of lying with me suddenly seems to alarm you.'

'It doesn't,' she denied desperately, thinking it might be a mistake to admit to any form of weakness 'It it's just difficult—on ship, with Jane and a crew never far away.'

'I agree. This is hardly a fit place for a tryst, but there are ways.' His fingers wandered lightly up her arm and his smile broadened into a rakish grin, more like the Tobias Rowena had known in Falmouth.

'What kind of ways?' she asked, immensely aware of the effect of his fingertips brushing her arm beneath the loose sleeve of her shirt and the magnetism his body was suddenly exuding.

'You'll see, and I don't think you'll be disappointed. Are you not the slightest bit interested, Rowena? Will you surrender to me willingly?'

She looked deep into his fathomless eyes. The memory of the time they had spent on the beach was still incredibly, vibrantly fresh in her mind, and the prospect of repeating what they had shared, just for a few hours, seemed irresistibly, sweetly appealing.

She nodded finally and softly said, 'Yes—as you wish.'

Chapter Eleven

The ship put in at the Gibraltar, which was a base for a British garrison. Here the crew would enjoy a brief dalliance with the raven-haired strumpets that hung around the harbour. Jane took the opportunity to acquire some decent European clothes, enabling her to discard the hated hijab. Rowena envied her, wishing she too could throw off her cabin-boy guise and present herself in feminine attire, but Tobias warned her against it. She had to be content with a new shirt and a hat to replace the one she had lost.

The town was enclosed by impressive walls, the oldest being those of the Moorish castle complex. Narrow passages and steps that climbed steeply between the buildings could be found in the upper part of the town. This was where Rowena accompanied Tobias one evening, when Jane had retired to her bed, complaining of a headache brought on by spending too much time in the hot sun—fortuitous for Tobias, for it gave him the opportunity to secrete Rowena away from the ship without questions being asked.

It was almost dark and the air was still as Rowena accompanied him towards the house set within its own grounds behind tall iron gates. They were admitted to the house by an elderly Spanish woman, who greeted them in broken English. They followed her into a small courtyard filled with tubs of exotic plants. Rowena paused for a moment, drawing deep breaths of the warm, perfumed night air.

'Where are we? Whose house is this?' Apprehension was creeping over her.

'Trust me.'

The woman gestured for them to follow, leading them through a series of elegant salons and down a short staircase to a lower level. Rowena's feet, shod in thin leather sandals, made no sound on the polished marble mosaic as she glided, ghostlike, beside Tobias. Now the air was thick and perfumed with musk and sandalwood and she could hear the tinkling of gently flowing water and voices hushed in conversation and laughter.

In the melancholy light of the candles a tall dark-skinned woman with the proud refined features of an Egyptian queen stepped from the shadows. She eyed Rowena with some curiosity and more than a little speculation, for she really did look like a pretty youth, and then she smiled.

'Welcome. You are expected. My name is Imelda.' Raising her arms, the long sleeves of her sleek, tubular wisp of a gown that could barely be given the name slipped down to reveal broad golden armlets. She handed Rowena a double-handed goblet. Rowena looked at Tobias. His eyes, a dark shade of blue in the subdued light, were watching her.

'Drink it. It will relax you.'

She obediently sipped the dark, herb-scented wine, before handing the goblet to Tobias to drink.

'Remember when you stayed with Ahmed and how you enthused over his bathing chamber?'

She nodded, something warm beginning to unfold within her, whether from the wine or the memory of that pleasurable experience she had no way of knowing, but she had no objections to experiencing it once more.

The woman conducted them to a large marble chamber that was a bath house. Deep in shadow, it glowed with a warm orange light from the lamps. In the centre was a tiled area with a sunken bath in which water was steaming. There was a brazier close by, towels to hand, along with flagons of oils and soaps—all a person could want for a luxurious wallow.

'Here we will have complete privacy,' Tobias told Rowena.

The warm, moist atmosphere was already beginning to get to her and she longed to pull at the cloying fabric that stuck to her damp skin. She went and stood at the shining blue-tiled rim, looking down at the water. Tobias came to stand beside her.

'This place was made for love, Rowena. I didn't bring you here to hurt you.'

The woman moved silently to the door and flashed

a dazzling white smile. 'I will leave you to your enjoyment. If you should need anything at all, please ring the bell.' Indicating the small object on a table, she left without a sound.

Alone with Tobias, Rowena was suddenly uneasy about the attention he was to give her. The pressure of his touch on her shoulder was light, but to her it felt like a steel trap. She began to seriously doubt her wisdom in coming here with him, but she owed him and she must see it through. Tomorrow it would be over, but she knew that nothing would be the same again. She would not be the same.

'It is hardly the place for a tryst I would have chosen, Rowena, but it's the best I could manage. It cost me nothing, only my service to Captain Ryan for helping to bring about Mason's demise.'

Rowena looked at him in alarm. 'He knows? You told him?'

He laughed lightly, his fingers lightly stroking the curve of her cheek. 'I merely told him I would like a night to myself on *terra firma* and would appreciate somewhere respectable to stay. Knowing of your fondness for cleanliness, I suggested a house with a bathing chamber would not go amiss. He was most happy to oblige.'

'Who does this house belong to?'

'Lord Charles Foley, who is attached to the garrison. Lord Foley and his wife are in England just now, so be assured we will not be disturbed,' he murmured, turning her to face him.

Rowena felt devoured by those burning eyes delving into her own. His voice was low and husky in her ears, and she had to reach deeply into her reservoir of will to dispel the slow numbing of her senses.

'Are you sure? There are servants in the house.'

'We are quite alone. You have my word on it.' Seeing a fleeting frown of bemusement cross her face, he said, 'Rowena, you are not afraid of being here alone with me?'

'Afraid? Have I need to be afraid, Tobias?'

'You need have no fear of me—but are you ready for what is about to happen between us?'

She looked at him steadily, at the half-curved lips with the low, intimate glow of the lamps moulding the handsome sculpture of his face with mysterious shadow. 'Yes. I—I wouldn't be here otherwise.'

Drawing her into his arms, Tobias slowly lowered his mouth to hers and kissed her gently. Her lips were moist and sweet against his. Rowena closed her eyes and slipped her arms around his neck.

'You'll have to show me how it's done,' she whispered against his lips. 'I've had no practice, you see, so I would not know.'

'I will teach you. I will waken all the passion in that lovely, untutored body. Are you ready to learn?'

His half-smile was so seductive it sent a thrill all the way down to Rowena's toes. 'Do you make a habit of deflowering virgins?'

'Not usually. Now, I want to see you—all of you. Let me help you with your clothes.'

A blush rose to her cheeks, but, though shy of him,

she was eager to proceed. Her heartbeat quickened as he removed her clothes, his sure hands warm when they touched her flesh. When she stood naked before him, her flush deepened. She was suddenly apprehensive, for she no longer had the guise of cabin boy to protect her from those eyes that touched her as she had never been touched before.

Slowly Tobias pulled off his shirt and cast it aside. Rowena took in the breadth of his wide shoulders, the clean sweep of his taut waist, her gaze moving lower, her body trembling with anticipation when he unfastened his trousers and stepped out of them.

'Well?' he asked softly, aware that she was holding her breath.

Her lips curved in a slow smile. 'There is no denying that you are a magnificent specimen, Tobias.'

He merely laughed softly in reply, capturing her hands when they reached out to stroke his flesh. They immersed themselves in the bath, enjoying the pleasurable sensation of the hot, scented water soothing their bodies. Tobias moved behind the woman he had wanted for so long, touching her neck gently, then caressing the smooth line of her back. She turned into his arms, her eyes wide and her soft lips trembling. The jolt of surprise she experienced had everything to do with the bold, manly touch of him, the alien hardness like a hot brand against her thighs.

Their bodies clung together, hers slender and silky, his hard, long and lean. Taking her face between his hands and threading his fingers into her silken hair, he kissed her mouth and trailed featherlight kisses down her neck to her breast.

'You are like a bird of paradise with a body made for love,' Tobias murmured, his breathing deepening as he felt her respond to his caresses.

They stroked and kissed, exploring each other and languidly enjoying the experience. But then Tobias drew her out of the bath and she found herself lying on a wide divan. Unable to shake off the lethargy creeping over her, she watched Tobias's tall, muscular figure move towards her and lower himself down. As he took her hand his expression was suddenly serious. Reaching up she caressed his cheek.

'What is it that makes you frown so, Tobias?'

'The bargain, Rowena.'

'What about it?'

'I know this is not the most desirable way of coming together. But despite what you may think of my insistence that our bargain will be fulfilled, I am not the kind of brute to trap you in a corner and force myself on you.'

'What are you saying?' she asked, bemused. 'That you don't want me?'

'Want you? Of course I want you. The very sight of you here with me makes my body ache to release the passion you arouse in me. Yet I must accept that you only agreed to my bargain out of fear for your sister. I placed you in an impossible position. I am giving you the opportunity to walk away, to forget the bargain ever existed, and accept that my services were freely and gladly given.'

'But I don't understand. Why did you not tell me this before we left the ship?'

'Because I wanted to see if you would hold to your promise.'

'You were testing me?'

'In a way. But now I am releasing you from the agreement, Rowena.'

'But I don't want to be released. If I were to walk away, I should for ever feel beholden to you. I don't want that.'

'Then what do you want?'

'To stay.'

'And what will pass between us will not be against your will, some noble sacrifice of martyrdom?'

'No.'

Tobias was stunned by the commitment she voiced and could find no worthy reply. He had not expected her to yield when he had given her the chance to leave, and now she was tearing down all the boundaries between them. What was he to think? And why did he suddenly feel like the conquered and less like a conqueror?

He breathed her name and bent over her to kiss her lips, skimming her throat with his kisses. She gasped and threw her head back. He was poised above her, his face hard and dark with passion, and a pulse was throbbing in his temple.

'You knew this would happen to me, didn't you, Tobias? You knew I wouldn't be able to resist you.' She ran her fingers through his hair, closing her eyes in rapture.

'So, you do want me, Rowena?'

'So much it terrifies me.'

'Then kiss me,' he ordered thickly.

And Rowena did. Curving her hand around his nape, she offered him her parted lips, kissing him as erotically as he had kissed her a moment before. He groaned with pleasure and deepened the kiss, almost losing control completely. She moved against him as his caresses grew bolder, exploring the secrets of her body with the sureness of a knowledgeable lover. He was gentle, infinitely so, his hand wandering with deliberate slowness over every part of her, as if savouring what he found, and she trembled beneath his touch. Rowena felt as if her body were on fire, melting and flowing, and a sob of startled pleasure escaped her.

Just when she thought she would surely burst from the feelings inside her, his knee parted her thighs and he lay on her and took her, and she held him to her, moaning and floating in a sea of mindless pleasure and pain. His body was as lean as an athlete's, bold, virile, thrusting and golden brown. Entwined, they merged together, the firm, slender body beneath his like a yielding, living substance as she gave all her desire, her passion and her love. They became one, fulfilling each other in a most sublime, exquisite act of love.

When it was over and Tobias dozed, Rowena had no immediate thoughts, only the memory of something immense, something important, of incredible joy, tremendous and wondrous, beyond which nothing was comparable. Opening her eyes, she wriggled on to her elbows and gazed at his face. It was more beautiful than she had ever known. She was saddened to the depths of her soul that she would never be anything to him other than what she was now, and in desperation she banished the chilling knowledge by reminding herself that for this one night he was hers.

A wave of rippling need for him washed over her. Moving closer to his warm, powerful body relaxed in sleep, she trailed a possessive caress with her fingers down his chest to his belly, so warm, so smooth, so firm, and then she kissed his cheek, gazing down at him. He was such a beautiful man and in this moment he belonged to her. She kissed his mouth, trailing her lips along his jaw and down his neck.

He moaned, waking, and burying his lips in hers he took her again, taking all the time in the world as he kissed her and loved her into mindless insensibility.

It was soft female laughter that awoke Rowena from her slumber. Raising herself on her elbow, she looked towards the door as it opened and two olive-skinned servant girls came in, one carrying a carafe of wine and the other a tray of fruit and sweetmeats. As they approached the divan, Tobias had the presence of mind to draw a silken sheet over them both. He sat up to block the servants' view of his Rowena, and she was grateful for his consideration, but it was too late, they had seen her. Inquisitive about the gentleman's companion, they cheekily craned their necks to take a good look.

'Thank you,' Tobias said, as they placed the trays on

a nearby table. 'It is much appreciated. Now will you excuse us? My—friend and I would like some privacy.'

To Rowena's irritation the girls giggled. 'Of course, sir,' one of them said in broken English. Picking Rowena's trousers off the floor, with raised eyebrows she placed them on the bottom of the divan.

'He—is very young—your friend,' the other girl commented, her eyes lighting with mischief.

Tobias's lips twitched with amusement. '*He* is a she—and, yes, she is *quite* young.'

They backed towards the door, their bare feet slapping on the tiled floor.

'Oh—we will not disturb you and your—*mistress,*' one of them said, covering her mouth with her hand to smother her giggles, which infuriated Rowena and raised the angry demon in her.

When they had gone, the lovers listened to the fading footsteps and laughter, then Rowena reared up and glared at Tobias accusingly.

'I agreed to spend this time with you, but I think you've carried it a bit far. How dare you let them think I am your mistress?'

Tobias shrugged indolently. 'If I let them think you are my mistress, they will not give you any more attention and they will have little to gossip about when Lord Foley returns. If they thought you were a lad—which is how you appeared to them when we arrived—then gossip they will and my reputation would be in question.'

'How very convenient for you,' she observed with arid sarcasm.

Tobias chuckled low, amused by her ire, but when he reached out to draw her into his arms and she dashed his hands away, he frowned with displeasure. 'Why do you flinch, when a moment ago you welcomed my touch?'

'Because I've suddenly decided I don't like being pawed,' she flared, angry with Tobias, angry with those silly, insensitive girls, but mostly she was angry at herself for having placed herself in this humiliating, shameful situation.

Tobias smiled crookedly at her, willing her to respond as she had just moments before, but there was no answering spark in her eyes. Her head came up and her soft mouth tightened, and he could see she had worked herself up into a fine temper.

'You will have to get used to it, my love, for when you are married to your rich and titled old man, you will have to accept your lot—and spend the rest of your nights yearning for a real man in your bed.'

The bright hue of Rowena's cheeks and flashing of her eyes gave mute evidence of his savage, cutting words. 'You beast!' she snarled, scrambling to her knees and glaring at him with feverish wrath. 'You said there was no bargain, but of course there was, and it was well met, but I can't help feeling there is something sordid about what we have done—what I have done. Suddenly I feel dirty, like the cheapest whore, and if I should find myself with child? What then? What shall I tell Lord Tregowan?'

He answered her question with another. 'And would you tell him?'

'I would be honest with him. I would not deceive

him into believing he was getting a chaste bride. What respectable man would want a woman with the morals of a whore?'

'You are too hard on yourself.'

'I don't think so. It will be me and me alone who must pay the price of this folly.' Flinging herself off the bed, she was about to reach for her clothes when Tobias sprang up and grasped her wrist, bringing her round to face him.

'You wouldn't be alone, Rowena. I would take care of you.'

'Why? What would you do? Marry me yourself? Make me your Mrs Searle?' Like a cold hand squeezing her heart, she heard him say quietly,

'No, not Mrs Searle.'

Rowena glared at him and snatched her wrist free of his grasp, her humiliation complete. 'Don't worry, Tobias. I'm not hankering after that. I don't want to be your wife any more than you want to be my husband. Besides, my father would not approve.'

'Why not? He might soften towards me when he sees he has Jane back.'

'He would not approve of the fact that I prostituted myself.'

'You did not prostitute yourself.'

'Then what would you call it? Whore! Harlot! Prostitute! What's the difference?' He towered over her, his overpowering presence so close that she was afraid her resolve would weaken. A gleam entered his eyes. He looked rakishly down at her and her breath held while his eyes boldly appraised her. He picked up her trousers and she snatched them from him. 'Leave it. I don't have need of your services. I can see to my own clothing.'

After pulling on her trousers she kicked the detested bindings aside and shrugged herself into her shirt, her fingers trembling as she fumbled with the buttons. 'Now the bargain is fulfilled, kindly take me back to the ship. You did me a favour in securing Jane's freedom. I have just returned the favour—in the basest way possible— payment for services rendered. How can any man respect me after that, when I don't even respect myself?'

Tobias stood back and leaned against one of the pillars that surrounded the bath. 'Ah, Rowena. Such anger. I have done you no wrong.'

'Of course you haven't,' she retorted sarcastically, 'You rescued Jane, didn't you?' He nodded. 'For a price,' she hissed, thrusting her face forward. 'For a price.'

Without more ado she turned on her heel and left him. Somehow she found her way out of the house and away from those detestable, giggling women and back to the ship and her cabin, where she could hide and lick her wounds, but not for long. Hearing a sound, she turned and saw Tobias in the doorway.

'You! What do you want?'

'Just to make sure you had got back safely.'

'I'm here, aren't I? Now go away. You have what you wanted, now leave me alone.'

They arrived in Falmouth on one of those days of dazzling clearness and an intensely blue sky. Billowing clouds floated above low green hills crowding close upon a golden strand of beach, which separated the land from the gently rolling surf that licked the naked shore. The air was warm and sultry as the *Cymbeline* came from her own white clouds, and her sun-bleached sails gleamed white in the brightness of the day.

Tobias came and stood beside Rowena at the rail. Their relationship had been strained since leaving Gibraltar, and Rowena had gone out of her way to avoid him.

Now she turned and gave him a speculative look. She truly did love this man. Why else would she be experiencing this painful yearning? She was finding it harder and harder to retreat into cool reserve when she was near him, especially when memories of his caresses, hot, wild and sweet, kept spinning around in her head.

'Well, Rowena, here you are—home at last.'

'I shudder to think what my father will have to say when I turn up looking as I do, with a face the colour of a burnt nut. I shan't be in any fit state to receive visitors for a while.'

Tobias stood back and regarded her for a long moment before he answered softly, 'I assure you your brush with the sun has done you no harm, and I have always found your attire most—provocative.'

She was unaware that her dark hair tumbling about her face from beneath her hat—having grown considerably since she had started out on this journey—was a hundred different shades and dazzling lights, from ebony to earth brown to lights of deepest red, as her brilliant, beautiful wide eyes flared to life. A smile began to curve his lips. His expression was unreadable, smiling, watchful, knowing—secretive.

'Are you glad to be back in England, Tobias?'

'I'm glad everything has turned out well. But time has a habit of passing, even though sometimes we would hold it back. I'm going to miss my cabin boy. There's not a cabin boy I know who moves like you do.'

'Like what?' Rowena laughed. 'Do I clump about— or perhaps I move like a galleon in full sail?'

'Good Lord, no,' he assured her. 'More like a siren's whisper in your bare feet.'

She flushed a delightful pink. 'Flatterer.'

'I do not lie, Rowena.'

It was the first time since leaving Gibraltar that he had complimented her or even looked at her as though she was an attractive woman. It brought a rush of heat to her cheeks, and suddenly she found it hard to hold his appraising stare. Her gaze was drawn to the fine dark hairs on his tanned forearm resting on the rail, and her heartbeat quickened at the masculine strength she saw there. She looked quickly away. There were times when Tobias Searle was too attractive for her peace of mind.

'Are you coming with us to the house?'

A light blazed briefly in his eyes, then was extinguished. He shook his dark head. 'Not now. Mark will go with you. Your father has a strong aversion to me, remember. But don't worry your lovely head. Confront him I shall, I promise you. We have unresolved issues that must be discussed.'

'Nothing is the same as it was. My father will know that and be for ever in your debt.'

'We shall see.'

Rowena gazed at him, her expression grave. 'What kind of man are you, Tobias Searle? I have often wondered, and despite being with you for many weeks—and having known you in the most intimate way a woman can know a man—I realise I have no idea at all.'

'And do you want to know?'

'Not if you don't want me to.'

His eyes gleamed. 'You will soon know all there is to know about me, Rowena. I promise you that.' He looked past her. 'Excuse me while I go and speak to Mark. Here is your sister.'

Rowena watched him walk away. Though it cost her every ounce of strength and will-power, and her own bloody-minded pride, she would not let him see how deeply their parting was affecting her, how much her heart was breaking, how much she cared. A slow realisation of what had happened to her, born in the moment so long ago now, it seemed, when he had followed her to the beach—perhaps even before that—was moving through her, making its way from her wounded heart to the rest of her.

Falmouth seemed to glow in a gilded light, which gave an aura of enchantment to the scene. Drinking it all in, Rowena realised how much she loved this place and how much she had missed it. Her heart soared—as high as the gulls circling overhead. She had been in a different world, and now it was time to get back to reality.

She looked for the *Rowena Jane,* but she was no longer at her moorings. She must have been sold. How much of the profit would her father have to pay to satisfy Tobias? But then her father was still beholden to the man he had wrongly accused of almost ending his life because he had brought his daughter back to him. It was a debt he could never repay.

There were few on the shore and in the harbour who did not pause in whatever they were doing at the sight of the new arrival, who did not recognise her sleek lines and the impressive pennant snapping from her mast in the breeze. It was three months since the *Cymbeline* had left Falmouth, and, just like Matthew Golding, they awaited the return of the vessel on which his eldest daughter had sailed to go and look for the lovely young Jane. Few believed she would succeed. Few believed she would return—including Matthew Golding himself, who had mourned the disappearance of his daughters as if they were dead.

One and all stood and waited, watching as the sails were dropped and the *Cymbeline* coasted to an easy berth on the quayside. The gangplank thudded down. Accompanied by Mark Dexter, Jane was the first to step ashore. A gasp escaped them and there were tears in some of the eyes that witnessed this momentous occasion. Little attention was drawn to the lad following behind, a straw hat pulled well down over his face.

Jane could barely contain her enthusiasm to reach her home. Rowena turned and looked back. Tobias was on the deck of the ship watching her go.

* * *

They were welcomed home with open arms. The reunion was a tearful one and Jane sobbed out her story to her father. It was later, when Rowena had stripped away her guise as a cabin boy and donned the clothes of a young lady—feeling strangely overdressed and restricted in female attire—that with a certain amount of trepidation she went to see her father alone. John, the man employed to look after his needs, had wheeled him out into the garden and he sat in the shade of a great elm tree as the sun's rays stretched long shadows across the lawn.

Rowena had been expecting a scolding, but instead her father received her with such an air of grief and relief to see her back safe that she was moved to tears.

'Well, Rowena, this time you have outdone yourself. There were times when I thought I would never see you or Jane again and it means everything to me to have both my daughters returned to me. I must make it clear that, however much I disapprove of your reckless actions, I am not above giving credit where it is due.'

'It is Tobias Searle you have to thank, Father. Without him we would not be here. He risked his life for Jane.'

He frowned and pursed his mouth and shook his head with a troubled countenance. 'So I understand.'

Rowena went on to explain what had prompted her to go after Jane, and how Tobias hadn't known she was aboard his ship until it was too late to turn back. Her father listened to all she had to say calmly and without interruption.

'Tobias had heard how the *Petrel* had been intercepted and that it was Jack Mason, turned pirate, who was responsible. Because of what had happened to his ship in Kingston harbour, he had vowed to track him down and saw his chance. It was Jack Mason who shot you, Father. He told me himself—before he died.'

Matthew nodded, accepting this. 'How did Mason die?'

'He was shot in a skirmish with a British naval vessel.'

Matthew became thoughtful. 'And good riddance. It would seem I have done Mr Searle a grave injustice. With good reason I truly believed he was the one who shot me.'

'He wasn't there. He had left to find the harbour master. You were right not to trust Jack Mason. He had every intention of inciting a mutiny and seizing the *Dolphin* for himself.' She leaned forward and took his hand. 'Father, where is the *Rowena Jane?* I looked for her, but she wasn't at her moorings.'

'No, I had a buyer.'

'Who?'

'Lord Tregowan. He—has been most generous.'

'Then the money from the sale must go to Tobias Searle.'

Matthew nodded. 'I am deeply indebted to him—in a way I can never repay.'

Rowena looked away, wondering what he would say if she were to tell him that the debt had been paid in full. 'So we are no better off, which is all the more reason why I must marry Lord Tregowan—if he still wants me.'

Matthew looked at his daughter, holding her gaze. 'You will see him?'

'Yes. He has not withdrawn his offer of marriage?'

Matthew averted his eyes. 'No—quite the opposite. He has been eager for your return. Tomorrow he will call on you.'

'I am surprised he still wants me to be his wife. I am under no illusions, for, despite my legitimate reasons for going after Jane, my reputation will be tarnished. There will always be gossip and speculation about me.'

Matthew chuckled softly and chucked her under the chin as he used to do when she was a child, showing something of his old self. 'And when did Rowena Golding ever give a damn about what others think? Never. Now go and get John to wheel me back inside. I feel a chill.'

Rowena was up early the next day. Feeling the need to set her eyes on the *Cymbeline* in the hope of seeing its master one last time before committing herself to another man, she went down to the harbour. Shading her eyes with her hand, she looked at the sea. Casually she scanned the wide expanse of water, looking at the ships at anchor and searching for the one she knew best, the one with a jaunty crimson-and-gold flag fluttering from its mast. But where was it? Panic set in and she became almost frantic. It had to be there—somewhere. Her feet took her towards the quay where she paused to ask a fisherman sitting on a cask smoking his clay pipe what had happened to the *Cymbeline.*

'Gone,' he informed her with a gesture to the sea with his arm. 'Sailed with the tide early morning.'

Feeling as if every drop of blood had left her brain, leaving her faint and sick, Rowena thanked him and began walking away from the harbour. Gone! Tobias had gone, and he had not even bothered to say goodbye. Oh, how could he do that—and how could she bear it?

Utterly dejected, she turned for home and her expected meeting with Lord Tregowan.

Everyone was on tenterhooks as they awaited Lord Tregowan's arrival. Rowena paced the hall, beset with apprehension, not knowing what to expect. When the moment finally arrived and the tall figure of Tobias appeared in the doorway, giving her his full attention, her shock was so great that her knees nearly buckled beneath her.

His face was shadowed, his eyes luminous. He seemed taller, bigger and more splendidly dressed, more magnificent than she had ever seen him. Wearing midnight-blue breeches and frockcoat, pristine white silk vest and a sky blue neckcloth at his throat, his black hair pulled back and tied at the nape, she was in awe of his lordly grandeur.

Her heart soared and beat with joy, for she truly believed he had sailed away. Why was he here? Had he missed her? Was he here to ask her to be his bride?

Tobias halted in front of her. Could this elegant young woman in her fetching periwinkle-blue gown, her hair elegantly coiffed, be the cabin boy he had come to know and love?

'Hello, Rowena. Have you missed me?'

Rowena stared, barely able to absorb it. Her heart pounded. She felt something inside her breaking free of its shackles, a rightness, an audacity such as she had never possessed.

'Tobias! Of course I've missed you. But—I was expecting Lord Tregowan.'

'Then I hope I don't disappoint you.'

'But—but what are you saying?' She could not form the question, though her mind raced frantically for a logical answer. 'But Lord Tregowan is…'

'What, Rowena? A doddering ancient?'

Bewildered she glanced about, unable to settle her misting gaze on any one thing while her mind flew in frenzy. 'Well—I don't know. We've never met, but I assumed…'

Tobias chuckled. 'My dear Rowena. You should never assume anything. Invariably you will be wrong. I am Lord Tregowan, and as you can see I am no ancient.' He reached out to take her hand.

'Don't touch me,' she flared, stepping back, tears beginning to run down her cheeks. She was absolutely furious. The identity of Lord Tregowan was more surprising, more unnerving, than she had ever imagined or even tried to prepare herself for.

'How could you? How could you do this to me? All this time you have let me believe you were someone else… You duped me—twice, for the first time I thought you were Mr Whelan. Next you duped me into believing I was to marry an old man. If you cared anything for me at all, you would have eased my fears and told me.' Unable to look at him a moment longer, she turned and stalked towards the window.

Tobias sighed and bowed his head as a heavy guilt descended on him. He moved to stand behind her, his heart wrenching with pain when he saw her slender shoulders tremble with her silent weeping.

'Rowena, my love…'

'Don't call me that. I am not your love!' She spun round, and her tear-filled eyes blazed at him as she choked on her sobs. 'You—you are a monster!' she cried, her voice ragged with emotion. 'You tricked me. You tricked my father. When I think of the time I gave myself to you—how you held me in your arms—how I love you… Oh, how you must have laughed at me, at my stupidity, my gullibility.'

She was glaring at him as if she could do him harm, and her fine-boned profile was tilted obstinately to betray her mutinous thoughts. Tobias truly believed she did not realise what she had just said, and his heart almost burst with thankfulness. He could not help but wonder at the substance of this woman. He had known no one like her, and the disturbing fact was that she seemed capable of disrupting his whole life no matter what character she portrayed.

'I never laughed at you. I wanted you, and I knew of no other way I could have you.'

'But you should have told me.'

'How could I? You hated me, remember? As did your father. Believing me guilty of almost killing him and refusing to listen to reason, he would never have allowed me anywhere near you, so I resorted to subterfuge. I could not have won you any other way. Both you and your father would have scoffed at my proposal.'

Dashing the back of her hand across her cheeks to wipe away her tears, she stared at him wide eyed. 'You mean—even then...'

'I wanted you, Rowena, so please don't berate me for using my wits to obtain that which I desire. Mason's apprehending of the *Petrel* was like handing you to me on a plate. You came to me for help because there was no one else who could. When I refused to take you with me, I did so out of concern for you, and when your father accepted my offer of marriage to you—without being aware of my true identity—I knew you would be waiting when I returned.' He grinned. 'How was I to know you had ideas of your own and would smuggle yourself aboard my ship in the guise of my cabin boy?'

Recollecting her father's attitude and suspecting something was not quite right, she said, 'Is my father now aware of who you are—and that it is you who purchased the *Rowena Jane?*'

'Yes. She will work out of Bristol, along with my other ships. My lawyer explained everything to your father after we left Falmouth—about Mason and what really happened on Antigua, but he swore him to secrecy, insisting that I be the one to explain everything to you on our return.'

'And—he didn't create a fuss?'

'Apparently not. He was so relieved I had gone to

look for Mason—and Jane—that he would have sold his precious ship to the devil.'

'But—your name—the Tobias Searle depicted on your flag?'

'Not Tobias Searle, Rowena. The S is for Searle, but the T is for Tregowan. I am Tobias Tregowan by birth, and Tregowan Hall is my birthright. When I was a child I lived in Bristol with my parents. My father—George Tregowan, a successful shipping merchant—died when I was but a babe. My mother married again—to James Searle. He was a fine man—a shipping merchant like my father. The two companies merged—which explains the pennant. To simplify matters, my mother thought it best that I was addressed as Searle.'

'But why did you not come to Tregowan Hall when Lord Julius died in the fire?'

'When my education was complete, on the death of my stepfather I took over the business, coming to Tregowan Hall only seldom to ensure the estate was being well run.'

'And now?'

'Now I have decided to live there permanently.'

'But the *Cymbeline?* I looked for it…'

'Its captain is taking it to Bristol. This is where I shall remain. It's high time I had a wife to give me ease and comfort and to bear my children in due course. I shall employ others to run the business—though I shall keep my finger on the pulse from here—and I shall visit Bristol often.'

'And my father's debt to you?'

'Will be cancelled on the day you become my wife.'

'What about the compensation owed to those men who were injured?'

'They will be taken care of. I accept Jack Mason was solely responsible for what happened, and no longer blame your father.' Moving closer, he cupped her chin in his hand with a soft beguiling smile. 'Marry me, Rowena. Don't hesitate. Know that I love you.'

She tilted her head to one side, a mischievous smile tempting her lips. 'And you're sure of that, are you, Tobias?'

'I have never been more sure of anything in my life.'

'But—in Gibraltar, you said you wouldn't marry me.'

'Not exactly. What I said was that I would not make you Mrs Searle. When we wed, you will become Lady Tregowan.' He grinned. 'You're the most stubborn, unconventional, argumentative woman I have ever met and I am sure I shall have a great deal of trouble with you, but it seems that I do love you—and I know you love me.'

'You do?'

'You've just told me.'

Her smile widened when she realised she had. 'So I did.'

'What do you say, Rowena?'

'Well, it's a strange offer, Tobias. If my memory of the time we spent in Gibraltar is correct, it shouldn't take you long to convince me that it's an offer I can't refuse.'

'No, you can't.' He cocked a sleek black brow and a crooked smile curved his lips. 'Our bargain is not complete.'

Surprise widened her eyes. 'It isn't?'

'You owe me one more night. When I offered to pay your sister's ransom, we agreed that payment would be made in kind—remember?'

Laughter bubbled to her lips. 'And I thought it must have slipped your mind.'

'I never forget what is owed, my love.'

'Then I suppose I shall have to settle my debt. When?'

'When you become my wife.'

They were married four weeks later on a warm and sunny October day. The bridegroom insisted on it and the whole of Falmouth and beyond was buzzing with it when it became known. A proud Matthew Golding— who had made his peace with his future son-in-law— was wheeled to the church to witness the union of his eldest daughter to Lord Tregowan. Jane looked radiant, the glow in her eyes enhanced because of the attentive presence of Edward Tennant, who had lost no time in calling at Mellin House when he heard she had returned.

Rowena and Tobias exchanged their vows in a church packed to the rafters with guests. The love they felt for each other and the strength of that love was there for all to see. It was a love that filled Rowena with wonder, which was often violent and passionate. It glowed and flamed with a fervour that stole their breath in its sudden spontaneity.

Afterwards the celebrations and toasts at Tregowan Hall went on into the night. Tobias danced his bride of several hours off the packed dance floor into the privacy of an alcove. Rowena smiled up at him. He looked positively dazzling in black velvet knee breeches and frock-coat, delicate lace cascading from his throat and spilling over his wrists.

Cupping her face in his hands, he placed his mouth carefully on hers and breathed her name and said something so quietly only she could hear.

'My darling bride, my love for you is endless. You are the most precious thing in my life—my treasure.'

Her laughter was so light and joyous it touched his heart. 'And you, my lord, are beginning to sound like a poet. Are you always so eloquent when you are in love?'

'How would I know that? I have never been in love before. Would you like another dance, my lady?'

'Have we not danced enough?'

His eyes narrowed and shone with a wicked gleam. 'Not the dance I like to do best—with its own music and its own rhythm. Shall we go upstairs?'

She placed her hand on his proffered arm. 'The guests?'

'Won't even know we're gone.'

Alone in their room his mouth covered hers, and they danced until dawn.

* * * * *

MILLS & BOON

Historical

On sale 4th September 2009

Regency

THE PIRATICAL MISS RAVENHURST
by Louise Allen

Forced to flee Jamaica in disguise, Clemence Ravenhurst falls into the clutches of the Caribbean's most dangerous pirate! Naval officer Nathan Stanier protects her on their perilous journey – and Clemence seems determined their adventure will be as passionate as possible!

The latest thrilling instalment of Louise Allen's
Those Scandalous Ravenhursts *mini-series!*

Regency

HIS FORBIDDEN LIAISON
by Joanna Maitland

Irresponsible and thoroughly charming, Jack Aikenhead never lacks female company. But Marguerite Grolier, delectable French fusion of strong will and subtle allure, may just be the lady to transform the reckless rake into an irresistible Lord – and honourable knave!

Third in ***The Aikenhead Honours*** *trilogy –*
Three gentlemen spies; bound by duty, undone by women!

MILLS & BOON®
Super
Historical

On sale 4th September 2009

LORDS OF SCANDAL
by Kasey Michaels

**Two eligible men
Two inconvenient wives!**

THE BELEAGUERED LORD BOURNE

Kit Wilde, eighth Earl of Bourne, pledged to enjoy all the willing female company London has to offer – not marry the first chit he kissed… Only Miss Jane Maitland, his impertinent, unwanted wife, is full of surprises – not least the passion in her eyes!

THE ENTERPRISING LORD EDWARD

Lord Edward Laurence must take a wife, and it seems that Miss Emily Howland is determined to protect her cousin from him, damning her own reputation as a result. Only his prickly new bride has no idea that *her* ultimate surrender is all Edward desires!

A Kasey Michaels Double Bill!

2 FREE BOOKS
AND A SURPRISE GIFT

We would like to take this opportunity to thank you for reading this Mills & Boon® book by offering you the chance to take TWO more specially selected titles from the Historical series absolutely FREE! We're also making this offer to introduce you to the benefits of the Mills & Boon® Book Club™—

- **FREE home delivery**
- **FREE gifts and competitions**
- **FREE monthly Newsletter**
- **Exclusive Mills & Boon Book Club offers**
- **Books available before they're in the shops**

Accepting these FREE books and gift places you under no obligation to buy, you may cancel at any time, even after receiving your free books. Simply complete your details below and return the entire page to the address below. You don't even need a stamp!

YES Please send me 2 free Historical books and a surprise gift. I understand that unless you hear from me, I will receive 4 superb new titles every month for just £3.79 each, postage and packing free. I am under no obligation to purchase any books and may cancel my subscription at any time. The free books and gift will be mine to keep in any case.

Ms/Mrs/Miss/Mr_____ initials _____

_____

Surname _____

address _____

_____

_____ postcode _____

Send this whole page to: Mills & Boon Book Club, Free Book Offer, FREEPOST NAT 10298, Richmond, TW9 1BR